A TOWN CALLED FURY
REDEMPTION

A TOWN CALLED FURY
REDEMPTION

WILLIAM W. JOHNSTONE
with J. A. Johnstone

P

PINNACLE BOOKS
Kensington Publishing Corp.
www.kensingtonbooks.com

PINNACLE BOOKS are published by

Kensington Publishing Corp.
119 West 40th Street
New York, NY 10018

PUBLISHER'S NOTE
Following the death of William W. Johnstone, the Johnstone family is working with a carefully selected writer to organize and complete Mr. Johnstone's outlines and many unfinished manuscripts to create additional novels in all of his series like The Last Gunfighter, Mountain Man, and Eagles, among others. This novel was inspired by Mr. Johnstone's superb storytelling.

ISBN-13: 978-0-7860-2691-3
ISBN-10: 0-7860-2691-X

First printing: July 2011

10 9 8 7 6 5 4 3

Printed in the United States of America

PROLOGUE

Oct. 29, 1928

Mr. J. Carlton Blander, Editor
Livermore and Beedle, Publishers
New York, New York

Dear Carl,
  Thank you so much for pointing me toward this Fury story! I know you didn't mean for me to get a "wild hare" (or is that "wild hair"?) and just go charging out to Arizona at the drop of your not-inconsequential hat, but that's exactly what I did. The story runs deeper than you could have known—or the sketchy reference books say, for that matter—and I found a number of the participants still alive and kicking, and best of all, talking!
  As you know, the story actually begins long before the events you provided me to spin into literary fodder. They begin in 1866, when famed wagon

master Jedediah Fury was hired by a small troupe of travelers to lead them west, from Kansas City to California. Jedediah was accompanied on this mission by his twenty-year-old son, Jason, and his fifteen-year-old daughter, Jenny, they being the last of his living family after the Civil War. Jedediah was no newcomer to leading pilgrims west. He'd been traveling those paths since after the War of 1812.

I have not been able to ascertain the names of all the folks who were in the train, but what records I could scrounge up (along with the memories of those still living) have provided me with the following partial roster: the "Reverend" Louis Milcher, his wife (Lavinia) and seven children, ages five through fifteen; Hamish MacDonald, widower, with two half-grown children—a boy and a girl, Matthew and Megan, roughly the ages of Jedediah's children; Salmon and Cordelia Kendall, with two children (Sammy, Jr. and Peony, called Piney); Randall and Miranda Nordstrom, no children, (went back East or on to California—there is some contention about this—in 1867); Ezekiel and Eliza Morton, single daughter Electa, twenty-seven (to be the schoolmarm) and elder daughter Europa Morton Griggs, married to Milton Griggs, blacksmith and wheelwright (no children); Zachary and Suzannah Morton (no children), Zachary being Ezekiel's elder brother; a do-it-yourself doctor, Michael Morelli, wife Olympia, and their two young children (Constantine and Helen); Saul and Rachael Cohen and their three young sons. There were a few other families, but they were not listed and no one could recall their names, most likely because they later went back East or traveled farther west.

The train, which contained livestock in the form of a number of saddle horses and breeding stock, a greater deal of cattle, goats, and hogs (mostly that of Hamish MacDonald and the Morton families) and, of all things, a piano owned by the Milchers left for the West in the spring of 1866. It was led by Fury, with the help of his three trusty hirelings. I could only dig up one of the names, here: a Ward Wanamaker, who later became the town's deputy until his murder several years later (which follows herein).

Most of the wagon train members survived Indian attacks (Jedediah Fury was himself killed by Comanche, I believe, about halfway west, several children died, and Hamish MacDonald died when his wagon tumbled down a mountainside, after he took a trail he was advised not to attempt), visiting wild settlements where now stand real towns, and withstanding highly inclement weather. About three-fifths of the way across Arizona, they decided to stop and put down stakes.

The place they chose was fortunate, because it was right next to the only water for forty or fifty miles, both west and east, and it was close enough to the southernmost tip of the Bradshaws to make the getting of timber relatively easy. There was good grazing to be had, and the Morton clan made good use of it. Their homestead still survives to this day as a working ranch, as do the large homes they built for themselves. Young Seth Todd, currently the last of the Mortons (and Electa's grandson) owns and runs it.

South of the town was where Hamish MacDonald's son, Matthew, set up his cattle operation, which had been his late father's dream. He also bred fine Morgan horses, the only such breeder in the then-territory of Arizona. His sister, Megan, ran the bank both before and after she married, she having the head for figures that Matthew never possessed.

For the first few years, everyone else lived inside the town walls, whose fortresslike perimeter proved daunting to both Indians and white scofflaws, and the town itself became a regular stopover for wagon trains heading both east and west.

But I'm getting ahead of myself. What concerns us here is the spring of 1871, the year that gunfighter Ezra Welk went to meet his maker. Former marshal Jason Fury (now a tall but spare man in his eighties, with all his own teeth and most all of his hair, and, certainly, all of his mental capacities) was very much surprised that I was there, asking questions about something "so inconsequential" as the demise of Ezra Welk.

"Inconsequential?!" I said, as surprised by his use of the word as its use in this context.

"You heard me, boy," he snapped. "Salmon Kendall was a better newsman than you, clear back fifty or sixty years!"

I again explained that I was a writer of books and films, not a newspaperman.

This seemed to "settle his hash" somewhat. However, it was then that I changed my mind about the writing of this book. I had planned to pen it pretending to be Marshal Fury himself, using the first person narrative you had asked for. However, in light of Marshal Fury's attitude (and also, there being other witnesses still living), I decided to write it in third person.

And so, as they say, on with the show!

Sincerely,
Bill

1

The black, biting wind was so strong and so fierce that Jason feared there was no more skin left on his upper face—the only part not covered by his hat or bandanna.

His nostrils were clogged with dust and snot, despite the precautionary bandanna, and his throat was growing thick with dust and grit. Whoever had decided to call these things dust storms had never been in one, he knew that for certain. Oh, they might start out with dust, but as they grew, they picked up everything, from pebbles to grit to bits of plants and sticks. He'd been told they could rip whole branches from trees and arms off cacti, and add them into the whirling, filthy mess, blasting small buildings and leaving nothing behind but splinters.

He hadn't believed it then.

He did now.

He could barely see a foot in front of him, and just moving was dangerous—his britches had turned into sandpaper, and his shirt was no better.

At last he reached his office—or at least, he thought it was—and put his shoulder into the door. He hadn't needed to. The wind took it, slamming both the door and Jason against the wall with a resounding thud that must have startled folks as far away as two doors up and down, even over the storm's howling, unending roar.

It took him over five minutes to will both his body and the door into cooperating, but he finally got it closed. Slouching against it, he went into a coughing jag that he thought would never quit. He would rather have been cursing up a storm than coughing one up, but when it finally stopped, a good, long drink from the water bucket put the world right side up. Well, mostly. He still couldn't breathe through his nose, but a good, long honk—well, six or seven—on his bandanna put that right again.

With the wind still howling like a banshee outside and flinging everything not tied down against his shutters and door, he thanked God for one thing: The storm was, at least, keeping everyone inside, which included Rafe Lynch—wanted for eight killings in California, across the river—and currently ensconced at Abigail Krimp's bar and whorehouse, up the street.

He didn't know much about Lynch, other than that he was clean in Fury, and for that matter in the whole of Arizona, and Jason was therefore constrained by law to keep his paws off Lynch, and his lead to himself. Actually, he felt relieved. He didn't feel up to tangling with someone of Lynch's reported ilk. Still, he was worried. What if Lynch tried to stir up some trouble? And what if he or Ward couldn't handle it? Ward was a good deputy, but he wouldn't want to put him up against Lynch in a card game, let alone a shoot-out.

He sighed raggedly, although he couldn't hear himself. Outside the jailhouse walls, the storm pounded harder and harsher. Dust seeped in everywhere: around the door and the windows, even up through the plank floor. Jason knew damn well that the floor only had two inches—or less—of clearance above the dirt underneath, and this occurrence left him puzzled.

He'd managed to make his rounds, although a bit early. It was only three in the afternoon, despite the dust and crud-blackened sky. Everyone was inside, boarded up against the wind and wrapped in blankets against the storm's detritus and the sudden chill that had accompanied it.

Couldn't they have just gotten a nice rain? Jason shook his head, and two twigs and a long cactus thorn fell to the desk. He snorted. He must look a sight. At least, that's what his sister, Jenny, would have said, had she been there to see him. But she was nestled up over at Kendall's Boarding House with her best friend, Megan MacDonald, or she was at home, madly trying to sweep up the dust and grit that wouldn't stop coming.

His thoughts again returned to Rafe Lynch. It gnawed on him that Lynch was even in town. In his town, dammit! Well, not actually his. The settlers had christened it Fury after his father, Jedediah Fury, a legendary wagon master who had been killed on the trail coming out from Kansas

City. He supposed the place's name was attractive to scofflaws, but they seemed (out of all proportion) drawn to the tiny, peaceful town in the Arizona Territory. Why couldn't they ride on over to Mendacity or Rage or Suicide or Hanged Dog or Ravaged Nuns?

He shivered. Now, there was a town he didn't want anything to do with!

His sand-gritted eyes were weary and so was he. He glanced up at the wall clock again. Three-thirty. No way that Ward was going to make it down here on time, if he came at all. It wouldn't hurt him to get a little shut-eye, he figured, and so he put his head down on his dusty arms, which were folded on the desk.

Despite the battering storm outside, he was asleep in five minutes.

Roughly twenty-five miles to the west of Fury, a small train of Conestoga wagons fought their way through the dust storm. Riley Havens, the wagon master, had seen it coming: the sky growing darker to the east, the wind coming up, the way the livestock skittered on the ends of their tie ropes, and the occasional dust devils that swirled their way across the expanses on either side of them.

But now the edge of the darkness was upon them, and if Riley was correct, they were in for one whiptail monster of a dust storm. He reined in his horse and held up his hand, signaling for the wagons to halt.

Almost immediately, Ferris Bond, his ramrod for

the journey, rode up on him and shouted, "What the devil is that thing, Riley? Looks like we're ridin' direct into the mouth a'hell!"

"We are," Riley replied grimly. "Get the wagons circled in. Tight."

"What about Sampson Davis? He rode off south 'bout an hour ago."

Riley didn't think twice. "Screw him," he said, and turned to help get the settlers, with their wagons and livestock, in a circle.

Down southeast of town, the storm wasn't as much sand and grit as twigs and branches, and Wash Keogh, who'd been working the same chunk of land for the past few years, was huddled in a shallow cave, along with his horse and all his worldly possessions. Well, the ones that the wind hadn't already taken, that was.

But despite the storm, Wash was a wildly happy man, because he held in his hand a hunk of gold the size of a turkey egg. It wasn't pure—there was quartz veining—but it sure enough weighed a ton and he was pretty sure that the mother lode was just upstream—up the dry creek bed, that was— just a little ways. If this damned wind would only stop blowing, well, hell! He might just turn out to be the richest man in the whole danged territory!

That thought sure put a smile on his weathered old face, but he ended up spitting out a mouthful of mud. The grit leaked in no matter how many bandannas he tied over his raggedy old face. Well, he could smile later. The main thing now was just to last out the storm.

Like him, his horse waited out the wind with his back to it and his head down. Smart critters, horses. He should have paid more attention when the gelding started acting prancy and agitated. But how could a man have paid attention to anything else when that big ol' doorstop of gold was sitting right there in his hand. He'd bet he would have missed out on the second coming if it had happened right there in front of him! And, blast it, he didn't figure Jesus would be mad at him, either! 'Course, he'd probably "suggest" that ten percent of it go to the Reverend Milcher or some other Bible thumper.

Fat chance of that!

He hunkered down against the howl of the storm to wait it out. But he was happy.

Very happy.

Back inside the stockaded walls of Fury—walls which had used up every tree lining the creek for five miles in either direction and used up most of the wagons, too—the wind was still whistling and whining through the cracks between the timbers. Solomon Cohen, who had been known as Saul until he changed it back to Solomon during a crisis of faith several months back, was huddled in the mercantile with Rachael, his wife, and the boys: David, Jacob, and Abraham. The back room of the mercantile was fairly tight, and so they had planted themselves there for the duration.

Solomon's crisis had come after a long time, a long time with no other Jews in town, no one else who spoke Yiddish, no one with an ancestry in common with himself or Rachael. Oh, there was her, of course, but it wasn't like having another Jewish man around to share things with, to complain with, to laugh with, and to spend the Sabbath with. How he wished for a rabbi!

And now Rachael was with child once again. He feared that they would lose this one, as they had the last two, and each night his prayers were filled with the unborn child, wishing it to be well and prosper. He didn't care whether God would give him a boy or a girl, he just heartily prayed that Jehovah would give him a child who breathed, who would grow up straight and tall, and who would be a good Jew.

Still, he wished for another Jewish presence in Fury. A man, a woman . . . a family at best! His children had no prospects of marriage in this town filled with goyim.

If they were to marry, they would likely have to go away to California, to one of the big cities, like San Francisco. It was a prospect he dreaded, and he knew Rachael did, too. They had talked of it many times. They had even spoken of it long before the children's births, when they first met in New York City, and Solomon spoke of his dreams of the West and the fortunes that could be made if a man was smart and handy and careful with his money.

It had taken him over ten years (plus his marriage to Rachel and three babies, all sons) to talk her into it, but at last she relented. Although he always remembered that she had cautioned him that they didn't know if the West held any other Jews that their children could marry—or even, for that matter, would want to!

As always, she had been right, his Rachael.

He looked at her, resting fitfully on the old daybed they kept down here, her belly so swollen with child that she looked as if she might pop at any second, and he felt again a pang of love for her, for the baby. She was so beautiful, his wife. He was lucky to have her, blessed that she'd had him.

The wind hadn't yet shown any signs of lessening, and so he slouched down farther in his rocker and carefully stuck his legs out between David and Abraham, who were sound asleep on the floor. Glancing over at Jacob to make sure he was all right, too, Solomon said yet another silent prayer, then closed his eyes.

Almost instantaneously, he was asleep.

The Reverend Milcher angrily paced the center aisle between the rows of pews. Not that they had ever needed them. Not that they'd ever been filled. Not that anybody in town appeared to give a good damn.

Even though he hadn't spoken aloud, he stopped immediately and clapped his hand over his mouth. From a front pew, Lavinia, his long-suffering wife, looked up from her dusty knitting and stared at him. "Did you have an impure thought, Louis?" she asked him.

"Yes, dear," he replied, after wiping more sand from his mouth. "I thought a sinful word."

"I hope you apologized to the Lord."

"Yes, dear. I did."

He began to pace again. They were running out of food, and he needed to fill the church with folks who would donate to hear the word of the Lord. That, or bring a chicken. He had tried and tried, but nothing he did seemed to bring in the people he needed to keep his church running. And now, this infernal dust storm! Was the Lord trying to punish him? What could he have possibly done to bring down the Lord's wrath upon not only himself, but the town and everything and everyone around it?

Again, he stopped stock-still, but this time his hand went to the side of his head instead of his mouth. That was it! The dust storm! Oh, the Lord had sent him a sign as sure as anything!

"Louis?"

"What?" he replied, distracted.

"You stopped walking again."

He pulled himself up straight. "I have had a revelation, Lavinia." Before she could ask about it, he added, "I need some time to think it through. Good night, dear." Soberly, he went to the side of the altar, opened the door, and started up the stairs.

Lavinia stood up and began to smack the dust out of the garment she'd been knitting, banging it over and over against the back of a church pew. She kept on whacking at it as if she were beating back Fury, beating back her marriage and this awful storm, beating back all the bad things in her life.

At last, she wearily stilled her hand and started upstairs.

When Jason woke, he still found himself alone, surrounded by unfettered wind whipping at the walls. And it was, according to the clock, ten forty-five. And there was no Ward in evidence.

He let out a long sigh, unfortunately accompanied by a long sandy drizzle of snot, which he quickly wiped on his shirtsleeve. Well, he should have expected it. He gave himself credit in fore-telling that Ward wouldn't brave the storm in order to come down to the office. Jason just hoped he'd found himself a nice, secure place to hole up in.

Jason reminded himself to hike up to the mer-cantile and see if they had any caulking. That was, when the storm let up. If it ever did. He was going to make this place airtight if it killed him. There was still dust coming in around the windows and the front door, and right up through the floor. He didn't want to see what was happening around the back door, but he knew it'd be bad. It wasn't nearly as tight as the front one.

Just then, a loud bang issued from the back room, and he shot to his feet, accompanied by the soft clatter of thousands of grains of sand falling from his body and hitting the floor.

Whispering, "Dammit!" he went to the door to the back room and threw it wide. He had expected to be met by the full force of the storm and the outer door hanging off its hinges, but instead he found Ward, struggling to close the back door.

He fought back the urge to laugh, and instead helped Ward. The two men succeeded in closing and latching the door, and Ward leaned his back against it, his head drooping, his hair hanging in his eyes. Jason grinned. "You look like you been rode hard and put up wet, man."

"Feel worse," Ward replied after a moment. Then he looked Jason up and down. "You don't much look like a go-to-town slicker yourself, either, boss."

Jason smiled, then led him into the main part of the office. "There's clean water in the bucket. You want coffee, you're gonna hafta make it yourself."

Ward went to the bucket and had himself two dippers of water, then splashed another on the back of his neck. "You ever seen a storm like this?"

Jason said, "I never even heard a'one." He hadn't, either, not one like this!

"Well, I heard about 'em, but this one's sure a ripsnorter. Don't believe I ever heard tell'a one lastin' so long or goin' so hard. Oh—what I come to tell you. One'a the Milcher kids is missin'. Found the reverend out lookin' for him, but you know him—he's like buttered beef in a crisis. Made him go on home."

Jason nodded. "When'd he go missing?"

"Sometime between seven and nine-thirty. The reverend thinks he's out lookin' for the cat. She's missin', too." During the passing years, the Milcher's original cat, Chuckles, had been replaced several times. The latest one was . . . well, he couldn't remember the name at the moment. But it was either a grandkitten or a great-grandkitten of Chuckles.

"Shit." Jason put his hands flat on the desk, then pushed himself up. "I reckon now's as good a time as any." He shook out his bandanna and tied it over his nose and mouth. "You rest up. Come out when you're ready."

But Ward was on his feet, his clothes dribbling sand on the floor. "Naw. I'll go with you. Four eyes are better'n two. Or so they tell me."

Jason nodded. "Appreciate it. Pull your hat brim low."

He opened the front door. He had a firm hold on the latch, but the sudden influx of wind shoved Ward off his feet and into the filing cabinets.

"You wanna warn a fella afore you do that?" he groused.

Jason didn't blame him. "Sorry, Ward."

Muttering something that Jason was glad he couldn't hear, Ward slowly got back to his feet, using his feet and hands and back for traction. He made it to the desk, and finally to the door.

Jason shouted, "We're gonna hafta get outside, then pull like crazy, okay?"

Ward nodded, and they did, each bracing a boot on either side of the doorframe. It took them nearly five minutes just until Jason lost sight of the wall clock, but eventually the door was closed and latched.

"Which kid was it?" he asked Ward over the howling wind.

"Milcher!"

"Which Milcher kid?" There were a bunch of them.

"Peter. The five-year-old!"

Great, just great. A five-year-old kid lost in this storm! A storm a grown man could barely keep his footing in, and that seemed intent on staying around until the end of time. Maybe it was the end of time.

But Peter was a tough little kid. If he had survived the trip out West in his mother's belly, he could survive anything. At least, that's what Jason hoped.

He tried to think like a five-year-old following a cat. . . .

"Follow me!" he said to Ward, and set off, staggering against the buffeting wind, toward the stables.

Up at the stable, they found several cattle and a couple of saddle horses standing out in the corral, all with their heads down and their butts into the wind. Jason wondered if they could get them inside once they found the Milcher boy.

It didn't take them long at all. Once they pulled the barn door closed after them and called out his name a couple of times, they heard soft sobbing coming from the rear of the barn. Well, it would have been loud wailing, if not for the roar of the storm. Ward heard it first, and Jason followed him back to a rear stall, where Jason uncovered the boy, hiding beneath a saddle blanket.

"Peter?" he asked.

"My daddy's gonna kill me!" came the answer. When the boy looked up, his face was streaked by the trails of tears through the crust of dust and grit on his face. "But I had to find Louise! She's gonna have kittens, and she's having them right now!" He pointed down next to him in the straw, and there was the Milcher's cat, with a third or fourth kitten just emerging.

"Get a crate, Ward," Jason said, and put an arm around the boy. "Don't worry, Peter. Your daddy's not gonna kill you. In fact, he was out looking for you, he was so worried."

Ward handed him an apple crate, in which he'd already placed a fresh saddle blanket.

"H-he was?" Peter asked.

"He was indeed. Now let's see what we've got, here. . . ."

Jason gently lifted the mother cat while Ward stooped over him, carefully bringing the still-attached kitten along, and they placed them in the apple crate. "Good," Jason said. "Now let's see who else is here."

He found not three, but four other kittens. Three were tabby and white, and one was all white. By the time the men got them all back with their mother, she had finished giving birth to the fifth kitten, had cut the cord, and was busy licking it clean. "Good kitty," Jason murmured, "good Mama." The kitten was tabby and white, too, although with more white than the others.

Jason and Ward stood up, and Jason held his hand down to the boy. "Guess we'd best get the lot of you back home!" Ward shifted through the

stack of saddle blankets and dug out a relatively
fresh one, covering the box snugly.

"But the baby cats can't go back!" Peter said as
he grabbed Jason's hand and pulled himself to his
feet. "Daddy doesn't like them. He says he doesn't
like the smell of birth."

"Reckon he's just gonna have to get over it,"
Jason said, trying to hide a scowl. He didn't much
like the smell of Milcher, either. And if Milcher objected to those kittens in his damned house, then
Milcher was going to find himself in jail. For something or other.

Jason lifted Peter up into his arms, then threw a
blanket over him. "You all snugged up in there?"
he asked.

A muffled, "Yessir," came from beneath the blanket, and with Ward carrying the box of kittens and
their mama, the men pushed their way out into
the storm again.

The wind hit Jason like a slap in the face, but
behind him, he heard Ward say, "Believe it's lettin'
up some!"

Jason didn't reply. He just forged ahead, toward
the Milchers' place. Thankfully, it wasn't far, and
when he rapped on the church door, Mrs. Milcher
threw it wide, then burst into tears. "Is he all
right?" she cried, pulling at the boy in Jason's arms.
"Is he—"

"I'm fine, Mama," Peter said after he wiggled out
of the blanket. And then he broke out in a grit-
encrusted grin. "Louise had her babies!"

Ward set the box down and lifted the cover. A

purring Louise looked up with loving green eyes, and mewed softly.

Mrs. Milcher cupped her boy's face in her hands. "Is that why you went out, honey? To find Louise?"

"Yes'm. And I did, too! She was in the stables."

Mrs. Milcher looked up at Jason. "She always wants to hide when she feels her time is here. What a night to pick!"

"Mrs. Milcher, ma'am? I know you've given away kittens before, and I was wonderin' if—"

"Certainly, Marshal! Any one you want!"

Jason smiled. "I kind of fancy the little white one. Got a name for him already and everything."

She cocked her head. "But you don't even know if it's a boy or a girl! Do you?"

"No, ma'am. Wasn't time to check. But I figured to call it Dusty. Name works either way, I reckon, and I'll never forget when he was born."

Mrs. Milcher smiled back at him. "No, I don't suppose you will! Thank you, Marshal, thank you for everything. My husband would thank you as well, I'm sure, but he has retired for the night."

Jason lifted a brow but said, "I see. Well, take care of young Peter, here, and watch over my kitten until it's ready to leave its mama." He and Ward both tipped their hats, and both stepped through the doors at once. But instead of the whip of wind that Jason was expecting, they stepped out into cool, clear, still air.

"What happened?" Ward said, looking around him.

"I guess it quit."

"Guess so. You wanna go up and get a drink?"

"Nope. Wanna go home and wash up."

Ward nodded. "Reckon that sounds good, too. Well, you go on ahead, Jason. I'll have a drink for both of us."

Jason laughed. "Just one, Ward. You're on duty, y'know."

Jason turned around and started the walk back to his house. The air felt humid, as if rain was coming. He hoped it was. Nothing would feel better right now than to just strip off his clothes and stand out in his front yard, naked. He chuckled to himself. Yeah, there'd be hell to pay if Mrs. Clancy saw him, but on the other hand, she wasn't likely to be awake at eleven at night, was she?

Jenny'd skin him, though. It was a terrible thing, he thought, to be ruled by women. Then he pictured Megan MacDonald. Well, there were exceptions to every rule, he thought, and grinned.

It did rain, and while Jason was outside, beaming and standing stark naked in his front yard with a bar of soap in his hand, miles away the wagon train was getting the worst of the dust storm. The wagons had been tightly circled and all the livestock had been unhitched and brought to the center, but the wind screeched through the wagons like a banshee intent on revenge.

Young Bill Crachit thought that maybe God was mad at them for giving up on the dream of California, and he huddled inside his old, used wagon, praying.

The Saulk family, two wagons down, held their children close, hoping it would just stop. Well, Eliza

Saulk did. Her husband, Frank, had the thankless job of trying to hold the wagon's canopy in place: The train had lost three already to the torrent of grit and dirt and cactus thorns. He was around the far side when, out of nowhere, an arm of a saguaro hit him in the back like a bag of nail-filled bricks. He went down with a thud, but was helped to his feet a moment later by Riley Havens, who yanked the cactus, stuck to Frank by its two-inch spines, free.

Blood ran down Frank's back in a hundred little drizzles, soaking his shirt, and Riley helped him back up inside the wagon. "Saguaro!" he shouted to Eliza. "Get those thorns out!"

Never letting go of the children, she moved back to her husband, gasped, "Oh, Frank!" and immediately began to ease him out of his shirt.

Riley left her to take care of her man and struggled next door, to the Grimms' wagon. Their canopy had blown off earlier. It had taken four men to chase it down and get it tied back in place. And that had been before the wind came up so damned hard. He doubted they could repeat their performance.

All was well with the Grimms, except that their dog wouldn't shut up. He was a cross between a redbone hound and a Louisiana black-mouthed cur, and the wind had brought out the hound side of him, in spades. While he yodeled uncontrollably, the Grimms had covered their heads with blankets and quilts, trying to hold off the noise of him and the storm. Riley hollered, "Shut up!" at him a few times, but it made no difference, and so he moved on to the next wagon and left the howling beast behind.

The raw wind still raked at his ears, even though he'd tied his hat down with one scarf, then covered his nose and mouth with a second one. But the crud still got through somehow, worked its insidious way up his nose and into his mouth. His eyes were crusted with it, and even his ears were stuffed. *I must look like hell,* he thought, then surprised himself by smiling beneath the layers. The whole world looked like hell tonight. He wasn't the only one.

The wind picked up—although how it managed, he had no idea—and one of the horses reared. He felt it more than saw it, because the horses were circled twenty feet away, in the center of the ring of wagons, but he knew what had happened. Somebody's gelding or mare had fallen prey to another of those thorny chunks of cactus that the wind seemed intent on throwing at them.

He made his way through the roar, falling twice in the process, but at last reached the distressed animal. Lodged on its croup was a fist-sized chunk of jumping cholla, which, in this case, might have jumped all the way from Tucson, as far as Riley knew.

He pulled it free, then pulled out what spines he could see. It was all he could do, but the horse seemed grateful.

Slowly staggering, he made his way to a new wagon to check in and give what reassurances he could. Which weren't many. He swore, this was the last train he was going to ferry out or back.

He was done.

2

Back in Fury, it was still raining come the morning, although it had settled into a slow but steady drizzle. And it didn't take much water for an Arizona inhabitant to forget the dust, Jason discovered. When he walked down the street to the office, he didn't pass a single water trough that wasn't filled to the brim. And grimy from all the gritty, dusty cowhands helping themselves to a free bath. Jason pitied the horses that had to drink from those troughs.

Surprisingly, there hadn't been that much wind damage. To the town, anyway. Ward Wanamaker told him, before he went home for the day, that the east side of the surrounding stockade wall looked like God had been using it for target practice.

Jason didn't feel like walking around the outside of the town, so he walked past the office and all the way down the central street, to the steps that would take him to the top of the wall. Every wall, his father had taught him, had to have places from which men could defend the interior, and this one did, around all four sides. When he reached the top, he stood on the rails that also ran around the inside perimeter, and looked down.

Ward had been right.

Cactus—clumps, arms, and pieces—covered the outside of the wall, and at the base was enough vegetation to start a small forest. If anybody in their right mind would want a forest of cactus, that was. And then he got to thinking that a forest of cactus just might be a good thing for the outside of that wall. He knew that cactus would just send down roots and take off, if you threw a hunk of it down on the ground. And they sure had a good rain last night, that was for sure. Hell, the stuff was probably rooted already.

He decided to leave it. It'd be just one more deterrent for Apache, and he was all for that.

He figured the stuff stuck to the wall would eventually fall off, leaving spines and stickers behind to discourage anyone who might try to climb in, too. If they made it past the cactus forest, that was.

"Oh, get a grip on yourself," he muttered to himself. "Stuff only blew in last night, and here you've got it six feet tall in your head!"

Shaking his head, he went back down the steps and started up toward his office. But he paused before going inside. He wondered if he should have a word with Rafe Lynch. He decided he should, but he put it off. Frankly, he didn't want it to turn into a confrontation and he was afraid that Lynch could do that pretty damn fast.

Actually, he was afraid that Lynch could rope, tie, and brand him before he even knew he was in the ketch pen.

So he turned and walked into the office, expecting one hell of a mess that'd need cleaning up. But to his surprise, Ward had spent a busy night with the push broom and the cleaning cloths.

Hell, Jason thought. *This place hasn't been this clean since we built it!* When he stepped out back, he found that even the bedding from the cells had been hung out in the rain and was now hanging damply from the lines!

"Wash and dry in one move," Jason said with a chuckle. "That's Ward."

Southeast of town, Wash Keogh was looking like mad for his gold vein, the one he was certain was going to make him rich, and the one from which he carried a turkey egg–sized chunk in his pants pocket.

He'd been searching all morning, but nothing, absolutely nothing had shown up. It wasn't raining now, but it had drizzled long enough after sunrise that the desert was still wet, washed free of its usual cover of dust. He had expected to find himself confronted with a shimmering wall of gold, the kind they wrote about in those strike-it-rich dime novels.

But no. Nothing.

Had somebody been in here before him and cleaned it all out? It sure looked that way. Maybe the chunk he'd found had simply been tossed away like so much trash. He growled under his breath. Life just wasn't fair!

"What did those other boys do right that I done wrong?" he asked the skies. "I lived me a good life, moved settlers back and forth, protected 'em from the heathen Indians! I worked with or for the best—Jedediah Fury, Whiskey Hank Ruskin, and Herbert Bower, to name just three. All good, godly men! I brung nuns to Santa Fe and a rabbi to San Diego, for criminy's sake, and I guarded that preacher an' his family to Fury. All right, I do my share of cussin', some say more. And I like my who-hit-John, but so do them priests a'yours. What more do you want from me?"

There was no answer, only the endless, clear blue sky.

Another hour, he thought. Another hour, and then he'd have himself some lunch.

He set off again, his eyes to the ground, keenly watching for any little hint of glittering gold.

It was Sunday, and Jason had let his sister, Jenny, sleep in. She was probably tuckered out from the storm. He knew he was.

The girls—Megan MacDonald was with her—woke at nine, yawning and stretching, and both ran to the window at the sound of softly pattering rain.

"Thank God!" Jenny said, loudly enough that Megan jumped. Jenny didn't notice. "Rain!" she said in wonder, and rested her hand, palm out, on the windowpane. "And it's cool," she added in a whisper. "Megan, feel!"

She took Megan's hand and pressed its palm again the pane, and Megan's reaction was to hiss at the chill. "My gosh!" she said, and put her other hand up next to it. "It's cold!"

Ever down to earth, Jenny said, "Oh, it's not cold, Meg, just cool. I wonder if Jason's up?"

She set off down the hall to wake him, but found his room empty except for an absolutely filthy pile of clothes heaped on the floor, dead center!

"He's gone," she said to nobody. Meg hadn't followed her. Turning, she grumbled, "Well, I hope he had the good sense to take a bath," and walked up the hall toward the kitchen, where she heard Megan already rooting through the cupboards.

A little while later, after both girls had washed last night's grime out of their hair and off their bodies, and had themselves a good breakfast, they walked uptown toward Solomon and Rachael's store.

The storm—long gone by now—hadn't shaken Jenny's hens, who had taken shelter in the low hay mow of Jason's little barn, and subsequently laid a record number of eggs. The girls' aim was to sell the excess eggs and find a new broom and dustpan, which Jenny had needed for a coon's age, but hadn't got round to buying yet. This seemed like the time, what with the floors of the house nearly ankle-deep in detritus.

They had barely reached the mercantile and were standing, staring in the window, when the skies suddenly opened again! Rain began to pelt them in huge, hard drops, and Megan grabbed Jenny's hand and yanked her. "C'mon!" she hollered.

But Jenny had put the brakes on, and just skidded along the walk behind Megan, the egg basket swinging from her other hand. "Wait! The door's back the other way, Meg!"

"Come on!" Megan insisted, and tugged Jenny for all she was worth. "The mercantile's closed, Jenny!"

"It is?" Jenny began to run alongside Megan then, and what Megan was headed for wasn't a very nice place—it was Abigail Krimp's. But any port in a storm, she told herself. It surely beat standing out here. Her skirt was already almost soaked!

Abigail was holding the door for them, and they ran directly inside, laughing and giggling from the race, not to mention where it had ended. It was the first time either one of them had so much as peeked inside a place like Abigail's—just the location made them giddy!

But Abigail was just as nice as Jenny remembered from the trip coming out. Why, she didn't look "sullied" at all! That's what Mrs. Milcher always called her. And then it occurred to her that she didn't even know what "sullied" meant. And Jenny had the nerve to call herself Miss Morton's assistant schoolmarm!

Abigail put a hand on each girl's shoulder and said, "Why don't you young ladies have a seat while you wait it out? I declare, this weather of late is conspirin' to put me outta business!" She led them to the first of three tables and sat them down. "You gals like sarsaparilla?"

Jenny's mouth began to water. It had been ages! She piped up, "Yes, ma'am!" and Megan nodded eagerly.

But Jenny's money sense moved in. "We don't have any money, Miss Abigail. But thank you anyway."

Megan looked at her as if she'd like to toss her over the stockade, and Jenny stared down at her hands.

"Not everything in here's for sale, you sillies!" Abigail laughed. "I thought we'd just have us a nice, friendly sody pop. Been forever since I just got to sit and socialize." And she was off, behind the bar.

Megan and Jenny exchanged glances, but Abigail was back by then, with three bottles of sarsaparilla, three glasses, a bottle opener, and a small bowl of real ice! The ice itself opened up the first topic of conversation, and Abigail told them that she had a little cellar dug far underground, under the back of the bar, where she kept a barrel full of ice when she could get it. This was the last of her current stash, which had come down from the northern mountains with the last wagon train to stop in Fury.

Jenny was transfixed, but Megan was halfway through her first glass. If you put enough ice in the glass, your bottle was enough to pour out twice. Jenny looked away from Abigail long enough to ice her glass, then fill it with sarsaparilla. It bubbled up into fizz when it hit the ice, and she was giggling out loud, which started Abigail, then Megan, who laughed out loud as well.

Abigail lifted her glass. "To old friends," she said.

Jenny and Megan followed suit, then clinked all three glasses together and drank.

Until her dying day, Jenny would swear that was the best sarsaparilla she ever drank.

"What the hell's goin' on out here? A hen party?" asked a new voice, male and jovial, but pretending to be cross.

Both Jenny and Megan twisted in their chairs to see the speaker. He was coming out of the mouth of the hall behind him, all clanking spurs and hip pistols and worn blue jeans and nothing up top except his long johns. And his hat, of course. Jenny didn't understand why in the West, nobody took off his hat, not even to greet a lady. Not even in church. Her brother aside, just a touch of the brim was the most she'd seen since they left Kansas!

But this man—whom Jenny liked already, just on general principle—not only took his hat clear off, but bowed to the table! Then he swept his hat wide, and said, "Good morning, ladies! I trust everyone came through the night in one piece?"

While the girls tittered, he looked at Abigail, raised his brows, indicating the empty chair at the table, and asked, "May I?"

"Certainly," she said. She was on the edge of laughter, herself.

The man sat down—right next to Jenny, who nearly fainted. He was tall—as tall as Jason, over six feet—had wavy, sandy hair, and it was cut fairly short. His eyes were blue, but not regular blue, like hers, nor sky blue, like Jason's. They were a deep, deep blue, as blue as she imagined the ocean would be if you swam down so far that your lungs were ready to burst. And he was, well, gorgeous, if you could call a man that.

"Allow me to introduce myself," said the vision sitting beside her. "My name is Lynch, Rafe Lynch, and I'd appreciate it if you'd call me Rafe."

Jenny stuttered, "Hello, Rafe. I'm Jenny Fury."

"Like the town!" He smiled wide. "Coincidence?"

She barely had her mouth open when she heard Megan say, across her, "Her father was the wagon master who started us West and her brother is our marshal, and I'm Megan MacDonald and my brother owns the bank."

Megan ran out of air, and Jenny just said, "Yes. What Megan said, I mean." She felt herself flush hotly and took a quick sip of her soda pop.

It was Abigail who saved her. She reached over and put a hand on Rafe's arm. "Can I get you somethin', honey?"

Rafe picked a little chunk of ice out of the bowl and ran it over his forehead. "A beer, if you wouldn't mind, Abby."

She said, "No problem at all," and stood up. Before she left, though, she said, "Rafe, honey, why don't you tell the girls, here, how you just beat the dust storm to town? I swan, I would'a been scared to death!"

He grinned. "Don't take much to scare you, does it, Abby?"

She laughed and he just kept grinning, even as

he turned back toward the girls. "How old are you two? Unless it's uncalled for to ask, I mean."

Megan said, a little too proudly, "I'm twenty-one. Jenny, here, is only nineteen."

Oh, terrific. Now she was marked as the baby of the group. She was going to have a word or two with Megan later. That was for sure! As calmly as she could, she said, "But I'll be twenty come June."

There. That was better.

"And your brother's the famous Jason Fury I been hearin' so much about?"

Jenny had never heard that he was famous, but she said, "Yes, I guess so. But he's just my brother."

Rafe Lynch ran the last of his ice over his forehead again, then popped it into his mouth. He pointed an index finger at Jenny and said, "You're funny. Why, I heard about him back in California! Somethin' about a couple'a Indian attacks. And yeah, somethin' else . . ." He smiled and thumped his temple. "It's gone right outta my head for the time bein'."

Abigail was back, and slid his beer across the table before she sat down again. "You tell 'em yet how you beat the dust storm?"

Jenny wanted to know what the other thing was that he'd heard, but held her tongue while Rafe took the first sip of his beer. Megan, she noticed, was leaning forward eagerly. Way too eagerly for somebody who was supposed to be soft on her brother, Jason, she thought. That was something else she was going to have to talk to Meg about later on.

Rafe started talking about the storm, how he saw

it coming on the horizon and nearly stopped. But then he saw signs of Apache far to the south, and hightailed it. . . .

Jenny listened as raptly as Megan. He was so handsome and charming, and had little lines that fanned out from the corners of his deep blue eyes when he smiled or laughed. Even his name was wonderful. She'd never known anyone called Rafe before.

She was smitten.

Over in California, near the Pacific coast and the upstart town of Los Angeles, Ezra Welk sat at the back of his room at Maria's place, listening to the morning birds singing over the desert while he smoked a cigar. He was a tall man, although he preferred to think of himself as compact, and studied the ash on the end of his cigar before he rolled if off on the edge of the sole of his boot. He was alone in the room, and had been ever since seven, when the little spitfire he'd spent the night with had left. Her name had been Merlina, he thought. Hell. She was probably servicing some caballero downstairs right now, behind the backbar.

That's where he'd found her, anyway. Quite the little bucking bronca, that gal.

He hoped her next "rider" was as satisfied as he was. He rolled the ash off the end of his cigar, in the ashtray this time—cut glass pretending to be crystal, he thought—and let out a sigh. He wasn't that tired. Well, maybe a bit tuckered out from

Señorita Merlina, but that'd pass. No, if he was tired of anything, he supposed it was just life itself.

That was a funny thing, wasn't it? He couldn't think of another way to put it, though, when a feller was sick and tired of, well, everything.

He took another drag on his cigar, then put it out before he stood up and gave his collar a tug. He supposed he'd best see about finding himself some breakfast, and then think about what to do.

This is all Benny Atkinson's fault, he thought un-pleasantly as he left his room and started down-stairs. *Why in hell did Benny have to show up in the first place?*

West of Fury, the wagon train sat forlornly, broken and wind-whipped. Two of the wagons had blown clean over during the night, killing the oc-cupants of one of them. The Banyons had man-aged to fall asleep somehow, Riley Havens guessed, and when their wagon went over, they were crushed by Martha's chiffarobe.

Ferris said it had taken two men with shovels to scrape up Darren's skull.

Three of the other men had set off to dig a couple of holes, and it wouldn't be very long before he was asked to come out and say some words over the dearly departed. What could he say? That Darren Banyon was the second to the cheapest cheapskate he'd ever met, but that he was a good man with his horses? And Martha Banyon . . . That she could be sharp-tongued and had already caused more than one blowup in the troupe, but that she could sing so sweet and pretty that it could make a grown man go all gooey?

He supposed he should just say the best parts. He'd leave the Bible-thumping to a couple of the other travelers. They sure enough had a crop of them on this journey, including a real Catholic priest.

But he supposed that Sampson Davis, wherever he was, leveled the field, good-and-evil-wise. There was something just plain nasty about the man. It wasn't in his voice or his looks or the way he carried himself, and so most people in the train liked him all right. But there was something . . . evil, that's what it was, downright evil . . . lurking behind those dark eyes. Riley seldom wished any man ill, but, may the good Lord forgive him, he hoped that Sampson Davis had died in the dust storm.

"Mr. Havens?" Young Bill Crachit, a sixteen-year-old on his own, and with his own wagon, stepped around to the tailgate, where Riley was sitting. "I guess we're ready for you, sir."

Riley hopped down, then ground out his smoke under his boot. "Thanks, Bill," he said as the two of them started toward the burial site. "Sampson Davis show up yet?"

"Oh, yeah," Bill said. "Rode in a half hour ago. Why?"

"No reason," Riley answered. "Just keepin' tabs on the train members, that's all."

They came to the site of the graves. Somebody had found the wood and twine to tie together some crude crosses, and the bodies had already been lowered. When the gathered crowd saw Riley and Bill coming, they stopped their low hum of conversation and looked toward Riley.

He took off his hat. "I'm not one for Bible verses," he said. "I'll let you, Fletch, or you, Father, take care of that part. But I can tell you about the Banyons. I didn't know 'em long, but long enough to know that Darren was the best I've seen for soothing a colicky mare or knowin' how to hitch his team just right, so they didn't never sore or come up lame. Martha was a beauty, and when it came to singin' a tune, I doubt anyone would say she wasn't the best they'd ever heard, especially in a wagon camp when people need some of the civilized things around them, fine things like music and manners."

Someone in the crowd tittered at that, and he cleared his throat. "Well, maybe I made a bad choice of words right there. But I think you all know what I meant. And now, if one of you more religious gents will take over?"

He stepped aside, and Fletcher Bean took his place between the head markers. Solemnly, he bowed his head, opened his Bible, and began, "Let us pray . . ."

Jason got up the nerve to go talk to Rafe Lynch around two in the afternoon, long after the girls had gone home. He found himself walking slower and slower as he neared Abigail's place, though, and had to mentally kick himself in the rump for being so scared. Lynch wasn't going to do anything, he told himself, not and ruin his harbor in a whole fresh territory!

That helped a little, so he was walking faster when he came up to Solomon's store. He knew full well that it was Sunday, but that had never before stopped Solomon from being open. Curious, he stopped and peeked in the front window, cupping a hand over his eyes to cut the glare.

What he saw surprised him. He saw the backroom door open, and Dr. Morelli step out and shake hands with Solomon, who'd been kneeling against a counter. The look on Solomon's face was ecstatic, and he pushed Morelli aside to go into the room, but Morelli blocked his passage, speaking to him very seriously. Solomon nodded just as solemnly, and then burst out in a fresh grin. He leapt up in the air, laughing, and finally Jason could make out some words through the glass.

"A girl! It's a girl!" Solomon shouted, and then gave Morelli one of those big bear hugs of his.

Morelli freed himself after a moment, and when he walked outside again, Jason was standing there on the boardwalk, smiling at him.

"Lived, didn't it?" Jason asked with a grin on his face.

The doctor allowed himself a small smile. "Yes, she did. I'm very happy for them, but . . . ."

"But what?"

"The baby isn't quite right, Jason. I think there's something wrong with her heart." Morelli shook his head slowly. "But it was a tad early. Sometimes these things just fix themselves with time, if there is any. This may have been what killed the boys, too, but since their religion prohibits any sort of postmortem . . ." He stared at the ground for a moment, then looked up. "Well, I must go. My wife's waiting dinner for me." He tipped his hat and cut across the street, making a beeline for his house.

Jason leaned back against the storefront, and shaking his head, muttered, "Well, I'll be dogged." He hoped Morelli was right about time fixing things. The last thing he needed was Solomon shooting up the place again.

He was just opening the doors into Abigail's place when someone fired a gun—and not too far from him! He whipped around and saw that it was Solomon Cohen himself, gun in hand, and screaming, "It's a girl! It's a girl!" He fired up into the air once again, then took off at a dead run, right down the center of town.

Jason took off right after him.

He caught up with Solomon only about six or seven steps later (Jason having the longer legs of the two, and not being nearly so giddy with joy), and wrested the gun away from Solomon.

"Yes, we know it's a girl! I reckon even the Apache, practically down on the Mexican border, know it, too!"

Solomon wasn't easily calmed or stilled, though. "But it's a girl, Jason, and she's alive!" he shouted, so loudly that it hurt Jason's ears. He blinked, and had to quickly shift his position when Solomon tried to take his gun back.

"There'll be none'a that, now. Why don't you come on over to the office, and we'll toast her with a cup'a coffee. I made it, Ward didn't," he added as an incentive. Ward made terrible coffee.

Solomon stood up straight. "Why, Jason! You're not goin' to arrest me?!"

"Just until you settle yourself down. I can't have you runnin' all over town, shootin' and maimin' folks."

"I'm not—"

"I know, Solomon," Jason said as he began to get them aimed toward the jail. "I know you're not tryin' to harm a soul. But you gotta admit that you're not the best shot. What if you was to shoot somebody by accident and they died? Think about how bad you'd feel then! And think how bad I'd feel, havin' to hang you after all we been through together!"

By this time, Jason had Solomon nearly to the office, and Sol wasn't fighting him. But in the half-second it took to let go of his arm and open the office door, Solomon snatched back the pistol, jumped away, and fired twice (down toward the open ground by the stockade wall), hollering, "Yahoo!"

Jason grabbed him from behind, shaking his wrist until the gun fell into the dirt. "Jesus Christ, Solomon, gimme a break, all right?"

"You shouldn't be taking the name of a prophet in vain," Solomon scolded.

"And you shouldn't be allowed anywhere near firearms when your wife's havin' a baby!" Jason shoved him back toward the jailhouse. This time, he got him clear through the front door and locked in a cell, then had to run outside again to pick up his gun.

The first thing Solomon said to him, once he came back inside, was, "So, I was promised coffee, already?"

Across the street, the Reverend Milcher sat alone in his church. Even Lavinia and the children were nowhere to be seen, and even the shooting and the shouted news that Solomon Cohen's child had lived—this time—wasn't enough to make him take his eyes from the broken clay-tiled floor.

Again, no one had come for Sunday service. No one except his family, and you could hardly count them.

How would he feed his children without some funding? How could he pass a collection plate when there was no one there to hand it to?

They had their milk cow, still, and she was heavy with calf. She'd calve any day, and then they could be sure of having milk. But he couldn't slaughter the calf until fall, until it had put on enough beef-weight to make it worthwhile. Lavinia had the few vegetables she could coax from the desert floor, but that was it. This was indeed the wilderness, but there was no manna from heaven.

3

By the time that Ward showed up to relieve him, Solomon had calmed down enough that Jason figured to let him go. Not his gun, though, just him. He could pick up the pistol tomorrow.

Jason walked with him as far as the mercantile, then said, "I've got some business to take care of next door." He indicated Abigail's place. "See you tomorrow, Solomon." Giving a last slap on the back to Solomon, he turned and walked over to Abigail's.

You were brave enough to do this before, you lug head, he said to himself when he paused just outside the front door. *It's only talk, right?*

He pushed open the door and walked inside.

There was no Rafe Lynch present. Just a few fellows from town and three girls, Abigail among them. He made no move to sit, but raised his hand to Abigail in a subtle wave. She came right over.

"What can I do you for, Jason?" she asked, more than surprised to see him. "A drink? A girl?" When he shook his head, she rattled on, "Your sister and

Megan were in this mornin', come in to get outta the rain. We had us a grand ol' time, had sarsaparilla and the last of the ice, to boot!"

Jason was shocked that the girls had set foot over Abigail's threshold, but instead said, "Rafe Lynch here?" Maybe he was up the hall with a girl.

But Abigail shook her head and looked annoyed. "Nope. He moved camp, down the street. To the saloon. I don't know what they got that I don't."

Jason thumbed back his hat, relieved. "Likely bigger card games, Abigail." If Lynch had changed his base of operation for the time being, there was less chance that Megan or Jenny would run into him. He didn't want his little sister or his gal, Megan, having anything to do with a murderer.

He rubbed at his arms. Just the thought of it had him broken out in gooseflesh.

Abigail wasn't paying any attention. Her eyes were on the three-man poker game a few tables away. Jason glanced that way, too, then cleared his throat to regain Abigail's attention.

When he finally had it, he tipped his hat and said, "Thanks, Abigail. I'll be goin' on home then."

"All right," she replied, looking back toward the poker game again. "Ward on duty?"

"Yeah. Why?"

"I might need him later on, that's all."

Jason cocked his head. "Why?"

She lowered her voice to a whisper. "Think I got a card cheat down there. Not sure yet, though." Then suddenly, she threw her arm around Jason's waist and turned him around, toward the door.

"You go on home and have some'a that good supper I know Jenny's cookin' up for you, okay?"

Somewhat reluctantly, he nodded. "You sure you don't want me to stick around for a while?" he muttered.

But she practically shoved him back outside. "You take care, now, you hear?" she called sweetly, and then she was gone, and Jason had nothing to look at but her outside wall.

Well, whatever it was—if it was anything at all—Ward could take care of it. He'd been wanting to make an arrest, single-handed, for ages now. And there wasn't anybody in there that Ward couldn't handle with one hand tied behind his back.

Jason shrugged and headed back up the street, toward home.

At home, the kitchen was buzzing with girl talk, giggles, and the clatter of pots and pans when Jason walked in. In fact, they didn't seem to notice his passage into the house and back to his room.

He was glad that Meg was staying for dinner. And he was even gladder to find that the filthy pile of clothes he'd left on the floor had been picked up and laundered, and presently lay neatly folded in his bureau.

But he hadn't escaped unseen.

Jenny appeared in his doorway, arms folded, and asked, "Well? Did you drag half the territory home in your clothes again?"

Jason played along. He doffed his hat and solemnly said, "No, ma'am, I decided to let Ward take a turn tonight."

"Good. It's only fair." She turned on her heel

and disappeared down the hall, calling over her shoulder, "Supper in ten minutes!"

Grinning, Jason hung his hat on the bedpost, and then slumped down into a sit. Jenny acted more like his mother than his little sister. But then, he supposed that came from a combination of her mother-hen instincts and his boyish looks and manner. He had never asked to be marshal. He'd never wanted to stay on, once everybody was settled in. His heart wasn't in Fury: It was back east at Harvard or Yale, back where fellows carried books, not guns, and the closest thing to an Apache attack was a stray spitball in the hallway.

His father had promised he'd send him, and Jason had promised he'd go, but Jason had since learned that a promise was just as fleeting as the air it was breathed into.

He pinched the brim of his nose to help keep himself awake. The kitten. He had to remember to tell Jenny. He'd forgotten all about it until just now.

Well, pinching his nose a few times didn't seem to do the trick, because the next thing he knew, he was stretched out on the bed and Jenny was back in the doorway.

"Are you coming or not?" she asked, her toe tapping.

"Oh." Supper, that was right, wasn't it? "Be right there."

She sniffed. "I swan, Jason Fury, I don't know what you'd do if left to your own devices. Sleep straight through until you were sixty, probably."

He raised his arm to make a point, but she

had already gone. Oh, she could be a saucy little wench, his sister, he thought with a smile. He sniffed the air. Chicken and gravy? His mouth began to water, and suddenly he was standing up and on his way down the hall. Jenny's gravy pulled at him like a magnet.

Things had surely changed since they left Kansas City, he mused. When they left, Jenny was more apt to blow up a kitchen than cook anything vaguely edible in it. But lately, she'd turned into one hell of a cook. Either that, or she'd just plain worn down his taste buds. . . .

He smiled as he sat down at the table. "Jenny, you've done it again. Smells great!" He snapped open his napkin and tucked it into his collar.

She carried a platter over to the table and slid it down beside him. Fried chicken, all right!

She muttered, "I can remember a time when you were afraid I was gonna blow up the kitchen every time I cooked."

Megan looked up from her plate at that, and Jason gave her a wink. "Well, Jenny, all I had to go on was past experience."

"One time! One time that happened, and that was clear back in Kansas City, Jason!"

He grabbed her around the waist, grinning, and said, "Now, sister, I admit it. You've improved tremendously! I actually look forward to coming home to your cookin', and that's the truth of it."

She relaxed, but said, "Don't go throwin' those college words around, you ol' show-off. 'Tremendously.' Honest to gosh!"

Jason tried to look innocent, but failed miserably.

He loosened his grip on Jenny, and she slipped away and into her chair. As she sat down and shook out her napkin, she said, "We almost had a guest for dinner. Besides Meg, I mean."

He helped himself to the chicken, then reached for the mashed potatoes. "How so? And Meg isn't a guest. She knows she's welcome here any old time, right, Megan?"

Megan didn't have time to do more than open her mouth before Jenny said, "It was the nicest man, Jason. We met him this morning, and he was just so . . . nice!"

"But we left before Jenny thought to ask him," said Megan.

"And when we went back, he was gone," Jenny said.

The girls were doing it again. They had him holding one conversation with two girls who seemed to be reading each other's minds. He didn't believe they even realized they were doing it!

"Who was he?" Jason asked as Meg handed him the gravy.

"Oh, he had the most beautiful name, too!" Jenny fairly squealed. "It was Rafe."

"Rafe Lynch," added Megan. "The first name's prettier than the last."

Jason froze, mid-pour. After the moment it took him to let this news sink in, he said, "You were at Abigail's when you met him." If he'd had access to a buggy whip, he would have taken it to Jenny right then and there.

Jenny, who seemed to be able to sense what he was thinking, said, "Now, Jason, don't be cross. We just ducked in to get out of the rain, and when we went inside, Abigail was the only one there!"

"Still, you know you're not supposed to be in there. Especially hangin' around with the likes of Rafe Lynch! He's a dangerous man, Jenny. And you pay attention, too, Meg. He's wanted for eight murders in California. Eight! He's a cold-blooded killer, and you're not to go anywhere near him again!"

Jenny started, "But, Jason . . ."

"No!" he shouted, cutting her off more firmly than he wished, but less vehemently than he felt. Damn that Lynch! Why did he have to choose Fury in which to stop over?

He remembered the gravy then, and finished pouring out his share. And when he looked up again, Jenny was close to tears. He reached to put his hand on her arm, but she snatched it away and said, "Don't!"

He switched his attention to Megan. "What?"

"You're terrible, Jason!" she said, shoving away from the table. "He was just lovely, really nice. There must be two Rafe Lynches, that's what it is, and Jenny and I met the good one! He couldn't possibly be a . . . a k-killer! He's well-spoken and he told us about beating the storm into town, and—"

"And he has little crinkles at the corners of his eyes!" Jenny added, as if this was a sure and certain sign of sainthood. Now, Jason knew full well that if there was more than one Rafe Lynch, this wasn't him. They had the real, honest-to-God Rafe Lynch setting up shop—now down the street, at the saloon—and he was a very bad man.

But in order to calm the girls, and also to avoid ruining a perfectly good meal, he decided to take the middle road. "All right. Maybe there is more than one Rafe Lynch. I'll check it out first thing tomorrow morning. Everybody happy again?"

Megan scraped her chair back toward the table, and Jenny took the gravy boat from Jason's hand. The situation was calmed, at least for the present.

However, it seemed that Jason was doomed to have a troubled suppertime. At just about the time that Jenny began to cut the apple pie into slices and serve it, the sound of arguing voices came to Jason's ears, followed directly by a fist banging on the door. "Who in the hell . . . ?" he muttered as he rose and walked to the front door, after cautioning the girls to stay put.

The banging, which had kept up since it started, suddenly stopped as Jason opened the door to find Deputy Ward Wanamaker, fist cocked back and aimed directly at Matt MacDonald, whom he held by the collar. And who was also the last person Jason expected to find in Fury that day. Ward was a tall, string bean of a man and had about four inches on Matt, and Matt looked, well, afraid.

Without taking his fist down, Ward said, "I already told him about twenty times that we ain't got no jurisdiction out at his place, but he kept shoutin' as how he wanted to talk to somebody in authority, not no stupid deputy. And so I brung him here. This here's the highest authority in Fury, Matthew," he added, punctuating the statement with a shake of Matt's collar that rattled the man's teeth.

Once again, Jason pulled on the cloak of peacemaker. "Let go of him, Ward."

Ward gradually loosened his grip and lowered his punching arm, and for just a second, Jason thought that Matt was going to rabbit. But he didn't. With a glare of unadulterated rage painting his features, he snarled, "I imagine you're gonna be as useless as usual?"

"If you got problems out at your place, you're right," Jason said. "What is it this time?"

"My cattle, godammit! Somebody stole two of my cattle!"

"Sorry to hear that, Matt."

"You're not sorry at all! You've got it in for anything or anybody attached to me, and I swear, I—"

"You swear what, Matthew?" asked Megan, who had just appeared at Jason's side, her napkin in her hand.

Matt simply stood there, boiling, and then he snapped, "You get yourself home, young lady, or there'll be hell to pay, you understand?"

"Don't move, Megan," Jason said quietly.

"Wouldn't think of it," she replied in the same light tone.

Matt glared daggers at her before he turned on his heel and marched, glowering, down the steps and across the yard to the street, where he turned and shook his fist. "I won't forget this, Fury!"

"I s'pose he wants to rename the town 'MacDonald,' too," Ward quipped.

Matt disappeared around the corner.

"He can be my guest," Jason said before he gathered himself and looked up at Ward. "What about his cattle, anyway?"

"Says somebody's swiped two of 'em. You ask me, it's a puma, or maybe a Mexican grizzly."

Ward was probably right. They both stood there, heads shaking, until Jason said, "You want somethin' to eat? Jenny did it again. Fried chicken and mashed, with gravy. Green beans. And pie?"

"Don't have to keep yammerin' at me, jus' git outta the way!" Grinning, Jason stepped aside and Ward walked past him, hollering, "Hey, Jenny! Set another plate, 'cause a man with a powerful appetite's comin' to supper!"

He heard Jenny laugh as Ward disappeared into the kitchen. He turned back to Megan, who was vacantly watching the empty road.

"Megan," he said, "I'm sorry."

She held up her hand, quieting him. "It's all right. I know he's a jackass. I've known it for quite a while, now. But he's my brother and I have to accept it. You don't, thank God. Now, let's go have some'a that apple pie!" She linked her arm through his and led him back to the kitchen, where Ward was already gobbling down fried chicken like somebody was going to toss it to the hogs if he didn't rush.

Before the sun went down, Ezra Welk made camp. He'd been riding easy most all of the day, which had been largely uneventful, save for the unusually large herd of pronghorn which had crossed his path this morning.

And all day long, even while he sat there, wrists crossed over his saddle horn while he watched those pronghorns slowly graze and amble their way north, he'd been thinking about that lame-brain, Benny Atkinson.

Whatever had possessed Benny to track him to Los Angeles, and why had he been dumb enough to call him out, right in front of God and everybody? It boggled him that anyone—even a so-called bounty hunter like Atkinson—would be dumb enough to try that. Especially when he had to know damn well that he was an inferior gunman to Ezra.

Well, apparently he hadn't, because he'd called out Ezra loud enough that they could have heard him down by the docks, and sealed his own fate, just like that.

Ezra had left him lying in the street, his pooling blood catching the dust sent up by Ezra's pony's heels as he beat it out of town. What law there was in Los Angeles didn't like him much to begin with, and he didn't figure to stick around and wait to see how they liked him now.

Now, Ezra had been riding out of Arizona, and it was a pretty dumb thing for Ezra to be headed back toward its border, but he was. At least Arizona was pretty much wide open. If you could steer clear of Indians and skirt the cities—of which there weren't many, unless you counted all those little-bitty, here-today-gone-tomorrow mining towns that popped up every sixty feet—you were in the clear. Same thing went for New Mexico and most of Texas, but then, he wasn't wanted in Texas. Yet.

Well, there was time. And he was still youngish, he thought with a snort.

Matt MacDonald made it home before nightfall and had one of the hands walk his horse, for it was sweating like it would never stop and lathered like a visit to a two-dollar barber. That's all he'd need right now, he thought. A messed-up horse, and all on account of that damned Jason Fury!

He slammed into the ranch house, then changed his mind. He walked outside again. "Send Curly up here!" he called to the human hot-walker, and then went back inside, the door banging behind him so hard that it broke one of the hinges.

The knock came less than five minutes later.

"Get your lazy butt in here, Curly!" Matt shouted, and Curly stepped in, grabbing the door by its latch and forcing it back up into position.

"What the hell happened, boss?" he asked, staring at the broken door.

"Never mind the damn door," Matt snapped. When Curly turned toward him, he added, "Got your attention, now?"

"Sure, boss. What you want?"

"Tomorrow, I want everybody to stop what they were workin' on and start buildin' a new corral next to the barn. A big one. I'm not going to lose any more cattle, you hear me? I want it big enough to hold every single cow, steer, and bull we've got on the place, with plenty of room for them to move around."

Curly screwed up his face. "What we gonna feed 'em, boss? I mean, out on the range they got forage, sorta. . . ."

"We're gonna feed 'em hay and corn, you dolt," Matt said. He was still angry, and he didn't think he was going to calm down anytime soon.

Curly looked like he knew it, and said, "Yeah, boss. First thing."

"All right then. You can go, now."

Curly tipped his hat, struggled once again with the door, and said, before he left, "You want I should send somebody up to fix this?"

Matt poured himself a glass of bourbon, took a drink, and barked, "Of course!"

"Yessir," Curly said as he closed the door. "Right away, sir."

And he was gone.

Matt sat down at the table, clenching his bourbon so tightly that the glass broke. Cursing, he found a cloth and wrapped it around his bleeding hand, then found another to pick up the broken glass and soak up the whiskey. It was all Fury's fault! Everything was Fury's fault, from the stolen cattle, to this mess, to the ingrown hair on his chin!

The glass picked up and the whiskey sopped, he threw the whole mess in the trash basket beside the sink.

And Megan, the ungrateful little wench! She was too old and too big to spank, but he'd think of something—something that would put her in her place for once and all. He'd had enough of her habit of hanging around with Jenny Fury, and worse, Jason. He'd had enough of her running his bank.

Well, on second thought, he'd best leave that one alone. Megan had a keen head for figures, better than his, and there'd been no complaints about her work. But he'd fix her wagon, all right, fix it so that there'd be no more back talk and no more crossing him. He'd show her!

But first, he had to gather in his cattle and he had to figure out what to do about that damned Jason! Why did Jenny have to be his sister? Why did she have to be related to him at all?

A new knock on the door caved it halfway in, and exposed a wide-eyed and blinking ranch hand. Matt noted the sky was dark behind him before he said, "Curly told you what to do?"

The fellow was still staring at the door. "Y-yes, sir."

"Well, get to it, then."

And then, his hand still bleeding into the wrapping towel, Matt stalked off to find himself some dinner. He thought Megan had made cookies or a cake or something the last time she was here.

He thought there was a chance it was still edible.

4

The next morning found Matt up bright and early, overseeing the work on the corral. There was still plenty of wood left over from the barn, and he had two men splitting it into usable sizes for posts and rough boards. Right at the moment, he was more concerned with getting the thing built than what it would look like.

His men didn't much agree with him, but they were smart enough to keep their opinions to themselves. They just went about their work with a distinct lack of enthusiasm.

Matt was still too het up to notice, though. He just kept pacing from man to man to man, hardly speaking, just staring at the ground and, every once in a while, glancing up at the work.

Blast that Jason Fury, anyway! He'd thought he could rustle up some men in town, at least; some volunteers, to help him find who was thieving him blind. Those cows weren't just cows, blast it! They were purebreds—well, mostly pure half-bloods— that his father had brought all the way out here.

Well, until he fell down the side of a mountain in the middle of nowhere, while they were on their way out.

And that was Jason's fault, too! In fact, to Matt's mind, there wasn't a single thing wrong with the world that wasn't Jason's fault! If the Lord kept a report card on Jason, he'd bet it was chockablock with F's.

And those F's didn't stand for "Fury," either.

His stomach rumbled. He hadn't eaten any breakfast, and it was almost lunchtime. He hadn't had much luck nosing around the kitchen last night, either. Meg had made a batch of ginger cookies, but they were so dried out that they were nearly impossible to eat. And the thing was, he knew that when she'd made them fresh, they'd been puffy and chewy and altogether wonderful. But he'd forgotten about them, just like he'd forgotten to pick up any groceries while he was in town.

Well, who could blame him? Again, he laid the fault at Jason's feet.

"Curly!" he snarled.

Curly trotted up to him, hammer in hand. "Yeah, boss?"

"Tell the bunkhouse cook to fix an extra lunch plate, and have somebody bring it up to the house to me."

Curly looked at him curiously, but all he said was, "Yessir."

"And have the boys light a fire under it. I want this thing finished and the cattle all brought in before I lose any more of 'em."

"Yessir," came the reply.

Matt turned his back and marched up toward the house, his stomach gurgling and thirst parching his throat. He hoped Cookie would get the lead out and slap him together some lunch, pronto. But first, he needed some whiskey.

A lot of whiskey.

Damn that Jason Fury, anyway!

Riley had started the train out early. At least, what was left of it. He just hoped that Fury had a couple of usable canvas covers that his two topless families could buy cheap, which wasn't always the case with these little upstart towns.

He had one of his "shank's mare" members driving the late Darren and Martha Banyon's rig, battered and tattered though it was. The other wagon tipped by the wind hadn't been mangled as badly, thank God, but the Banyons' looked like it had been to hell and back, then run through a wringer.

Several of the fellows had shored up the rear axle, broken in the terrible clash of wind and desert, and done their best to patch up the broken wheel, but they were just temporary fixes. As it was, the wagon just lurched along. He hoped that Fury had somebody who knew his way around a Conestoga, too. He may have lost the Banyons, but he'd by God get their belongings back to their folks!

He was staking a lot on Fury, he realized. He prayed that the fellow he'd run across in that bar back on the coast had been right, and that Fury was "a nice, friendly, little town."

He heard somebody riding up behind him, and turned to look.

It was Sampson Davis, the big, burly fellow who'd joined the train at the last minute and gone missing during the storm. At first, he'd been happy to have the extra man—and muscle—and glad for the money he paid. But then, something about Davis began to bother him. He couldn't put his finger on it, but something just didn't smell right. He'd told himself he was full of hooey, and that there wasn't anything wrong—nobody could really be as evil as he felt Sampson Davis was—but with each passing day, the feeling grew stronger.

Sampson reined his bay in next to Riley, and began to pace him. "How long till we hit Fury?" he asked. No salutation, no greeting of any kind, just that question. It was delivered with the usual scowl, of course.

Riley let out a disgusted huff, then said, "Before nightfall, I reckon." He was going to add, *What's your hurry?*, and more to the point, *Where were you last night?*, but Davis had reined his horse around and was galloping back to the train before Riley had a chance to open his mouth again.

"Prick," he muttered before he spat down into the brush, and then turned his attention back to the rugged landscape that lay ahead of him.

Despite any evidence to the contrary, Wash Keogh was still searching for the vein of gold that had spat out the turkey egg–sized nugget that was wearing a hole in his pocket. He wouldn't leave it back in camp, no sir! Who knew who might just come along and accidentally "find" it? Nope, he was keeping it on his person, even though it felt as if it was adding ten pounds to every stride he took.

Hell, he thought. *It probably is.*

He sat down for a minute, to catch his breath and grab a drink from his canteen. He'd gone through his whiskey supply already: finished it off the day he found the gold rock. But he figured he was entitled to it. When a man found something like that, he had best get himself good and drunk!

He took a slug of water, swished it around in his mouth, then swallowed. He was almost out. He supposed he'd have to go back up into town to replenish his supply, and mentally flogged himself for not catching some of the rainwater. He could have done it. There was some canvas to trap it in.

But the canvas had gone unused, and now he was running low. He figured that maybe he could stay put for the rest of the day and part of tomorrow. There were plenty of barrel cactus between him and town, and he could always raid a couple of those if he got desperate. Of course, he'd have to be pretty damned desperate to do that. Water from a barrel cactus tasted like, well, like water from a barrel cactus. Unconsciously, he made a face.

He stared at his canteen for a long minute before he lifted it to his lips once more and took another drink. And then he stoppered it and slung it back over his shoulder, standing up slowly.

"All right, gold. You'd best quit hidin' from me.

This here's Wash Keogh, and I means it!" he half-shouted at the desert, before he took a deep breath and started off again, his diligent eyes to the ground.

In his office, Jason was struggling with a letter to the U.S. Marshal's office up in Prescott.

He still didn't know what to do with Rafe Lynch, who was still in town, and whose presence he thought the Territorial Marshal should be aware of. At least, he'd want to know if he were the Territorial Marshal.

He wrote that down, then reread it, balled the paper in his hands, and pitched it into the wastebasket. It joined roughly twenty other crumpled pieces of paper, his whole afternoon's work. Every letter he had started to write had turned into what sounded to him like begging. Or worse, whining. He didn't think that was a very professional way to contact the marshal's office, but he couldn't keep the fear out of his writing.

He had just taken a new piece of paper and written the salutation, when the office door banged open and Ward burst in. Startled, Jason looked up.

"They're comin' in!" Ward said, and his excitement was plain.

"Who's comin' in?"

"It's a whole new wagon train, with goods to sell and folks wantin' to buy stuff!"

Ward was right to be excited. A wagon train always brought good news to Fury, in the form of new settlers and fresh trade. Jason smiled for the first time that afternoon. The day wasn't a total loss, after all.

Ward leaned across the desk and jerked Jason's sleeve. "C'mon! They're pullin' up now, and you gotta make a whatchacallit. An official presence or somethin'."

Jason put his pen down and stood up. Whatever would take him away from this blasted letter was something to celebrate, he supposed.

They walked up the street, then down to the south gate, which Ward had already opened. Sure enough, wagons were pulling into place and lining up outside, all down the south wall. The people in the front, who had already set their brakes and climbed down from their seats, were coming forward to glad-hand him. The first among them was the wagon master, who introduced himself as Riley Havens.

Jason made a quick assessment as they shook hands. Havens was sandy haired and tanned, and about thirty or so, he guessed. He had brown eyes and a tan line across his forehead (which Jason glimpsed when Havens doffed his hat to a passing lady), the latter of which denoted a fellow who worked outside in the sun for a living. He took a quick liking to the man, who said, "Pleased to meet y'all. You fellas, you just call me Riley, okay?"

"All right, Riley," Jason replied. "I'm Jason, and welcome to Fury. Lookin' for anythin' special, or are you folks just glad for a place to camp near what we laughingly call 'civilization'?"

Riley laughed. He said, "Both, I reckon. We're in need of canvas. That big storm the other day yanked the tops clean off'a couple a wagons. Reckon they're in the Pacific by now. And we're in need of a wheelwright and an axle man, if you got one."

Jason rubbed at his chin before he said, "Reckon we used up most of the canvas already, but there might be a couple of wagon covers tucked away someplace. And as for your wheel and axle man, we've got one who'd be happy for the business."

Ward, beside him, nodded happily. "Yessir, we sure do! Jason, you want I should ride out to the Morton place and get Milton Griggs?"

"Tomorrow morning'll be soon enough, Ward," Jason said. Behind him, in the stockade, he could hear the town waking from its siesta, rattling its shutters and dusting off the welcome mats. "In the meantime, Riley, y'all c'mon in and grab yourself a drink. Water, whiskey, beer, whatever you want!"

He was about to take his leave of Riley and go back to face the letter, when a big, burly man, stepped up. "You the sheriff?" he asked in a bark.

"Yeah," said Jason. "What of it?" He noticed that Riley had taken a step back.

"I'm lookin' for somebody. Rafe Lynch is his name. The sonofabitch in town?"

Jason didn't like the looks of him, and stalled a little. "Might I ask who's wantin' to know?"

"I'm Sampson Davis, and I'm here to kill the rat bastard."

* * *

Even down the street, walking back toward the safety of the office, Jason and Ward spoke in guarded tones. It was one thing to have a killer in town, but another entirely to have two of them!

"Look, that Sampson guy, he's sayin' right out that he's gonna kill Lynch, but Lynch ain't done a dang thing wrong here in Fury," Ward was saying.

"And if he kills him in Fury, he'll hang for murder, just like anybody else would."

"Take a mighty stout rope to hang a big, muscled-up fella like that, Jason," Ward mused.

"I'll keep that in mind, Ward," Jason said, and opened the door to his office. They both stepped inside, and ran smack into Rafe Lynch.

Jason had been wanting to talk to him, but he would rather have been the one to pick the time and place. He had only glimpsed Lynch in person, and seen his poster, and now he decided that the poster hadn't done him justice. No wonder Jenny was so taken with him.

He said, "Lynch. What brings you to Fury in general, and my office in particular?"

Beside him, he heard Ward utter a low gasp and felt him take a discreet step to the side, then halt, rock solid as usual. It was good to know Ward had his back.

Lynch said, "Guess you already know my name. And I know yours, too. You're Marshal Jason Fury, brother to the charming Miss Jenny Fury, and son of the late, lamented Jedediah Fury." He stuck out his hand and Jason reluctantly took it.

"And you're Ward Wanamaker," Lynch went on, "unless I miss my guess. Have I?"

Next, Ward took his hand and gave it a half-hearted shake. "I'm Wanamaker, all right," he said, a little stiffly.

"You'll pardon my deputy," Jason said when Lynch arched a brow. "Like me, he's just wonderin' what a fella wanted in California for killin' eight men is doin' here in Fury."

One corner of Lynch's mouth crooked up. "Well, you boys ain't nothin' if not direct." He turned around and pulled out the chair opposite Jason's desk. "You mind if I set myself down? I got a feelin' this is gonna be a long palaver."

Jason said, "Help yourself," moved around to his chair on the other side of the desk, and wished he'd finished that damned letter and sent it out yesterday. At least the wastebasket didn't look disturbed. Lynch hadn't been snooping, which left Jason feeling oddly relieved.

Ward moved across the room and took a seat in front of the cells, where he could keep an eye on Lynch's gun hand.

Jason crossed his arms on the desktop and leaned forward. "So, why Fury? How come we're blessed—or damned—with your presence?"

Lynch gave him that crooked-up smile again. "Because you're close enough to California that I can make it in a day's ride, and because rumor has it that you run a friendly little town. Am I right?"

Jason tipped his head, then nodded. "So far," he said.

And Lynch laughed! Still cackling, he said, "I like you, Fury! You got a by-God sense of humor!"

But Jason didn't return Lynch's smile. He said, "I mean, how long are you plannin' to stick around? You waitin' for somebody or what?"

"Tryin' to tell you," replied Lynch, still holding that amused expression. "I'm not meetin' anybody, or makin' plans for anything, and there ain't nobody here I wanna hurt. All I want is safe harbor, like those sailor boys say. I promise to mind my P's and Q's while I'm in town. Hell, while I'm in the whole territory!"

Despite himself, Jason was warming to Lynch as he spoke. He could see why Lynch would want—and need—a safe place. And he didn't seem like such a bad fellow. Of course, he'd killed all those men. That mattered. That counted against him in the most serious way!

Jason said, "And what about all those men you killed? They probably could'a used a 'safe harbor' somewhere, too."

"I ain't gonna go into it now, but there's a good reason attached to each one'a those killin's."

Behind him, over by the cells, Ward let out a loud "Hmmph." Both Jason and Lynch ignored it, each for his own reasons.

Lynch stood up, startling Jason, who rose, too. Lynch said, "Well, I just wanted to check in and let you know I ain't lookin' for any trouble. I'm stayin' across the street at the saloon, in case you wanna get hold of me. I liked it at Miss Abigail's, but there ain't much of anybody in there to get up a decent poker game with." He paused. "The gals who drop by are a bit on the tender side, too," he added, with a wink to Jason.

"I imagine they are," he replied, without expression. He was glad, though, that Lynch had taken up residence at the other end of town, in the saloon. And he also hoped that Lynch kept true to his word, and stayed out of trouble.

They'd taken a few steps toward the door before Jason remembered, and stopped. "Wait," he said, grabbing Lynch's arm. "There's a fellow in town. Just rode in with the wagon train, and he's lookin' for you. Says his name is Sampson Davis, and that he's gonna—"

Lynch's grin widened. "Gonna kill me?"

When Jason nodded, Lynch added, "I knew he was gonna catch up with me sooner or later. Just sorry it had to be here. You tell him I was in town?"

Ward said, "Already seemed to know. Nasty sort of fella."

"Yup," said Lynch. "That's Davis. Well, I'll be on the watch for him. Thanks, fellers."

He tipped his hat and walked out. Jason watched through the window as he looked up the street, toward Abigail's, then down it toward the saloon. Finally, he set off for the saloon, walking at a casual clip.

Beside Jason, Ward said, "He's sure somethin'."

Warily nodding, Jason said, "Yeah. He surely is."

Finally satisfied with the content and phrasing of his letter to the U.S. Marshal (which included the fact that Fury had not one, but two gunslingers in town), Jason sealed the envelope. "I'm leavin'!" he called to Ward, and exited using the front door.

Up the street he went toward Solomon's store, after checking to make sure the end of the street with the saloon was quiet. Everything was calm, aside from the burble of trading coming from outside the gates. He momentarily wondered if Jenny had been out to buy anything edible, and if there'd be a treat for supper. It didn't last long, though. He put his hand on the latch to Solomon's mercantile and went in, accompanied by the jingling little bells attached to the door.

"Solomon?" he called when he saw no one. "Hey, Sol, are you around? It's Jason!"

He heard some rustling from upstairs, then Solomon's voice. "Hold on to your skivvies. I'm coming, already!" Then footsteps on the staircase.

Solomon himself came around the corner with a wide smile on his face. "Jason!" he said. "What can I do for you on this fine day?"

Jason grinned back at him. At least he wasn't holding a grudge about the earlier lockup. He reached into his pocket and pulled out the letter, then into another and pulled out some change. "Got a letter to go out," he said, sliding the envelope across the counter.

Solomon looked at it. "To Prescott?" he said. "Be thirty-five cents. Sorry it's so much, but there's hardly anything else goin' out, and Grady won't take his confounded horse out of the stable for less than a dollar."

Grady was the young man who ferried the mail to Prescott and back.

"Well, you tell Grady that there's another dollar in it for him if he gets that letter to Prescott in less than two days, all right?" Jason counted out the money.

"You're paying?"

Jason laughed. "I'm paying."

Solomon nodded. "I'll tell him. And by the way, did I tell you? Rachael and I, we have a houseguest!"

"I'd hardly call your new daughter a house guest, Sol!"

"No, no." Solomon laughed. "A real houseguest and a Jew to boot. He turned up this afternoon looking for something kosher to eat, and we asked him to stay. Rachael, she's not up to cooking yet, but I made him the best and biggest kosher meal he'd had in a long time. We're celebrating Sarah's birth, you know," he added, as if to excuse the excess.

Jason grinned at him. He knew that Solomon had been longing for some Jewish company, and he hoped this fellow would stay. He'd certainly perked Sol up, that was for sure!

He said, "Congratulations again, Solomon! Glad you finally have somebody Jewish to talk to. Well, you know what I mean. And you've already named the baby?"

"Yes, we have and I certainly do! And thank you, Jason, my friend."

Jason nodded and grinned.

"She is quiet and calm, and he is a little on the quiet side at first, too. But I think he'll eventually open up and be hearty company!"

"I'm sure he will." Jason pushed the change for the letter across the counter, tipped his hat, and said, "We'll be seeing you, Solomon! I'd best get home and see if Jenny remembered to fix me some supper."

As he turned, Solomon called after him, "If she didn't, you come back here. We have some fine kosher brisket left over, if I say so myself!"

"I'll keep that in mind," Jason replied, turning slightly back to face him, then opening the door. "See you!"

He had walked halfway home before he realized he'd forgotten to ask Solomon what his guest's name was.

Oh, well.

It'd wait till tomorrow.

When he walked in the front door, the first thing Jenny asked about was the Cohens' baby, and Jason dutifully reported. He also reported that they had a houseguest, but couldn't give any more information on the subject.

Jenny had been up to the wagon train, as had Megan, judging by Jenny's pretty new hair bow and Megan's new shoes. He said, "They let out school early today?"

Jenny grinned. "Yeah. Miss Electa Morton let everybody go at two-thirty—"

"—and I closed up the bank at three—"

"—so we went together!" Jenny finished.

"There's still a lot we didn't see," Megan began.

"So we're going back in the morning!" Jenny finished.

Jason clapped his hands over his ears. "You two don't stop doin' that, you're gonna drive me to the asylum!"

Jenny just laughed and slid a plate of beefsteak in front of him. Megan sat across from him, chin planted primly on the backs of her hands, while she grinned.

"Very funny, the both of you," Jason said before he sliced into his steak. It was cooked perfectly: pink and juicy on the inside, slightly charred on the outside. It seemed like everybody else in town liked their beef cooked to the consistency of shoe leather, but not him.

Home was the only place where he could get a steak cooked right!

Ezra had camped early again that night, satisfied that nobody was trailing him.

He'd already settled in his horse, and cooked and eaten his own supper—roasted jackrabbit, fresh biscuits, and canned peaches—and was presently engaged in nothing but watching the stars. He'd once ridden for a while with a man who said the old-time Greeks or Romans or somebody had made up pictures by drawing imaginary lines from star to star, but Ezra never saw the sense of it. How the hell did a bunch of dots of light in the sky look like a horse with wings or a dragon or a pretty woman, anyway?

Still, he liked looking at them. Sometimes, they seemed like the only constant thing in his life.

5

The next morning found Jason and Jenny and Megan all up bright and early, and outside the stockade, taking in the sights of the wagon train. Most of its members were just plain folks, trying to get back to Kansas City, but a few had fancy goods and the like.

One of them, Mrs. Judith Strong, had a wagon packed nearly to the canopy with all kinds of yard goods and an assortment of notions, and she sold both the girls the material to make one new dress each.

While they were jabbering with her, Jason busied himself talking to Riley, the wagon master, and strolling down the line. "Where's Sampson Davis this mornin'?" Jason asked. He hadn't seen the man.

Riley shook his head. "I dunno. Lost him last night. Figured he was stayin' at your hotel or somethin'."

Jason shook his head. "Already been there. And it's a boardinghouse, actually."

"Whatever."

They kept walking.

Riley began, "About that axle and wheel man . . . I wondered if—"

"Ward rode out first thing," Jason said with a smile when he cut Riley off. "Ought to be back early this afternoon. Give him time. It's a ways."

Riley nodded. "No offense."

"None taken," Jason said, and grinned at him. Riley grinned back. "All your folks make it through the storm all right? Except the ones that lost their lids, I mean."

"Two of us didn't make it," Riley said gravely. "Wind took their wagon and rolled it a couple times. They got crushed under the weight of their own belongings."

Jason shook his head. "Shame. They linger?"

"Nope," Riley replied. "Died instantaneous."

Jason nodded. Some things were best when they were over quickly.

Riley didn't speak. He just nodded alongside Jason.

A boy came walking toward them, a boy whose heels were tagged by the goofiest-looking hound dog that Jason had ever seen. Well, he thought it was a hound, anyway, or maybe part hound. He nudged Riley and tipped his head toward it. "What the hell is that?" he asked.

"Up there? That's Bill Crachit.

"I mean, what's that thing followin' him?"

"Oh! That's the Grimms' dog, Hannibal."

Jason sighed. "I mean, what's his breeding?"

Riley laughed. "Oh. Accordin' to Tom Grimm,

Hannibal is half Louisiana Black-mouthed cur, and half Redbone hound. 'Course, you couldn't prove any of it by me."

It was Jason's turn to laugh this time. "No wonder I was confused!"

Riley said, "Join the party, Marshal."

When Bill Crachit and Hannibal neared them, they stopped and Jason said, "Can I see your dog?"

Shyly, Bill said, "Sure, mister."

While Jason bent to the dog—a houndy-headed, droopy-eared beast, colored and ticked like a redbone, but coarser-haired and bushy-tailed—Riley said, "Jason, here, isn't just a 'Mister,' Bill. He's Marshal Fury."

"Sorry, Marshal," said Bill after a gulp. "I-I didn't know."

Jason looked up from the dog, which was happily wagging his tail. "That's all right, Bill," he said. "You just call me Jason. Say, this is a right friendly dog you've got here. Or I guess he's the Grimms' dog, right?"

Bill glanced quickly at Riley, then said, "Yessir, he is."

"Don't believe I've ever seen . . . anything quite like him."

Bill smiled for the first time. "Neither had anybody else on the train. He's a oner, all right." His hand dropped down to scratch the dog's head, and Hannibal complied by leaning his body against the boy's leg and nearly knocking him over.

Jason shot out a hand to steady him: A lucky thing, or he would've been knocked into a wagon. Or maybe under it.

"Thanks," Bill said, once he got his balance back again.

Jason noticed that the dog hadn't moved a muscle, except for his eyelids, which were drifting closed. He decided he could really get to like this dog.

A new fellow, soberly dressed, came walking up from the rear, behind Bill Crachit. He stopped and tipped his head to Riley. "Good morning, Mr. Havens." His hand went to the boy's shoulder. "You, too, young Bill."

Riley nodded, and Bill said, "Mornin', Mr. Bean." Turning to Jason, Riley announced, "This is one of our men of God, Jason. The Reverend Mr. Fletcher Bean. And Fletcher, this is Jason Fury, marshal of Fury."

Jason stuck out his hand and Mr. Bean took it, adding, "God bless you, son."

Not exactly sure what to reply to something like that, Jason simply said, "Uh, thanks." And then he quickly added, "The same to you, Reverend!"

Their little group soon turned into a larger one, with folks walking up and down the line of wagons to introduce themselves. Jason shook hands with over a dozen people, although later, he'd be dogged if he could remember any of their names.

Well, he guessed he wouldn't have to, unless some trouble came up. And right now, it was looking like any trouble would be inside Fury itself.

Giving a last pat to Hannibal, Jason excused himself and started back up to the town's entrance and the sheriff's office. He passed Jenny and Megan, who seemed to be dickering with somebody over something, and waved as he passed.

When he went through the gate, he wondered if he should stop by the mercantile and meet Solomon's company, then decided against it. There would be time for that later, and right now he was thinking that he'd better talk to Rafe Lynch. He had seen neither hide nor hair of Sampsom Davis, and just hoped that he hadn't found Lynch first.

The piano was tinkling out a slow song and there were several girls in evidence, although it wasn't yet nine in the morning when he got to the saloon. To the bartender, Jason said, "Seen Rafe Lynch this mornin'?"

Sam, the barkeep, replied, "Oh, it's way too early for him, Jason. He might wander down around ten or so. Probably later. Got a message you want passed along?"

Jason shook his head, then changed his mind. "Tell him I wanna talk to him. He doesn't need to come to the office, though. I'll come back down here. Oh, and Sam? Anybody else comes lookin' for him, you tell 'em he ain't here."

"Anybody?"

"Anybody."

"Will do," said Sam, and went back to polishing bar glasses.

"I'm telling you, Solomon, I don't like him!" Rachael hissed again, her head under the covers.

"But he's a Jew!" Solomon whispered back. For him, that overrode anything else, despite the fact that Sampson made him a little nervous, too.

"I don't care if he's a rabbi! I want him out of here and away from the children!"

"Shhh!" Solomon hissed. "Do you want he should be hearing you?"

Rachael tempered her tone, then said, "I don't like him. I think he is a bad man. Solomon, try to act like your namesake. Don't be blindly accepting him just because of his race."

Solomon pursed his lips. "Rachael, I don't know how to answer. My head pulls one way, my heart pulls the other."

"Think about it. And while you are doing this thinking, you had best get ready to go down and open the store. The tempus, she is fugiting." She leaned over and brushed his lips with a kiss, then gave him a playful shove.

Solomon rose and stretched his arms, saying, "Women. They are never happy. You go right, she says left. You go up, she says down. You take brisket, she says the corned beef is better. You ask for—"

"Solomon?" she cut in sweetly. "The store?"

Muttering, "Oy," he began to dress for the day.

When he left the bedroom and walked into the open space that comprised the rest of their quarters, all three of the boys and their new baby sister were still soundly sleeping in their beds, but Sampson Davis was nowhere to be seen.

Solomon scowled. Where on earth could he have gone to? And then he slapped himself alongside the head and muttered, "The wagons, of course." Sampson had left something necessary in his wagon, and had gone back for it. Oh, well. Solomon had been looking forward to a morning prayer with him, but it would wait. God was patient.

He pulled off a hunk of brisket, put it between two slices of Rachael's home-made bread, and headed quietly down the stairs, to the mercantile.

Back in his office, Jason went through the files, searching in vain for anything on Sampson Davis. But he'd known he'd find nothing, and he wasn't disappointed. He only had a little information on California criminals—just what the Territorial Marshal's office deemed fit to send him.

Once again, he wished they were on the stage route. Well, he didn't see why they shouldn't be, for they had lodgings and water and a stable for the stage horses. They could sure use the steady influx of folks coming and going, and the steady mail service, too. All of which reminded him that he'd forgotten to check and see if Grady had made it out of town yet.

He poured himself the last cup of coffee and slouched down at his desk. He'd walk up to the mercantile later, but first he needed a sit-down and a drink. Files were tiring things!

He had just taken his second sip of coffee when he happened to glance out the window and see Jenny across the street. She frequently ran errands for Electa Morton and was emerging from Salmon

Kendall's printing shop with a stack of papers in her arms, so he didn't think much about it. Until moments later, that was.

She started toward the jail, walking across the street, when suddenly, Rafe Lynch came vaulting off the sidewalk where she had been and shoved her over, knocking her and her papers to the ground! Before Jason could stand up, a runaway driverless wagon flashed right over the place where his sister had been walking, and Rafe Lynch was helping her to her feet again.

"Jesus," whispered Jason. "Sweet Jesus!" He got to his feet and rushed outside, running to Jenny's side.

But when he got there, she was actually laughing!

He grabbed her by the shoulders and said, "You could have been killed if Rafe hadn't pushed you out of the way! Don't you know to look both ways before you cross a street? Have you lost your senses?" And then he suddenly hugged her to him so tightly that before he knew it, she was struggling and he realized she couldn't breathe.

He loosened his grip and allowed her to push away. When she caught her breath again and finished coughing, she said, "Does this mean that if I don't succeed in killing myself, you'll do it for me?"

He laughed so loudly that one of the Milcher kids opened the church door and peeked out. "Precisely, precisely!" And then he remembered the kitten, probably because of just seeing the Milcher kid. "Jenny, I've got a present for you, but it won't be ready for six or eight weeks," he declared impulsively.

Jenny clapped her hands as best she could with an armload of papers. "What, Jason? What is it?"

He smiled slyly. "I call it Dusty."

"Dusty? What's a 'dusty'?"

"Yeah," said Rafe, who Jason had completely forgotten was there. "What is a 'dusty'?"

Jason stared at him for a moment, and then relaxed back into a smile. The man had just saved his sister's life, after all! He said, "A 'dusty' is the name of something small and white and fluffy and incredibly sweet—just like you, Jenny—that was born just a few nights ago."

Jenny squealed, and Jason noticed that when she did, Rafe made a pained face. That was good. Jenny wasn't paying any attention, though. She cried, "The Milchers! You got one of those new kitties for me, didn't you, Jason?" He nodded, and she added, "Oh, I could just hug you!"

"Best wait until you deliver those papers to Miss Morton!" he joked.

Jenny laughed, as gaily as if she hadn't just been nearly killed. There was a kitten in the picture now, and everything was right with the world. Jason had guessed as much.

"Well, congratulations, Miss Jenny!" exclaimed Rafe. He looked as happy for her as she did for herself.

"Hadn't you best run those papers up to Miss Morton?" Jason asked.

"Oh! Oh, gosh, I almost forgot!" She blinked rapidly, turned to Rafe and said, "Thank you so much! Come to dinner tonight!" Then she fairly ran up the street. Well, as close as a lady could come to running. When she stopped outside the schoolroom door, she paused, turned, and tossed a kiss to Jason, who made a show of catching it and then pressing it to his heart.

He and Rafe stood there a minute, until Jason thought to get out of the street. Davis could be anywhere. He said, "Let's get outta the line of fire."

"Your office or mine?" Rafe asked, and that half-crooked smile was back on his face again.

"Yours, I think," Jason said with no humor. This was no time for jokes.

He saw the runaway team being led back around the corner at the end of town, and shouted, "Everything all right, Jed?"

Jed Dawson hollered back, "Yeah. Your sister okay?"

"Yup. Doing fine!"

Jed crossed himself, then called, "Praise the Lord!"

"Whatever," muttered Jason as they stepped up on the boardwalk and he followed Rafe inside the saloon.

It was a lot more lively than it had been the first time Jason had been in that day, and he tagged after Rafe, who led him to an empty table.

"This'n all right?"

Jason allowed that it was, and the men sat down.

After the libations arrived and both men were comfortable, Jason asked the question.

"Why is Sampson Davis after you?"

Rafe looked him square in the eye and said, "Because I shot his no-account brother-in-law. I only shot him in the shoulder. Wasn't my fault it went septic and he died. And I shot him because he murdered my daddy over some gold shares Daddy had, just outright murdered him in cold blood. At least I had the gumption to call him out into the street to answer for it in a fair fight! So now I got Sampson Davis doggin' me everywhere I go. The whole damn family should'a stayed back East."

Rafe took a long drink of his beer, as if the telling out of his story had exhausted him. Jason, surprised but finally educated, followed suit.

Frankly, it wasn't what Jason would call a murder. He wondered if it was one of the ones listed on Rafe's poster, and he asked him.

"Yeah," came the answer. "California's real nit-picky about that stuff. You want another beer?"

Jason looked down at his glass, which he had emptied, much to his surprise. "Yeah," he said.

Rafe looked over at the bar, somehow caught Sam's attention, and held up two fingers. Sam nodded, and before they knew it, a blond girl in a fancy green silk dress was sliding the drinks onto the table.

Jason started to dig into his pocket, but Rafe stopped him. "It's on me. My office, after all." He smiled, full faced this time. "By the by, in case you're wonderin', my name's spelt R-a-l-p-h. My mamma was from England and Daddy was from Ireland, and Rafe is how they pronounce it over there. Don't ask me why," he added with a wave of his hand. "I got no idea."

Jason thought back to what he knew about England, and said, "Yeah, those English got their ways about 'em. They call B-e-l-v-o-i-r 'Beaver'—that's a castle I read about once—and Grosvenor 'Gruvner.'" Bemused, he shook his head and took another drink of beer.

"And Cholmondeley, they call 'Chumly.'" Rafe laughed, and then Jason, after swallowing his gulp of beer, joined in.

He had a feeling that everything was going to be all right. For the moment, anyhow.

6

That afternoon, after a scanty lunch consisting of bread and water, Reverend Milcher sat upstairs at his desk (which, by some miracle, had managed to escape the flames several years back), lost in thought.

He had to figure out what to do to bring the people in, to bring them to God! Didn't they know that their mortal souls depended on it? Hadn't he preached enough fire and brimstone on the journey from Kansas City out to their current residence in the wilderness of Fury?

He put his head in his hands and prayed, once again, for guidance. Nothing came of it, however, and he dropped his chin to his chest and sighed deeply. He became aware of a deep, soft, rumbling sound, and realized it was the cat—Louise was her name, he thought—nursing her kittens in a box beneath his desk. His initial anger quickly fled, though, once he saw her and the pile of gray, tabby, and white that was the kittens.

It struck him that she was caring for her brood

in the same manner that he had promised the Lord he would look after His people. There was joy in her heart just to have them near her, and joy in their hearts that she was close, so warm and comforting. And it occurred to him that he needed to minister to his flock's needs and wants like a mother cat.

"I need to be more mannalike and less lecturing," he muttered. "More comfort and fewer claws. My message needs less barbs, and perhaps my demeanor could be softer, as well."

Just then, there came an enormous clap of thunder that nearly startled him from his seat. As it was, he fell to his knees and clasped his hands before him. "Is that You, great and holy God? Have You given me a sign?" he asked with trembling lips.

The "answer" came in a second, distant clap of thunder. It was not as loud or as jarring as the first, but it was enough for him. He lay prostrate on the floor, arms outstretched, his face in the rag rug, muttering, "Thank You, Lord, thank You. Praise be to Your name . . ."

He would be softer, he vowed, more kindly and less prickly. He would be a friend to his parishioners, not a judge.

Up north, Ward Wanamaker and Milton Griggs, Fury's blacksmith, were nearly back to town. Ward had ridden north at dawn and arrived at the Morton place at around noon, his horse having thrown a shoe on the way up there. Milton fixed it for him, and was thrilled to hear that he was needed in town.

He was still babbling excitedly when Ward first spied the town stockade in the distance.

Ward hadn't much been listening, though. He'd been thinking about Jason, down there with those two gunfighters. Down there, all alone. And Ward had come to a conclusion. They needed at least one more man, one more man that was good with a gun and wasn't afraid of nothin'.

They needed old Wash Keogh, that was who they needed.

Ward turned in his saddle, slightly. "Milt, you go on in, straight to the marshal's office and check in with Jason. He'll get you pointed in the right direction."

"Sure," said Milt, with a nod. "What about you?"

"Tell Jason I'm goin' to fetch Wash Keogh."

Milton, who'd actually been listening to Ward while he was telling the story about the gunfighters and the wagon train and the storm, nodded his understanding. "He down southeast?"

"Right, workin' a claim. Tell Jason I'll be back."

Before Milton had a chance to answer him, Ward tore off at a fast lope toward the eastern corner of the walled town. Before Milt went much farther, Ward had disappeared around it, and all that was left to show his passage was a small cloud of dust rising up over the stockade wall.

After the corral was finished, Matt MacDonald sent all the hands out (save two, who were still painting the fence) to round up every last head of his cattle and get them started home. He actually felt a little better, knowing he'd soon be able to see, all at once, his entire herd. And Cookie's good lunch hadn't hurt his mood, either.

By five, they started to come in. He stood out on the porch and watched them wander down the hill. They were heavy with calf, most of them, and he'd told the men not to rush them too much. He didn't want a pen full of aborting cows.

When at last the final cow had been ushered into the large corral and the gate closed behind her, he noted that only one cow was missing—not two, as he had previously thought. But one was enough to make him want to call in the cavalry. However, the cavalry had seemed loathe to respond to him in the past. He could see no reason to expect any more action now.

Curly rode up to the house from the corral, and said, "That's all we could dig up, boss."

Matt nodded. "Tell the boys they did a good job, Curly. And break out a round of whiskey for 'em. They deserve it."

Curly nodded. "Yessir, boss. The men'll sure 'preciate that."

Matt's eyes weren't on him, though. He stared past Curly, toward the southern hills. His forehead furrowed.

Curly asked, "Boss? What is it, boss?"

Matt raised his arm, finger pointed to the horizon. "Do you see what I see?" His voice trembled slightly, which he hoped went unnoticed by Curly.

"Kinda hard to see much in this light, boss."

"There! There, man, look!" What Matt saw on the distant horizon was smoke. Or dust. He couldn't say which, but it couldn't be good. "Apache, man, Apache!" he shouted, jumping down off the porch and running like sixty for the barn to get his horse.

Curly stood there, shaking his head. Sometimes he just plain thought the boss had lost his mind. First off, he figured that everybody—including old ladies and dogs—knew that Apache didn't attack at night. By the looks of that dust in the distance, it'd take whatever was making it three, maybe four, hours to get this far. He'd never in his life heard of an Apache attack commencing at ten in the evening! It was most likely just a bunch of dust devils again.

But by then, the boss was already galloping past him on the way to town, whipping his horse like crazy. If he were that horse, Curly thought, he'd dump Mr. Matthew MacDonald in the nearest patch of cactus, and then trot on back home.

Back up in town, Jason was just sitting down to dinner, along with the girls and Rafe Lynch. He'd had Lynch come up around the back of the sheriff's office and they'd taken the back way home— out of the sight of prying eyes, he hoped.

But the girls were thrilled!

Jenny had made a pot roast for the occasion, complete with what he remembered his mother using: cut-up potatoes, carrots, and onions. She'd gone all out and baked biscuits, too, and they were so light that he nearly had to stab his fork through them to keep them from floating to the ceiling! A plate of fresh-churned butter and jars of mesquite honey and her cactus jelly completed the feast, and they all made good and satisfying use of it.

At last, Rafe leaned back from the table. "Miss Jenny, that roast was so good and tender and flavorful, it nearly wore me out! And the potatoes and onions? Lord have mercy! I ain't et this good in a coon's age!"

And Jenny replied as she had to most of Rafe's comments during the meal: She flushed right up to her hairline, stifled a giggle, and stared at her lap. *Oh, she is sure as shootin' gone on Rafe,* Jason thought, and not for the first time.

Oddly, the idea didn't bother him as much as he'd thought it would. He, himself, was growing to like the man more and more, and after hearing Rafe's explanation of the Sampson Davis matter— and another, different slaying on the way home— he was beginning to see Rafe as a victim of circumstance. Rafe's rescue of Jenny earlier that day hadn't hurt, either. Jason was enough of a lawman, though, to avoid going with the idea completely.

But he didn't have time to give it further thought, because just then somebody started in pounding on the front door, and it wasn't Ward this time. Or at least, he was fairly certain it wasn't.

He ripped the napkin from his collar and, cursing under his breath, marched toward the front door. He could hear the voices growing louder as he neared it, and when he threw it open, the clamor had him throwing his hands over his ears.

He looked at the dozen or so people gathered—and arguing—in his front yard, and shouted, "Shut up!"

The mob, with heads pulled back and eyes blinking, quieted immediately. That was, until Salmon Kendall spoke up. "We want you to do something about Matt MacDonald!" he snapped, then crossed his arms over his chest as if that was the answer to everything that was wrong with the world.

He wasn't far from the truth, Jason thought, but he wearily said, "What's he done *this* time?"

Hattie Furling, one of their latest additions, piped up, "He's runnin' up and down Main Street screamin' 'Indians! Apache!' and 'Come out, you cowards!'"

Salmon cut in, "Gus Furling went up on the stockade and said he couldn't see a thing!"

Hattie nodded vehemently in agreement.

"That's right," said Dr. Morelli, with his dinner napkin still tucked into his collar. "Nothing. I went up myself and checked."

"Where was Ward during all this?" Jason asked.

"Nobody knows," replied Salmon. "We can't find him."

He was likely still out looking for Wash, or up at Abigail Krimp's, Jason thought, taking care of her card-cheating problem. He said, "All right. Lemme tell Jenny where I'm headed."

* * *

After hearing a very shortened version of Matthew MacDonald and what he currently believed to be his "problem," Rafe insisted on accompanying Jason on his short jaunt to town. Jason had mixed feelings about this, but with Megan's brother being the cause of the ruckus and a front yard full of townsfolk about to equip themselves with weaponry, he didn't have the time or the energy to pull Rafe aside and explain things. He just went, and Rafe tagged along.

After they turned the corner and headed down toward Main—now followed by twenty or so irate citizens—Jason turned his head and said, "Salmon, run down to the office and see if Ward's turned up yet. If he hasn't, you're in charge till I tell you different. I'm gonna check Abigail's."

He didn't look back. He trusted Salmon. Instead, he forged ahead to Abigail's place, turned the corner, and swung wide the doors. Rafe entered right behind him.

Abby turned round at the sound of their entry, and said, "Good evening, Jason, Rafe. You two decide to go slummin'?"

Jason stepped to the fore. "No, Abby, no. We were just searching for Matt MacDonald, that's all."

"Well, the sonofabitch ain't in here, that's for sure." She flipped a glance toward the three men at the poker table.

Politely, Jason muttered, "Yes, ma'am," grabbed Rafe by his other arm, and exited Abby's. "C'mon," he said to Rafe once they were outside. "We've gotta find Matt before somebody kills him just for bein' a jackass."

"Just on general principle, you mean?"

"You been hangin' around me too much."

Rafe grinned. "Mebbe so."

And then, quite suddenly, the crowd behind them quieted. From clear down at the other end of the street, they saw Matthew MacDonald backing out of the saloon, and yelling, "Bunch'a lily-livered cowards, that's what you are! I thought Fury had some real men livin' in her!"

"I think that'll about do it," said Jason, and began marching down the center of the street with Rafe following along, aping his speed as well as the disgusted expression on his face. Halfway down the street and mid-stride, Jason called out, "MacDonald! Matt MacDonald! Hold it down!"

Matt stopped, turned, and looked, and hollered up the street, "Well, if it isn't Marshal Chicken-shit and Deputy Dog Turd!" He hadn't recognized Rafe, and Jason had the sense to leave well enough alone.

They had kept walking toward Matt during his tirade, and were quite a bit closer now. "You wanna go to jail for disturbin' the peace, keep on hollerin'," Jason said, just loud enough to be heard. He stopped walking and so did Rafe.

Matt's mouth snapped shut with an audible click.

"Well, then," Jason began, "now that we've got everybody calmed down, what seems to be your problem, Matthew?"

"What's always my problem?" Matt snarled. "I've got trouble out at the ranch and nobody'll help!"

Jason closed his eyes for a minute, then said, "What trouble? Apache?"

"Yes!" Matt shouted. "I can't get it through anybody's head! By now, they're probably swarmin' the ranch, killin' off all my hands, makin' off with all my livestock, and nobody gives a good goddamn!"

He put his head in his hands, and suddenly both Megan and Jenny, whom Jason hadn't realized had joined the following crowd, ran past him and to Matt's side. He couldn't make out what they were saying, but both girls were talking to Matt in whispers, soothing him. Then Jenny looked up and straight at Jason.

"Jason, you go out there," she said. "Don't go as the marshal. Go as my brother."

"But, Jenny . . ." he began.

"Don't you 'but, Jenny' me! Just go! Now!"

He'd been about to tell her that Apache didn't raid at night, but he could see that right now she wasn't going to hear anything he had to say. He was stuck. "All right," he said grudgingly. "But I hope you'll feel stupid when we don't turn up anything!"

"And you'd best save us some dessert!" Rafe added, grinning.

"You're going?" Jason asked, amazed.

Rafe shrugged. "Gotta work off some'a that good dinner 'fore I treat myself to any more of these ladies' vittles."

Jason shrugged. "Your funeral."

When he glanced over and saw Salmon Kendall leaning out of the marshal's office's front door, he said, "Salmon, you stay here and watch over the town." He turned back toward the stable. Then he stopped, looked back over his shoulder and said, "Move it, Matt!" when he saw that a stunned MacDonald was just standing there. However, the call woke Matt from his trance, and he dogtrotted to catch up with them.

They got Jason's palomino and Rafe's bay tacked up and ready, and set out, with Matt leading, toward the south and the Double M ranch.

Jason felt like a fool. He didn't know what Rafe was thinking (and told himself he didn't care), but he considered himself a Class-A Idiot for humoring Matt, especially during the evening, and especially during his dinner!

Women. If it hadn't been for Jenny and Megan, he would've just shot Matt and gone home. No, he wouldn't. He'd probably be riding out here anyway, if to do nothing but shut Matthew up.

And so here he was, loping south, thinking foul thoughts about MacDonald. He gave his head a shake, and rode on.

7

They came in sight of the ranch, and Matt almost looked disappointed when it sat quietly on its site, with a big new corral filled with livestock, and Curly standing outside against the ranch-house porch railing, smoking a cigarette.

"Quiet sort'a raid, ain't it?" Jason heard Rafe mutter.

"The kind ol' Matt usually gets out here."

"Now, just a minute, Fury!" Matt barked. "They might not be here yet, but they're coming! There were signs, I tell you, signs!"

"Think we oughta go down and look, just in case?" Rafe asked around the cigarette he was lighting. "Gotta start coolin' these horses down, one way or the other." He was right. The horses were lathered and blowing, a fact abetted by Matt's having pushed them into an all-out gallop once they got clear of town.

"I suppose," Jason admitted, and started his horse walking toward the ranch.

"Finally!" Matt muttered, just loudly enough that

both Jason and Rafe heard him, and exchanged glances. Apparently, a walk was too slow for Matt, and he kicked his gelding into a canter.

Jason shrugged. He and Rafe held it down to a walk.

Matt reached the porch ahead of them, and immediately started hollering at Curly. He kept it up until Jason and Rafe were within three lengths of them, and then Rafe did the unthinkable.

Quicker than lightning, he pulled his sidearm and fired. It nearly scared Jason to death and he was about to draw on Rafe when he realized that nobody was dead or even injured.

Except for a fat, six-foot sidewinder, thrashing its last in the dust three feet from Matt's right boot.

"Hate them damn things," Rafe said by way of explanation. "Sorry if I scared anybody, but by the time I saw it comin' into the lantern light . . ." He shrugged.

"Thanks, Rafe," Jason said, and his words were echoed by Curly and a grudging Matt. The snake, in its death throes, lashed Matt's leg, and he vaulted up on the porch.

While Jason stifled a grin, he heard Rafe say, "You gotta watch them suckers. They'll keep thrashin' around for a hour, sometimes, even if you shoot the head clean off."

Jason leaned forward and squinted through the dim light at the snake. "Believe you shot the head clean off that one, Rafe. Good goin'."

"Try to do what I can," Rafe said, and swung

down off his horse. Jason followed suit, and hid his chuckle behind his saddle.

"You got somebody to walk these horses out, Matt?" Jason asked. He'd be damned if he'd ridden clear out here on some fool's errand only to end up with a colicky horse for his trouble. And come to think of it . . . "I think we could all use a drink, too."

"Best idea I heard all night," said Rafe. And after he roared, "Get a hot walker up here, now!" down toward the barn, he added, "Y'know, I believe I could use a couple'a whiskeys, too. I'm pretty dadgum parched! Chasin' ghost Apache wears me out. Don't it wear you right down to a nub, Matt?"

He handed his reins to Curly, climbed up on the porch, and put his hand on Matt's arm, like Matt was his new best friend. "I heard rumors in town that you're purty well-stocked out here, Matt. Hope they were right!" And he proceeded to lead a confused Matt inside the house.

Jason and Curly just looked at each other until Curly shrugged and took Jason's reins from him. "Man wants a hot walker, he gets a hot walker. Steve!" he shouted toward the barn. "Come up here and get these horses!"

To Jason, he said, "Have one for me while you're in there. Y'know, I don't believe I'm ever gonna understand him so long as I live."

Careful to avoid the dead snake, Jason stepped up on the porch. "You're in good company, Curly," he said, then turned and followed Rafe and Matthew into the house.

* * *

Two hours later, a drunken Rafe and an only slightly more sober Jason threw wide the door to Matt's house, and stepped out on the porch (or, as Matthew liked to call it, his veranda) and took a couple of good, deep breaths of the night-chilled desert air. Jason came away from the experience still thinking that Matt was an asshole of the first order. He didn't know what Rafe thought. He was one tough fellow to read.

Their horses had been properly walked out, then watered, and stood tied to the porch railing, dozing. Rafe said, "Let's walk or jog 'em back, all right?"

"Good idea."

They both checked their girth straps and their bridles, and mounted up, while Jason puzzled over what had just happened. And then, out of nowhere, Rafe said, "He's sure one peckerwood box'a tricks, ain't he?"

Jason laughed out loud. "That he is," he said when he could. "That he is. Just never heard it put quite that way before. The only reason we didn't get a bigger crowd at the house was that everybody else owes him money."

"Oh, yeah. He owns the bank, don't he?"

"Yup."

"And his sister, Miss Megan?"

"She runs it for him. Does a damn good job of it, too!" Jason was proud of Megan, and sniffed at people who thought women should stay out of business. He knew that Matt sure couldn't do the job!

Rafe nodded. "I think she told me that. Strange job for a female, but if you're good at somethin', you ought'a do it, I figure." He rolled himself a cigarette as they rode along, which put Jason in the mood. He pulled out his fixings bag, too.

When they were both smoking, Jason asked, "Rafe, how'd you get started on your so-called life'a crime, anyhow?"

Rafe shrugged. "That thing with my daddy, I reckon. That was the first. And once there was paper out on me, it seemed like there was some dumb cluck hidin' behind every tree tryin' to kill me for the bounty. Didn't seem fair, somehow." And then he paused for a half second. "Shit. My smoke went out."

As he dug into his pocket for a new match, he said, "After I killed a couple of bounty-happy kids in self-defense, I got to thinkin' what I just told you. Y'know, if you're good at somethin', do it. So I hired myself out to a rancher who was havin' troubles with cattle thieves." He stopped again, to light his cigarette.

"What happened?" Jason asked him.

"The trouble with the rustlers stopped. They don't get put on wanted posters, y'know, unless they're on 'em already. I mean, unless they get tagged for doin' some other crime. My boys were fairly new to the trade, I reckon. That, or fairly good at not gettin' caught."

"How many?"

"Three. Killed the bossman and his ramrod, sai

down with the kid helpin' 'em and threatened to castrate him if I ever caught him thievin' cattle again." Rafe smiled. "He agreed, and I let him go. You ain't never seen such a quick exit in your life as that kid made!" He broke out into laughter again, just picturing it.

Jason smiled, his head shaking. If he'd been that kid, he would have beat it, too!

The rest of the ride into town proved uneventful, except that by the time they came in sight of Fury, they had both sobered up to a large extent. Several of the people who'd been at the house came up while Rafe was putting his gelding away, asking if there'd been any Apache, and all received the same answer.

When Rafe had seen to his horse, he walked along back to Jason's house, where Jason put his palomino up alongside Jenny's.

"*Two* palominos?" Rafe asked, surprised.

Jason shrugged. "Well, Jenny needed a horse, and she'd always admired Cleo, so . . . I thought I'd keep it in the family, y'know?"

"So, what Jenny wants, Jenny gets, right?"

Jason nodded and laughed. "That's about right. Now, if we don't get up there and demand dessert pretty damn fast, there's gonna be hell to pay. At least for me. You get to run off and hole up down at the saloon, but I have to live here!"

They found the girls in the living room, playing checkers.

"Well, it's about time!" Jenny said before Jason had time to open his mouth.

Megan looked up. "No Indians?"

Jason said, "Nope," and she looked satisfied when he did. He continued, "Jenny, we're here for some of your world-famous dessert!"

"You're lucky I didn't toss it out," she said as she stood up.

"Miss Jenny," Rafe interjected, "seems to me that you got a lot of attitude for somebody who made her brother ride out there on some fool's errand. Jason, if I was you, I think a visit to the woodshed would be in order."

Well, that shut Jenny up! Not only did she not utter a word while serving them dessert, but she gave them extra-large portions of what turned out to be apple crumb cake. Jason reminded himself to buy even more dried apples come fall. She worked magic with them!

However, Megan made up for Jenny's silence by asking questions. She particularly enjoyed the part about Rafe shooting the snake and her brother vaulting the three steps up to the porch. In fact, she laughed until tears were rolling down her cheeks, and Jason, caught up in her infectious laughter, was roaring, too.

"Hell!" marveled Rafe. "Didn't think it was *that* funny."

"Oh, you would if you knew Matt," Megan managed to blurt out.

She wiped at her eyes, then fell back into laughter.

Jenny spoke for the first time since Rafe had embarrassed her. "I think you're all too hard on him," she scolded. "He's just trying to protect what's his, that's all. And you, Megan! You're his sister! I'd be ashamed if I were you."

Rafe's mouth quirked up as he listened. He said, "I think it's healthy for at least one person in a family to have a sense'a humor. That was sure a fine dessert, Miss Jenny. Hope you'll invite me again sometime." He wiped the last traces of apple crumb cake from his mouth, then smoothed his napkin out on the table.

He pushed back his chair, but before he could get all the way up, Jason said, "Coffee, Rafe?"

Jenny glared daggers at him.

But Rafe said, "I thank you for the offer, Jason, but I'd best be gettin' back to my no-good ways, which means playin' cards and drinkin' up to the saloon." Both men had taken off their hats when they entered the house, and now Rafe took his from the hat rack, swept the hand holding his hat wide and to the side, and said, "Ladies, Marshal, it's been a pleasure."

Jason called after him, "Best take the back way, Rafe. And tell Salmon that everything's all right out at the Double M."

Rafe's reply was another bow, then a swing of his hat to the top of his head, with a tip of the brim to the ladies.

Jason closed the door behind him and went back to the kitchen. Slouching in his chair, he said, "What's wrong with you tonight, Jen?"

"Me?! What's wrong with *me*?" she fairly snarled at him.

He could only stare at her, blinking.

"You're the one who wanted to kill him just a few days ago. You're the one who was all het up just because Megan and I just talked to him at Abigail's! You're the one who—"

Jason held up his hands, palms toward her. "If you're gonna get up a lynch mob, just do it and quit jabberin' at me. I'm the marshal, you know, and I had a right to be concerned about that little meeting, not only as a lawman, but as your brother. And I didn't want to kill him so much as I just wanted him out of my town. We still don't know what element he'll attract, though we've got one gunslinger after him already."

Jenny just stood there with her arms folded, practically the definition, Jason thought, of the word "resolute."

"It's why I told him to take the back way to the saloon."

Jenny still didn't speak. He glanced at Megan, who was fiddling with her coffee cup (just to keep out of it, he figured) and didn't look up.

Jason shoved back his chair and stood up. "I'll take my leave of you ladies, then. Good night." He turned on his heel and without another word, headed for his bedroom.

Solomon came up the stairs, having closed the store and locked the doors for the night. "Did you hear what Jason did, Rachael?" he asked when his head came level with the second floor. "Oy, this is rich!"

He heard her quietly say, "Hush, Solomon. You'll

wake the children." His two oldest boys were still awake, noses buried in the dime novels he'd gotten for them yesterday. But the youngest boy and, of course, baby Sarah were sleeping soundly. And so, it seemed, was Sampson Davis. He half-sat, half-lay on Solomon's favorite chair, his head on his barrel chest, black hair hanging in his eyes, roweled spurs digging angled holes into Solomon's ottoman.

"This, I will not have!" Solomon said under his breath, and continued his climb up the staircase. But by the time he reached the landing, his hospitable sense was taking over. Perhaps this was how they behaved in Sampson's family. Maybe they all went to sleep in chairs and put their boots up on the furniture, with their spurs on, no less!

He greeted Rachael and the boys before he did anything else. He dutifully admired Abraham's school project—a catapult—and helped David with a mathematics problem. And then he turned toward Sampson.

And discovered that Sampson was not only awake, but on his feet and standing in the kitchen.

Solomon started. "My goodness, Sampson! You scared me to death!"

The faintest hint of a smile showed briefly on Sampson's face, then vanished. "What's the time?" he asked, although he was standing right next to the clock.

Solomon scowled, then said, "Eight-thirty. Why?"

The big man said, "I have an errand to run. Can I get a key to the store so's I can let myself back in?"

The scowl was still on Solomon's face. Who had errands to run at eight-thirty of an evening? And give him a key to the store? There were so many things wrong with that idea that Solomon couldn't even begin to list them! But, despite a sidelong glance from Rachael, he dug into his pocket and pulled out the key. He handed it over, saying, "Be certain the door is locked after you go through it." He forced a smile.

Sampson tossed the key into the air, then grabbed it again, sticking it into his breast pocket. "Will do," he said.

And then, without further ado, he started down the same stairs that Solomon had just climbed up.

Solomon and Rachael just stood there, watching him disappear down the staircase. And when they finally heard the click of the door unlocking, the jingling of the bells, and then the thud and click again as the door was closed and relocked, "Get him out!" Rachael hissed. "Solomon, I am your wife! Does that mean nothing to you?"

"What? You're not making sense!"

"When you are not here, he orders me around like I am his wife, or his maid. It's always, 'Make me a sandwich,' or 'Don't you have any knishes?' or 'Give me the beef brisket.' Do I look like a short-order cook to you, my husband? And when he is not eating, he is asking all sorts of funny questions about the town and the people. I am telling you, Solomon, this man has none of my trust!"

But Solomon was stuck back on her previous sentence. "What sort of questions?"

"I don't know. Just odd questions. He asked where people in town rent rooms, and that one,

I was glad to hear because I thought he was thinking about moving out. But then he asked about the saloons and where they were, and if I'd ever heard of somebody or other . . . Rafe something. I can't remember. And then he wanted knishes and I said we didn't have any right now, and he says, 'What kind of household is this, anyway?' and I said the kind that doesn't make knishes at the drop of a hat. And he cleans his guns all the time. Around the children! This afternoon I caught him about to hand a loaded pistol to David!"

"Stop already," Solomon said, holding up his hands. "I get the picture." He did, too. He thought this was something he should talk to Jason about, and as soon as possible.

He glanced at the clock. Almost nine. Salmon Kendall had dropped by earlier and told him about Jason riding out to the MacDonald ranch. With somebody called Rafe Lynch. He had agreed with Salmon that there probably weren't any Apache (other than those in Matthew's mind), but when he'd asked who Rafe Lynch was—thinking Salmon would say he was just someone from the wagon train—Salmon surprised him. He said he was sworn to secrecy, and couldn't say any more, but that Solomon could ask the marshal for himself.

And then he paid for his purchases and left. Rather hurriedly, as Solomon recalled.

He wondered if Jason was back yet. And then he wondered if it was too late to go knocking on the marshal's door.

"Solomon?" Rachael was staring at him curiously, but with concern, too.

"Don't worry, Rachael," he soothed. "I need to go out, too, to go to Jason's house. If Sampson gets back before me, do not tell him where I've gone, all right?"

She nodded.

"And I promise you, he'll be gone very soon, our houseguest."

He kissed her lips, and then trotted down the stairs to fetch his extra key from the cash register.

Jason had just blown out his lamp and was in the process of getting his pillow just right, when the knock came on the front door. He decided he'd made it up and punched his pillow again when a second knock sounded. Followed by, "Jason! Jason, are you still up? It's important!"

He knew the voice right away and went to his window, which overlooked the front yard. "Sol? Solomon, that you?"

"Yes, it's me, already, and I have something important to tell you!" There came the sound of feet scuffling through dusty grit and gravel, and then Solomon's shape appeared. He didn't waste any time. He came right to the window Jason was leaning out of and rapidly told Jason of his conversation with Rachael.

"I'm worried," he said. "What sort of man have I given shelter in my home?"

"The worst kind," Jason replied, mentally kicking himself for not having earlier asked the name of the Cohens' houseguest. "You'd best get him out of there, first thing tomorrow. Send him down to the boardinghouse or somethin'."

"But how—"

"Make up some excuse or other. Tell him Rachael or one of the kids is sick."

"But—"

"And don't give me any of that crud about lying being a sin. God'll forgive you on this one, trust me. Did you say he went out tonight?"

"Yes, and he has a key to the store!"

"That's the least of your troubles. Now go on home and act like everything's normal, just fine. Okay? And for God's sake, don't mention the name 'Rafe Lynch' around him. He's here to kill him."

Solomon put his hands to his throat. *"Mein Gött!"*

"Yeah, what you just said. Now get going. I gotta put some clothes back on and get up to the office!"

Solomon backed away into the darkness and Jason plopped back onto the bed and rolled over until he was next to the lamp. He felt for—and found—a match, lit the lamp, then stood up and scrambled into some clothes.

He had to find Rafe before Sampson Davis did.

8

Jason, hurriedly dressed, left the house and took the back way—which was rapidly becoming an alley—over to the marshal's office, and burst through the back door. "Salmon!" he called, "Salmon, we've gotta keep Sampson Davis from findin'—"

He burst through the second door. And found Mayor Kendall sitting at his desk with his legs up, and across from him, calmly smoking a cigarette, sat Rafe Lynch, slouched in a chair.

"Rafe Lynch," Jason finished lamely.

"Sampson Davis on the hunt for him?" asked Salmon Kendall, much too calmly.

Jason nodded. "Actively."

Salmon stretched his arms. "Yeah, we saw him walk past the window 'bout a half hour ago. Went into the saloon."

"Probably still in there, givin' those fellas a hard time," Rafe added.

Salmon nodded. "Probably. If he gives 'em as

hard a time as Matthew did, he's liable to find himself tarred and feathered."

Rafe broke out in a laugh.

Jason scratched at his chin, thinking. Finally, he said, "I got an idea—for tonight, anyway—but I doubt you're gonna like it too much, Rafe."

Both Rafe and Salmon, who seemed to have taken quite a liking to Rafe, waited with heads tilted and curious expressions.

Jason forged ahead. "Rafe, tonight I talked to Solomon Cohen. He tells me that Davis may be closer than we thought to bushwhacking you. I think you ought'a spend the night right here, in the jail." Leaning back against the wall, he folded his arms, prepared for the verbal onslaught he was about to take.

But much to his surprise, Rafe said, "You got yourself a smart marshal there, Mayor."

Salmon nodded. "Good idea, Jason."

Well, either he'd gone crazy or everybody else had. He'd expected a pitched fit from Rafe and some solid objections from Salmon, but not this. Well, praise the Lord for like minds finally thinking alike! He said, "Salmon, you can go on home, now. I'll hold the fort tonight."

"Where's Ward, anyway? You didn't say."

"Oh, he got this harebrained idea that the only thing that was gonna save the town was ol' Wash Keogh. Rode out to his claim to find him."

Salmon nodded while he pulled his long legs down off Jason's desk. "Well, I wish he'd hurry and dig him up. Or else come on back alone. Feel better when you got someone to back you up."

Jason almost said he did, almost indicated Rafe, but stopped himself just in time. Despite all the evidence so far to the contrary, he still couldn't bring himself to trust Rafe all the way, still couldn't admit to liking the man. It was odd, because Rafe had done nothing in town that he could even vaguely suspect as being illegal. He was funny and bright, and agreed with Jason about Matt Mac-Donald, which, especially, went a long way in his favor. But still, he couldn't bring himself to pardon Rafe for all those killings. The taking of any human life was too great a thing, too important, to take lightly, or worse, ignore. Especially for a lawman, which was what Jason, despite all his protests and attempts to the contrary, was becoming.

"Don't worry, Salmon," he said, standing. As he walked Salmon to the door, he said, "I'll be fine. Don't give it a second thought."

"How about a third thought? I'm thinking this will make a great story for the weekly!" Salmon said, referring to the *Fury Titan*, the scrawny excuse for a newspaper that he put out once a week.

"Maybe," said Jason, shaking his head. "We'll have to wait till the end of the week to see what happens."

Behind them, from his chair, Rafe said, "Hope the story don't end in my obituary."

"Yeah, sure," Jason scoffed as he closed the door behind Salmon. "As if anything is gonna happen in Fury, of all places!" Actually, it was the perfect place for trouble, but he wasn't going to let Rafe know that. And he especially wasn't going to let it slip to Sampson Davis!

"Sure, you say that now," mused Rafe. "Way I see it, a town called Fury is just askin' for whatever trouble it can suck in. Benevolent: now that's a name for a town. Or Peaceful. Like that." And then, after a pause, he said, "Don't be lookin' at me like I'm full'a sheep dip, Jason. I'm older'n you. I've been places and seen things."

Unaware that he was making any expression at all, Jason said, "Like what, for example?"

"I been to war, for one thing. You were probably too young. I fought for the North. A Johnny Blue-Coat, that was me. I seen men dyin' right and left, seen 'em cut up by butcherin' sawbones, seen 'em left to die when even the sawbones wouldn't carve 'em up. Seen the look on the faces of the defeated, seen 'em rounded up like cattle, seen 'em all dressed in rags with those hollow eyes and missin' arms and legs or an eye, sometimes all three. Weren't pretty."

Jason wanted to say that his older brother had been in the fight, too, but that wasn't like saying you'd been there yourself. He took the wiser path and kept his mouth shut.

Rafe asked, "You want I should keep goin', or you got my point?"

Jason shook his head. "I got the point. But don't see what that has to do with the names of towns."

Rafe just shook his head, then stood up. "Let's see. Cell number one or cell number two?" He looked back at Jason, who shrugged.

"Cell number one, then," Rafe said, and swung open the door. "And without further goin' on, I bid you good night, Jason." He walked as far in as the bunk, then turned round. "Say, you got any whiskey in the place?"

Jason, who was sitting behind his desk by this time, pulled open a bottom drawer and lifted out a bottle of whiskey and two glasses.

"Jason Fury, you are my savior," Rafe said, and took no extra time getting back across the room and sitting down opposite Jason. He took the glass Jason had poured out for him, and took a slug of it before he said, "Now, if you had a deck of cards hangin' around, my life would be complete."

Grinning, Jason reached into the same drawer and pulled out a deck of playing cards, bound up in one of Ward's broken shoestrings. "Play for matches?" he asked as he untied the deck and began to shuffle.

"Hell, at this point I'd play for imaginary penguins!"

Jason laughed, then began to deal. "Five card draw okay by you?"

"Perfect," said Rafe.

Southeast of town, in the starlit dark of the desert foothills, Ward Wanamaker was camped near a stand of prickly pear cactus.

After giving up for the day, he had made a small fire, cooked himself a rabbit, and now he drank the coffee he'd been brewing. He only had tomorrow left to look, because he was about to run out of water, even with rationing.

Where in the hell could Wash be? He'd looked everywhere he could think of, and a few other places, too, but no Wash. He'd found his campsite—recently used but completely vacant—and came to the conclusion that either he'd moved, or he'd gone back to town. He was beginning to think he'd gone back to town, because he sure as hell wasn't here. He'd followed the various tracks and trails Wash had made through the brush, and some of them led pretty damned far, too. But in the end, they always ended up back at the now-deserted campsite.

Over his coffee, he suddenly shouted, "Blast your hide, Wash Keogh! Where'd you get to, anyway?"

And then, in the distance, came a thin cry. "I'm right here, you blamed idiot!"

Ward stood up, spilling his coffee. He looked out onto the dark distance and called, "Wash! Wash Keogh! That you?"

"Well, it ain't U. S. Grant, that's for blamed sure." The call came from closer by, this time. "You got coffee?"

"Yeah!" Ward answered excitedly. It was Wash. Wash was coming, and now they could go back to the relative safety of Fury. "Yeah, I do! Got a bite of rabbit left, too!"

"Well, you don't need to shout, Ward," came Wash's voice, surprisingly close.

Ward whirled to his left, his hand automatically going to his gun. But it never even left the holster, for into the firelight stepped Wash Keogh, himself, leading his horse and looking beat to a dried-out husk. He said, "You promised coffee."

"Sure, Wash, sure!" Ward scrambled to pour him out a cup, which Wash took with trembling hands.

He finished the first cup, then a second, then a third, before he thought of his horse. "Holy Christ!" he yelped as he stood up. "You got any horse water?"

Ward went to his gear and pulled free a canvas bag partially filled with water. He opened it as he walked over to Wash, who took off his hat and held it out, upside down.

Ward knew what he wanted, and poured water directly into the hat. Wash offered it to his grateful horse, who drank it down to the bottom. "You'll hafta wait a bit for more, ol' girl," he said, patting her neck, then returning the hat to his head. A bead of leftover water ran down his face and neck.

Ward grinned. "You're leakin' a little bit, Wash."

"Don't I know it, and don't I love it!" Wash replied. He went back and sat beside the campfire. "You say somethin' about rabbit?"

Ward pointed to it, and Wash inhaled it almost before Ward noticed that he'd picked it up. "You got more?" Wash stared at him, grizzled brows raised.

Ward shook his head. "'Fraid not. Sorry."

Wash waved a hand. "Don't be sorry. Not your fault I come draggin' in here in such a pitiful condition. What brings you out this way, anyhow?"

"You."

Wash's face screwed up. "Me? Why?"

"We got a gunfighter in town. Rafe Lynch is his name. Heard of him?"

Wash shook his head.

"Well, he's wanted for killin' eight folks over in California. And we got another one gunnin' for him!"

"Whoever said Fury was a quiet little town sure didn't live there long. . . ."

"Yeah. Now, Jason didn't send me out here or anythin', but I thought of you right off. If ever we needed a man who was good with a gun to back us up, it's now. You game?"

Wash didn't hesitate. "I'm game, all right! Just lead me to 'em and point 'em out."

Ward heaved a sigh of relief, held in too long. Surely, with Wash Keogh on board, they could fight off anybody!

The next morning, Solomon didn't have to make up a story of sickness to get rid of his houseguest. Baby Sarah truly was ill, and when Sampson woke up, Dr. Morelli was there.

"She's just not thriving, Solomon," Morelli was saying. "I'm so sorry, Rachael." She stood at Solomon's side, weeping, incapable of speech.

"But what is it?" Solomon demanded tearily. "What's wrong with her? What does she have that could make her so sick, so fast?"

"She's been sick since she was born, Solomon. I'm afraid it's her heart."

"But how? Why?" He struggled to cope with this news, and part of him blamed it on Sampson Davis, the unwanted houseguest. Could he have slipped something into her? Just a little of some poisonous desert herb, tucked into her mouth. She could have swallowed it. He could have poisoned her! "Was it something she ate? Could someone have done this to our baby?"

But Morelli shook his head. "I'm sorry, Solomon. It's what we call a 'birth defect.' Now, she may surprise us and grow out of it. Sometimes they do. But I thought you ought to be prepared."

Solomon dipped his head. "Thank you for your honesty, Dr. Morelli."

"I'm so sorry, Solomon, for both you and Rachael. . . . And I'm sorry to say it, but I think it's best if no one foreign is around the baby, at least for a few weeks." He turned and eyed Sampson. "Sorry, sir, but it's best for the baby."

Sampson, burly and barrel-chested, stood up, and for a moment Solomon thought he was going to hurt Dr. Morelli. But all he said was, "I can take a hint, Doc," and began to gather up his possessions and toss them into his saddlebags.

Morelli said, "Thank you, sir. You can find excellent lodgings at Kendall's boarding house, just a half-block down the street." He turned toward Solomon and Rachael again. "Don't despair. There's always hope." Then he added, "I'll be back to check on her later this afternoon, all right?"

Solomon felt himself nod in the affirmative and then heard himself say good-bye to Dr. Morelli. He was vaguely aware of Morelli going down the steps, and then of Sampson, telling them good-bye and grudgingly following along after Morelli.

And then Rachael was in his arms, sobbing, and he forced himself back to reality. "There, there," he murmured into her hair. "We will ask for God's help. He will help us. He must."

And then he, too, broke down in tears, hugging his Rachael and silently praying, and trying to tell himself that if they had not come west, their baby would have been all right, or at least there would have been a heart specialist who could help her. Poor Sarah, his poor little Sarah!

Rachael broke away from him and went to the baby's crib-side. He watched as she leaned over the tiny child and scooped her up into her arms.

"Don't listen to what that man said, Sarah," she said softly. "And don't you worry, not a tiny bit. You're going to grow up into a beautiful young lady, my precious angel, and love God . . . and drive all the boys wild."

Solomon sat down in the closest chair and, silently, he began to pray.

Ezra Welk sat on the west bank of the Colorado River, trying to figure out whether he could safely ford it here or not. He had remembered there being a ferry here. Maybe not. Maybe it had been a few miles upstream or downstream. The only thing he knew for certain was that it sure as hell wasn't here.

He snorted out air through his nose. Well, crap. He'd try upstream first, he decided, and reining his horse to the left, began to backtrack the current.

Almost a half hour later, just when he was about to give up, he came across it: signs of a wagon train's crossing. It hadn't been that long ago, either.

A few days or better, according to his take on the bent grasses on the shallow bank. Could be army, could be civilian, but he figured civilian. The wagon tracks were too sloppy for a military caravan, and it looked like they had some livestock with them. A few cattle and pigs, plus the usual horses and oxen.

He couldn't tell if the water had gone up or down since their fording, although it looked as if it had been windy as hell. A dust storm, most like. He shuddered involuntarily. He hated them almost as much as he hated Apache.

And that was saying quite a bit.

He took a deep breath, crossed himself, and started down the riverbank, headed directly for the Arizona Territory.

9

Outside the walls of Fury, Mrs. Judith Strong, the woman who had sold Megan and Jenny their yard goods, was getting ready for the day. And she made sure to choose an outfit that was soft, yet businesslike: There was work to be done this day.

When at last she felt she was ready, she grabbed her pocketbook from a dresser drawer and climbed down to the ground. She had forgotten how she had hated the journey west with Linus. Well, that had nothing to do with Linus. He made everything acceptable, everything fun. In the two years since his passing, she had at last grown weary of mourning, weary of crying herself to sleep at night and, well, weary of herself. Linus had brought out her sense of humor, and she'd lost that, too.

It seemed that Linus had been her everything. It was time, she'd decided, to learn to be everything to and for herself.

And so she had decided to leave California behind, leave the dirt and grit of the mining camps, and the hopelessness that had finally finished off Linus—even though he hadn't done badly for himself, it wasn't what he had pictured, what he had hoped for or dreamt of.

She walked up the lined wagons, thinking about her husband's fantasies of wealth and palaces. Such a dreamer he had been! How many times had she been swept up in his enthusiasm for this thing or that, only to end up disappointed—not in Linus, never in him, but in the dream of the moment. Why, she wondered, wasn't he like other men, who always thought the worst?

Oh, well. It was a puzzlement, and one she might never figure out, let alone have a grand revelation standing in the stockade gates of a dusty little town called Fury. She had considered whom to talk to about the property, and had finally settled on the sheriff. He seemed a nice enough fellow, anyway, even if he was despicably young. But if anybody would know what was what in town, it was him.

She adjusted her light jacket and checked the angle of her hat, pulled up her chin, and proceeded down the street, toward the marshal's office.

When the knock came at the door (Jason having locked it, just in case, before he went to sleep), it startled him awake, and clear out of his chair and onto the floor. Whoever was out there, he was glad they hadn't seen that. Rafe was laughing loud enough for two men, as he watched Jason try to get his spur free from one of his desk drawers.

He finally did—after the person at the door knocked two more times—and hissed, "Shut up, Rafe!"

He opened the door to find a well-dressed, middle-aged woman, who was preparing to knock again. When the door swung inward, she smiled and said, "Marshal Fury?"

"Yes, ma'am! Sorry about the delay. I, uh, fell asleep at my desk." And then he added, by way of explanation, "My deputy is out of town at the moment. What can I do for you?"

"You can do quite a bit, actually," she said, and started to come into the office. Now, Jason had hoped to keep her where she was. He didn't much like the idea of advertising Rafe's presence. But he had no choice but to move out of her way. Fortunately, she went straight to his desk and sat down in the chair opposite his, entirely ignoring the cell area.

He followed suit by going to his desk, upending his chair and sitting down. Which wasn't such a good idea. One of the legs had broken in his fall, and he took a second tumble, this time catching himself on the edge of his desk—with his chin.

The woman sprang to her feet. "Are you all right, son?"

Jason nonchalantly waved his hand, once he was halfway standing. "Stupid chair. Keep forgettin' to have it fixed. Now. Let's start over. I'm Marshal Jason Fury—the town's named after my father, not me—and you're with the wagon train, right?"

The woman cocked her head. "Your father isn't Jedediah Fury, is he?"

Jason nodded. "Yes'm. Or at least he was. He died while we were ferrying the main part of the town, here, out from Kansas City. The folks, I mean."

Genuine sympathy filled her face. "I'm so sorry to learn of this. I knew your father. He ran the wagon train that Linus and I—he was my husband—took passage with back in '49. He got us to the California goldfields in fine shape. We spoke of him often."

"And now you've lost your husband." He didn't phrase it as a question. The pain that had overtaken her face told him what he needed to know.

After a moment of staring out the front window, and not at him, she turned back to him. "Yes, I have. And I'm sorry, I'm Judith Strong, and I'm looking to settle in Fury."

Jason's face lit up. "Well, we'd be glad to have you, Mrs. Strong, and welcome to the Fury family. We're a little rough around the edges, but we try."

"Sounds like I'll fit right in. I've got a few rough edges, myself. A woman doesn't spend over a decade moving from mining camp to mining camp without developing somethin' of an attitude."

Jason chuckled. "I imagine so."

"To get right down to brass tacks, Marshal Fury, I'm a dressmaker and a milliner, and I intend to find a place here in your town to set up shop. I've been looking over properties for the last couple of days, and I believe I've found one that will suit me. If the price is right, that is. And what I need to know from you is who owns it."

"Which building are we talking about, Mrs. Strong?"

She pointed out the window. "Right there. The one next to the newspaper office or print shop or whatever it is. And please, call me Judith."

"And I'm Jason. I'm fairly certain that Salmon Kendall owns that property—Salmon's our mayor and he has the newspaper office and the boarding-house, too. He's the man you should talk to."

"Well, thank you, Jason," Judith said, rising. "You've saved me a lot of trouble."

He stood as well. He'd been sitting on the edge of the desk. "No trouble at all, Judith. That's why we're here." He grinned at her despite his aching jaw, and walked her to the door. "Any more questions, you just come see me." He meant it, too. She put him in mind of his mother.

"Thank you, Jason," she said. "I'll do that!" Then she stepped through the door.

He stood there, watching, as she crossed the street and entered the newspaper office. He hoped Salmon would sell her the place. He could use the money, Jason knew. Hell, they all could.

He turned back toward his desk, moving what had been her seat behind it. It would do until he could get another one.

"Seemed like a nice lady," said Rafe, startling Jason. He'd almost forgotten Rafe was still there, in the cell.

"You know, you got a real knack for spookin' the bejesus outta people," Jason said.

Rafe sat up. "Why, thank you very kindly, Mr. Chair Crusher. How's your chin? And your leg?"

"My leg?"

"Don't try to hide it. I seen you limpin'."

"It'll be fine. Just bruised it, I think." Jason took a seat in his new chair, still warm from Judith's backside. He slung his leg up on the desk and pulled up his pantleg. Oh, he was going to have a bruise all right. An area the size of a silver dollar, centered on his shin, was already turning from an insulted red to an accusing purple.

"Got coffee?" Rafe was standing on the other side of the desk.

Jason nodded toward the potbellied stove. "Might still be some left from last night."

Rafe managed to find half a cup still left and sipped at it. "Just the way I don't like it. Too strong and too cold."

Jason started to open his mouth, but Rafe beat him to it. "I know. Beggars can't be choosers. Crap. What time is it, anyway?"

Jason pointed toward the clock, which read seven-thirty. And was then treated to a line of expletives by Rafe, who was only stopped by the opening door.

It was Ward, and he wasn't alone. Wash Keogh was with him, and they both looked worn to the bone. "Don't worry, Wash," Ward was saying. "They'll be fed and put up just fine."

"Talkin' about the livery?" Jason asked.

Ward nodded, and Jason added, "Yeah, don't give your mare a second thought, Wash. They know what they're doin'. I let 'em see to my Cleo all the time. And this," he said, waving toward Rafe, "is undoubtedly the reason Ward rode out there to fetch you. Wash Keogh, meet Rafe Lynch."

Rafe took a step forward and held out his hand.

Wash looked leery, but he moved forward, too, took it, and gave it a shake. "Can't say as how I'm pleased to meetcha, Rafe. I don't know yet."

"That's understandable, Wash. I'm real pleased to meet you, though."

Wash's face scrunched up. "You are? Why come?"

"Are you kidding?" asked Rafe, incredulously. "Why, you're famous! I been hearin' about Wash Keogh this and Wash Keogh that since I was a kid over in California!"

Wash stood up a little straighter, and the dust on his shoulders shifted, cascading to the floor. "Californy, you say?"

Rafe nodded. "Yes, sir! Don't know how much of it was the truth once it got to us, but if even half of it was right, you're a whatchacall, a living legend!"

"Imagine that!" Jason said softly—just loud enough to keep the story going and Rafe talking. He figured that Rafe was just shining-on Wash, but it was sure winning Wash over. Even Ward, leaning against the wall, looked a tad awestruck. It was as if he were seeing Wash in a whole new light!

"Imagine that!" Wash echoed, in a rare grammatical moment that lasted that—only a moment. "All the way to Californy! Jason, I'm famouser than I thunk! And wait till you see . . ." He dug down into his pocket. "I found it afore the dust storm kicked up. Ain't she a beaut?"

He held up the rock, and just the sight of it staggered the other three men. They all stood there for a few moments, not knowing what to say.

And then Rafe said, "Is that for real, or did you have it painted up to fool us?"

Jason punched him in the arm.

But Wash said, "Nope. Found 'er 'bout thirty feet from where I was diggin', almost took me a piss on it, as a matter'a fact, and I spent the next couple'a days tryin' to figure out where the hell she come from. Ain't she a beaut?"

"That she most certainly is, Wash," Jason said, then tentatively held out his hand. "Can I hold it?"

Carefully, Wash put the turkey egg of a nugget into Jason's hands. The gold was surprisingly heavy, but felt cool, very cool, to the touch. A few thin veins of milky quartz ran through it, but it was primarily solid gold. Anyway, so far as he could tell. He didn't know how long he stood there, transfixed by it, but then he heard Wash say, "Jason?"

Reluctantly, he handed it back. "Man!" he said at last. "That's really somethin'!"

Ward held out his hand next, and like Jason, seemed mesmerized by the huge nugget. And then Rafe broke in, "May I?" and took it from Ward.

"Good Lord," he said, turning it over in his hands. "This is one more thing to add to your legend, Wash. And something for Jason and Ward to tell their grandkids about, just that they touched it." He handed it back to Wash. "Seems to me a thing like that ought not be melted down. Ought'a be on display in a museum or somethin'. What do you think, Jason?"

Numbly, Jason felt his head shake no. "Don't ask me. It ain't mine." And then he gave himself a little, shivery shake to bring himself out of it. He stood up straighter and said, "Wash, you'd best get that thing up to the bank and get it put in the safe.

And I mean now! There's people in town who wouldn't mind guttin' you for it."

Everybody looked at Rafe, of course, but Jason said, "Get real, boys. He ain't wanted for robbery."

"No, just murder," Ward added flatly.

"Aren't you off the clock?" Jason asked.

"I reckon," Ward answered after a moment, and he looked at Jason as if Jason had lost all sense of reality.

"Don't worry, Ward," Jason said with a reassuring smile. "I ain't lost my marbles. Why don't you walk Wash on up to the bank, then head on home and get some sleep. You look like you could use it! And tell Megan hello for me?"

Most of the worry drained out of Ward's face, Jason noticed, and he said, "All right. See you tonight, buddy."

Ward made his exit with Wash Keogh in tow, and Rafe turned toward Jason. "Don't suppose we know where Sampson is, do we?"

"Not a clue." Jason walked back around his desk and slouched down into the chair. He hadn't noticed before, but his leg was killing him. "Figured I'd take a walk on over to the saloon first, and check it out. I know he was in there last night— well, I suspect that I know—but he hadn't left before we finished playin' cards and went to bed."

Rafe was staring out the window. "Who's that? Don't believe I've seen him before." He pointed toward the hitching rail across the street, where a well-dressed, dark-haired man was just dismounting.

Jason shook his head. "Never seen him before. Might be a cardsharp, lookin' for a game."

"Maybe. Maybe not." After a short pause, Rafe, ever impatient, asked, "Were you goin' across the street?"

Jason hauled himself out of his chair. Some people were worth a lot less than others, and right now, he felt at the bottom of the heap. He limped to the door, grabbed his hat off the rack, and settled it on his head. "I'm goin'," he announced, and stepped out onto the boardwalk. And immediately realized that he had to piss like a racehorse.

A little side trip to the alley set that right, and then he was off to the saloon.

Riding slow and taking his time, Ezra Welk, long dry from his ride across the river, continued to follow the wagon train's trail. Except now his keen tracker's eye had picked up a new rider, one who had more recently followed in the wagons' path.

Wherever these wagons were goin' is sure a popular place, he thought. And then he thought long and hard about avoiding it. After all, he was still wanted in the territory for killing that blacksmith . . . Jacobs had been his name, he thought. Well, it'd served the bum right for shoeing his horse off-kilter like that. Cost him the horse, in fact! Old Berry fell and busted his leg—dang near busted Ezra's, too—not a day out of that piddling little town, and Ezra had to shoot him.

Maybe he should've held off on killing Jacobs, he thought angrily. Maybe he should've let him carry all of Berry's tack and gear four days through the desert to the next town. And *then* shot him. Ezra's mouth quirked up into an unconscious smile.

But then, he thought, he'd never heard of a town being out this way. How old could it be, anyway? Hell, it might be nothing more than a stage stop. And stage stops didn't have sheriffs, but they almost always had whiskey. And sometimes, they had women. Still smiling, Ezra kept on following the wagons' path, and the path that another rider had followed before him.

10

West of Fury, riding at a slow jog and taking his time, Teddy Gunderson rode through the desert brush, following the track the wagon train's recent passage had provided. He had just ridden past the site of two fresh grave markers—travelers killed in that nasty dust storm, he figured—and by his reckoning, was about a day's ride, more or less, from his destination.

Which was Fury, a little squirt of a town that had popped up in the Arizona Territory about four, maybe five years ago. That pretty much encapsulated his knowledge of the town, and the only reason he knew that much was that he'd spent a lot of time pumping a drunk, in a bar back in Los Angeles, for information about a fellow named Rafe Lynch.

Three hours, six beers, and as many whiskeys later, he'd found out that little snippet about Fury, but more about Rafe Lynch. He'd already known the man had twelve thousand—maybe more—on his head, and that was reason enough to pique his interest, and to make him "play nice" with the old sot who'd given him the information he needed. He'd even found out about the wagon train, which had left a day earlier.

Plying drunks might turn out to be just one more cost of doing business.

Gunderson was a bounty hunter, although fairly new to the trade, having captured and turned in only two men. But they had each paid him well enough that he wanted to keep on doing it. Hell, if he could get Rafe Lynch, he'd be set for life!

He couldn't take him in town. He knew that much. As badly as California wanted Lynch, he was as clean as a whistle in Arizona. Killing him on this side of the river would make him a murderer, and put a price on *his* head!

He sure didn't want that.

He figured to wait until Rafe was out of sight of the city, and then shoot him. Or at least, kidnap him and take him to the other side of the Colorado River, and *then* shoot him.

Teddy was a clever man. At the moment, he had no idea how he'd get Lynch alone outside the walls of Fury, but he was convinced that he'd think of something. He always did.

There was one thing he hadn't taken into consideration, though, and that was Rafe Lynch.

Jason finished up over at the saloon and thanked the barkeep, who told him that Sampson Davis had finally given up on Lynch at about two a.m., and gone on home. He was staying at the boardinghouse, which Jason was relieved to hear, and the men at the saloon hadn't seen hide nor hair of him since last night.

After a quick stop over at the office, where he told Rafe that it was safe to go on across the street, Jason told him to stick to his room as much as he could. Sampson seemed to have figured out where he was staying, and he was bound to be back.

Next, he took it upon himself to see how Solomon was doing—and find out how he had got rid of Sampson Davis. He assumed it had been without bloodshed, but then, you could never be too careful.

When he arrived at the mercantile, the youngest Cohen boy was sitting out front, back in the shadow of the building, huddled on a bench with his knees drawn up and his head buried in his arms.

"Jacob?" he asked. He didn't know if he'd gotten the name right—the boys ran together in his mind—but the kid looked up at him with tear-stained eyes. Concerned, Jason asked, "What's the trouble, son?"

"The doctor was here this mornin'. They thought I was asleep, but I heard 'em talking, and he says my baby sister's gonna probably die." The boy broke into a new round of sobs, and Jason sat down next to him, pulling him close. The boy immediately threw his arms around Jason and hugged him for dear life, leaving Jason uncertain about what to do next.

But after a moment, he asked, "Jacob? The doctor didn't say for sure, did he?" He knew Morelli didn't pull his punches.

The boy pulled in tighter and said, "No, but he said she might." This seemed reason enough to set him off, once again. Jason felt the boy's hot tears soaking through his shirt.

He dipped his head to the boy's ear and said, "You know, I think that Dr. Morelli said that just in case. He told me that in a lot of cases, just the passing of time can heal a body. You know, like, you remember the time I got shot?"

Against his side, the boy nodded.

"Well, I didn't die, did I? After enough time passed, I was up and around, and feeling a lot better!" *And stuck being the marshal of this place,* he added silently. He gave the boy a little hug, then extricated himself and stood up. "I'm gonna go in to see your father now. He around?"

The boy mumbled, "He's here. Marshal? Please don't tell him I was listening?"

"Your secret's safe with me," Jason said, smiling. He put a hand on the boy's head—he still wasn't sure which one he was—and ruffled his hair before he went inside.

The bell jingled when he closed the door, and he stood there a few minutes, waiting for someone to respond. Now wasn't exactly the time to holler for help. But a few seconds before he turned to go back outside, he heard someone coming down the stairs. A few moments later, Solomon poked his head around the staircase corner.

"What can I do for—" And then he looked up and a weary smile broke out on his tear-stained face. "Ah, Jason," he said. "How kind of you to stop by."

His voice told Jason that Sol was about to burst into a fresh onslaught of weeping, so he quickly said, "Solomon, I just stopped by to ask you how the devil you managed to get rid of Sampson Davis."

He'd thought it was a safe question to ask, but he was obviously wrong. Uncontrollably, Solomon began to openly weep. When Jason took a step toward him, he held out his hands, as it warding Jason off, and stepped behind a counter, putting it between them. Then he turned his back and wept a bit more, got himself under control, and sheepishly turned back to face Jason.

"Good Lord, Sol," Jason said softly, and reached across the counter to touch Solomon's arm. Remembering the child's plea to keep Solomon from learning what he'd overheard, he said, "Is it that bad?"

Ambiguous, but comforting, he thought.

"It's little Sarah," Solomon said hoarsely. "She's dying."

"Surely not!" said Jason. If she'd been born with half her parents' strength and tenacity, it was an impossibility. This, he truly believed.

But slowly, Solomon repeated what Morelli had told them this morning. Jason had to admit that it didn't sound good at all. But he said, "Solomon, I believe that your baby's going to be fine. I believe that she's going to be better than fine. Any child who had the nerve to be born during—and live through—that storm is strong right down to her heart and soul. I believe that with all my heart."

There was a pause before Solomon said, "Thank

you, my friend." He sniffed several times. "Thank you for listening, and for being a kind ear to talk to. Thank you for being my friend." And then he broke down again.

Jason stayed in the mercantile for a long time, and—after he pushed Sol into the storeroom—even waited on a man who came in looking for nails and chicken wire.

Hours later, Jason stood outside on the boardwalk, staring down the street toward the boardinghouse. It was past noon. He knew that much, because the sun threw his shadow in front of him as he began to walk east, down Main Street. All this time to prepare, and he still didn't know where to start with Sampson Davis.

But he knew he was going to have to start with him, at least. Solomon had told him enough about the man, in teary little dribs and drabs, that he felt he sort of had a handle on his character. Enough to open up a conversation, at any rate.

Cordelia Kendall was serving lunch when he entered, and a quick glance at the diners didn't show him Sampson.

"Ma'am?" he said, instead of clearing his throat. He thought it was more polite, her being a lady and all.

She turned toward him. "Why, Jason!" she exclaimed, setting down the gravy and moving toward him. "How nice to see you! And to what do I owe this honor?"

Jason grinned. He liked Salmon's wife. They'd

been together on the wagon train coming out to Fury, and had since settled in admirably. He said (after he remembered to take off his hat), "No honor, ma'am, unless it's mine. I was lookin' for Sampson Davis."

"Mr. Davis is still sleeping. I understand he got in quite late last night." She lifted a brow, as if to ask a question.

"Don't disturb him, then," Jason said, partly relieved and partly annoyed. "I can talk to him later."

"Well, then," she said, as if he'd satisfied her curiosity. "You're most welcome to stay to luncheon, you know."

She was a famous cook, and he was tempted, but he said, "My sister packed me up a lunch, and if I don't rave about it in detail, she'll have my hide. Another time?"

She laughed and said, "Of course! Any time at all. Shall I send Sammy over to your office when Mr. Davis rises?" Salmon, Junior, was nearly old enough to take a wife, but she still insisted on calling him Sammy—as did his father.

He put his hat back on. "I'd be right pleased, ma'am."

She shook her finger at him. "You know, you're getting so you talk like a Texas field hand! We're going to have to usher you back East to college, one of these days!"

He silently wished she'd hurry it up and end his misery, but he said, "Yes'm," and "Thank you, ma'am," and took his leave. He crossed the street and entered his office. It was quiet, and it was empty—at first glance, anyway.

Rafe Lynch rolled over at the sound of the closing door, and sat up on his cot, yawning and stretching.

"Thought you'd be long gone by now," Jason said. He began rooting through his desk drawers for his lunch, which Jenny would have dropped off sometime during the early morning, on her way to school.

"Too tired," Rafe answered. "Went back to bed. Is that lunch?" he asked, eyebrows raised.

Jason had finally found the sack in the bottom drawer on the left, and hoisted it up on the desk. It was heavy! "Yeah," he said, his mouth watering. "Mine."

He peeked inside and saw . . . two of everything: two thick chicken-and-tomato sandwiches, two servings of potato salad, and on and on. He looked back at Rafe, now standing in the doorway of his cell and putting his hat on. Jason sighed. "Take your hat back off. Jenny put in two, apparently, of everything in the whole blasted kitchen."

Rafe hurried over, dragging a spare chair behind him and tossing his hat on the rack. "What a gal!" he said as he swung the chair around and sat on it backwards. And he said it again, when he took the first huge bite of his chicken sandwich.

Jason just shook his head and got up to start some fresh coffee brewing.

Sammy Kendall came running across the street a couple of hours later, bearing the news that Mr. Davis was up and demanding lunch. Which, of course, his mother had already served. He said that Davis was headed up the street to grab a bite at the café, and if the marshal wanted to see him, Sammy figured he'd best light a fire under it. All this, Sammy said in one long, quickly spoken, run-on sentence, with hardly a breath to break it up.

Actually, it rather took Jason by surprise. Rafe was long fed and gone to the saloon, and he'd been sitting there, writing up reports of the past week's activities. He'd been smack in the middle of the latest MacDonald false-Apache attack (riveting reading, that, he wryly thought to himself), when Sammy burst in and started spewing words like a Daniel Webster Gatling gun—if there were such a thing.

However, he was glad for the break, if a little nervous about talking to Davis. But it was time to—what had his father always said? "Man up," that was it.

Time to man up, Jason, he told himself. And he said, "Thanks, Sam. Thanks to your ma, too," as he pulled his hat down off the rack and settled it on his head. "You've done your civic duty for the month," he added with a wink.

"Marshal?"

"Yeah?" Jason was surprised the boy was still there.

"Could I follow along and just, you know, listen to what you say to him?"

Jason felt his brow knit. "Why?"

Sammy shrugged. "Just curious. About your profession, I mean."

Jason thought quick, but he thought hard, and

he finally said, "Sam, I'm honored that you want to learn more about the law business, but this fellow is a pretty dangerous sort. Part of being a marshal is knowing when you have to say 'no,' and this is one of those times. I'm sorry."

Sammy looked a little downhearted, but he mumbled, "Okay. I guess."

Jason elbowed him in the ribs. "Tell you all about it later."

Sammy's face lit up again, and he beamed. "That's great! Thanks!"

"All right," Jason said. "Get along back home with you."

Very quickly, he found himself alone again, and walked through the front door, which Sammy had left open. "It's now or never," he muttered to himself, and began to stride up the street to the café.

Sampson Davis had just ordered something he thought he could eat—the beef stew—although he was pretty sure the beef wasn't kosher. Times like these, though, you had to figure out what was more important: filling your gut or getting your man. Right now, his stomach was voting for filling his gut.

He'd been after Rafe Lynch for a long time—long enough that he could be patient now. At least he'd learned where Lynch was hanging out—the saloon at the end of the street. Hell, he hadn't even known it was there until he overheard two cowpokes talking about it. He'd thought that Abigail Krimp had the only action in town.

Well, she sure had the location. When you came into Fury, it looked like it was all cafés and boarding houses and general stores and the mercantile, with Abigail's being the only source of pleasure in the whole town. That was sure enough wrong! Down at the other end of town, that was where all the important stuff happened. And where he'd learned his man, Rafe Lynch, was staying. Usually. Nobody knew where he was last night. Or if they knew, they wouldn't admit it. It made him think that maybe he shouldn't have announced his reason for being in Fury in the first place.

A waiter brought him a plate of beef stew, complete with a side order of biscuits and honey, and he'd taken exactly three bites of it—and it was very good—when he looked up to see Marshal Jason Fury standing opposite him at the table.

If this upstart of a lawman expected him to jump or be startled, he was going to be disappointed. Sampson calmly set down his fork and said, "Howdy-do, Marshal. Somethin' I can help you with?"

"Yes, there is," Jason said flatly. "Leave town." He looked like he meant it, too, but Davis wasn't easily cowed. He huffed.

"Leave town? Hell, I just got here! Can't a man enjoy your little oasis here, when he's not causin' any trouble?"

"That's just it, Sampson. You intend to cause trouble, and in a big way. You've already announced your purpose, and I will stop you, no matter what it takes. If you so much as harm a hair on Rafe

Lynch's head, you'll face trial, and very possibly a noose. Got me?"

Well, if this young pup of a lawman was nervous, he didn't show it. Sampson would give him that much. But he'd come here with a purpose, and he had made up his mind that his purpose was going to be fulfilled. Maybe not today, maybe not tomorrow, but here, in Fury. He didn't answer the kid's last question. He'd heard threats before. They didn't scare him.

He said, "Don't intend to muss his hair none." And then he took another bite of his stew.

"Don't take this warning lightly," said the marshal. "Lynch isn't wanted in the Arizona Territory. Leave him alone, and leave town."

With that, the boy marshal turned on his heel and exited the café. Sampson noted that all the other patrons had gone silent, and only when he stared at them did they pretend they hadn't been listening, and tried to resume their former luncheon conversations.

Well, the kid has balls, Sampson thought. *Too bad he has to die right along with Rafe Lynch.*

11

After what seemed an endless afternoon of switching his attention back and forth between the reports he was trying to write and looking out the window, checking for any signs of Sampson Davis, Jason was about to rip out his hair. He'd done well with Sampson, he thought. At least, he hadn't wet himself, which was what he'd felt like doing most of the time he was in the café. But he wasn't at all certain that Davis had taken his warning seriously. In fact, he was pretty sure it had fallen on deaf ears, and that Sampson's new unspoken intent was to kill not only Rafe, but him, too.

It wasn't the most comforting thought.

He was about to try to refocus on his paperwork when the door burst in.

"What?" he half-shouted.

It was Ward, and despite his refreshing day's sleep, he looked like they were going to be wiped out by Apache within the second. Nervously slamming the door behind him, he exclaimed,

"Another one! We got us another one and he's over to the saloon right now!"

"Another what?" Jason said, rising from his chair. "What the hell are you talkin' about?"

"We got another one, I tell you! Wash Keogh just sent word. He's been down at the saloon all day, and he says that the man just come in, askin' about Rafe Lynch! Well, come on, Jason! We gotta get over there. Now!"

"All right, all right," Jason muttered, thinking that if Wash had been at the saloon all day, he was likely to be seeing elephants riding duck-billed platypuses. As they hurried across the street, he asked once more, "We've got another *what*, Ward?"

"Gunfighter!" Ward threw a glance at him that told him Ward thought that was the single most stupid question he'd heard in a long time. "Teddy Gunderson, from over California way. He's a bounty hunter," he added, only slightly more patiently.

"Says Wash." Jason was still dubious.

They stepped up onto the boardwalk outside the saloon.

"Says Wash! Come on." Ward pushed open the batwing doors and led the way in.

Jason spotted Wash first, and made his way over to his table. "Mind sharin'?" he asked. Wash nodded, and Jason sat down, followed directly by his deputy.

"So, what's goin' on, Wash?" Jason asked, pushing back his hat and crossing his arms on the table.

"Thought Ward was gonna tell you," Wash slurred, then turned his head toward Ward. "Sammy get you the message?"

"Yeah. Guess the marshal wants to hear it all over again, firsthand," Ward said disgustedly.

"That's enough, Ward," Jason said. "Tell me, Wash."

"Well, you're too late, anyways," Wash said. "He up and left 'bout fifteen minutes ago. He kept pumpin' Sam for information and Sam wouldn't give him none, so—"

"What do you gents want to drink?" asked a pretty girl in a low-cut red dress.

"Nothin'," said Ward, and Jason echoed him.

But Wash said, "'Nother boilermaker, Ruby."

She winked at him, said, "Sure thing, Wash," turned on her heel, and wended her way back to the bar.

Jason said, "You seen Rafe, Wash?"

"Nope, not since he come in. Went straight to his room and ain't stuck his head out since." He pointed to his eye and missed. "Been watchin' his door."

Jason glanced up at the row of doors strategically placed along an open, second-floor hallway that was barricaded only by a wooden rail along its outside, with a staircase at either end. It was usually used by the girls and their customers, but Sam occasionally let rooms out to special guests.

Rafe, it seemed, qualified.

Jason said, "And what about this Teddy . . ."

"Gunderson," said Ward.

"Thanks. Any idea on his story, Wash?"

"Nope, but I can tell you what he looks like. Six feet, mayhap a tad over. Narrow build, kinda lanky. Got kinda sandy-colored hair, mustache but no beard. Youngish. But then, everybody seems young to me these days." His boilermaker arrived, and he thanked the waitress before he turned back to Jason. "Where the hell was I? Oh, yeah. Youngish. Good lookin', I s'pose. The gals in here were gaga over him, anyways. And that's all I know." With that, he picked up his shot glass, dropped the liquor ceremoniously into his beer mug, and chugged half of it down in one long gulp.

Jason leaned back in his chair, and a hint of a smile crept over his face. "Wonder if he's stayin' up at the boardinghouse?" Maybe he and Sampson Davis would kill each other! It sure beat the other alternatives, which were one of them killing him, or vice versa.

Neither one was very pleasant to think about.

Father Micah Clayton was inside the town that afternoon, visiting families of the faith, and taking confessions. He was amazed at the number of Catholics in Fury, as well as their long lists of sins to confess. It seemed that a priest had never visited there before, and so the lists of sins went back five or six years. Sometimes longer.

He was startled at their creativity, too. In fact, there were several occasions when he had felt the need to hide his face during confession, lest he break out in laughter. The things some children— and parents!—thought were sins!

Of course, there were serious incidents, too: enough Catholics and enough sins to make him believe that Fury wasn't just in need of the occasional ministering touch that would be provided by a traveling Father or Brother. No, they needed a church, to whose bells they could harken, and where they could find a priest, day or night, to comfort and instruct them in time of need.

Also, he understood that there was competition in the form of the Reverend Milcher, from whose church he now stood across the street, and who he also understood was in trouble. It seemed that the reverend—who several people had confided in him was not ordained, but only a layman—was losing his flock. Or had already lost it, according to who was doing the talking at the moment.

Fury needed a church, and God was sending him signs that he was to build it. Father Micah didn't know if the Lord would call on him to tend its flock forever, or just until a new priest came, but he was to do the building of it.

He didn't imagine he could pull off something grand, like the Spanish had erected all over Mexico and the southwestern United States, but God didn't mind. All he need was a building to shelter the faithful while they prayed and listened and took communion. And donated, he thought, somewhat selfishly. He was one to freely pass the plate when it came to donations. The church would cost money to build, and he had to live, didn't he? Christ, Himself, would have understood his dedication to the wine decanter.

No, the good folks of Fury could support him while he lent them the spiritual grace and comfort they pined for. Now all he had to do was find a proper place to erect his church.

His church. He liked the sound of that.

And the second he realized what he was thinking, he rammed his fist against the adobe-coated post next to him.

Thou shalt have no other Gods before Me, Micah, the voice in his head boomed, putting him in his place. He scowled before he examined his bleeding knuckles. *Especially not thyself.*

He went back to his Conestoga and said five Hail Marys and three Our Fathers—much as many of those whose confessions he'd heard today were doing—and petitioned the Lord to grant him humility.

That afternoon, at about four o'clock, another rider was approaching Fury. He was a big man—tall and stocky, but not fat—with dark brown hair under his battered hat, a clean-shaven face, and a deputy U.S. marshal's badge pinned on his worn leather vest. He rode a blue roan gelding, the same one that had hauled him over half the territory for the past few years, and which he wholeheartedly hoped would last another few. The horse's name was Boy, and the man was U.S. Deputy Marshal Abraham Todd, down from Prescott.

He scouted the landscape ahead of him, which included not only the fortresslike town walls, but what looked to be a wagon train parked outside its southern perimeter. The wagons were calm, although there were people moving around, and the horses had been unhitched and placed in a corral closer to him, opposite the open doors of the wall.

He gave a close look to the lead wagon and wondered if anyone he knew was leading it. Probably not. These days, the West was somewhere a lot of people wanted to go. The Lord only knew why.

He reached the gate, tipped his hat to two ladies walking back in from the wagons—both carrying bundles—and asked where the sheriff's office was. They looked at him oddly, but a voice from behind him said, "Just down the street, sir."

He twisted to see a comely woman, standing outside in front of the schoolhouse. She pointed east, down the main street. She had dark hair, pulled back into a bun, and wore a deep blue dress, and he was taken with her right away.

"Thank you, ma'am," he said in a gruff voice (that most people found kindly, rather than abrasive), nodded, and moved Boy on down the street.

He'd gone about a block's worth when he had to smile and chuckle. *They musta knowed I was comin'*, he thought when he saw the sign on the building up ahead. The sign read MARSHAL'S OFFICE.

He reined the roan into the rail outside, dismounted, banged his hat on his leg a couple of times, and opened the door.

Nobody was there, so he figured the "marshal" was off on rounds or something. He went back outside, leaned against the rail, and rolled himself a smoke.

He could wait. He had time.

A few moments later, Jason and Ward exited the saloon with Wash Keogh propped between them.

He had finally drunk himself into a stupor, and Ward had volunteered to put him up for the night if Jason would help carry.

Ward didn't have to ask him twice.

However, they were only two steps outside the saloon when Ward stopped suddenly, yanking on Wash and nearly pulling Jason, on the other side, to the ground.

As Jason managed to get back his balance, Ward said, "Who's that?"

Jason looked up. "Where?" he asked before his eye stopped on the tall man standing in front of his office, having a smoke next to a blue roan horse. "In front of the office?" he asked before Ward had the time to answer him.

The late afternoon sun glinted off something metal on the man's chest.

"Is this our man from Prescott?" Excitedly, Jason began to walk across the street, hauling Wash and Ward along with him. He surely hoped so. This thing he was dealing with could go off any second, he figured. At least he still knew where Rafe was holed up, but he was clueless as far as Teddy Gunderson's whereabouts. He just kept telling himself that Sampson Davis and Gunderson would cancel each other out.

He fervently hoped so, anyhow.

When they had crossed the street, dragging Wash between them, Jason went right up to the stranger and stuck out his hand. "Jason Fury, Marshal. Pleased to meet you."

The marshal took his hand and gave it a shake.

"Howdy, Fury. I'm Deputy U.S. Marshal Todd. Your letter sounded urgent."

"And I'm Deputy Ward Wanamaker," Ward interjected, sticking out his right hand, which was the only one not holding up the drunken prospector.

Marshal Todd took it and shook.

"Things are worse than when I wrote you boys," Jason said as he and Ward guided Wash into the jail.

"Stick him a cell for now, Jason?" Ward asked, once they were inside.

"Yeah. I don't think he's gonna mind, let alone remember." He turned back to the deputy marshal and began listing the town's current woes. As he talked, Todd grew more and more serious.

And when he'd finished, Todd said, "I think I've got it. You got a town overpopulated with gunmen and a nutcase rancher who sees Apache behind every cactus. Right?"

Jason's jaw hung open. Todd had boiled it down to one sentence, more or less. He finally got control of his speaking parts and said, "Basically, yeah."

Ward, standing by the file cabinets, muttered, "Now, don't he make it sound simple. . . ."

"Always best to tackle the problem one step at a time, deputy," Todd said without turning around, despite the fact that Ward was standing across the room, behind him.

Todd leaned forward, putting his elbows on Jason's desk. "Now, first off, I gotta tell you that I know Rafe Lynch, and I like him. I'll get back to why in a second, but when you get right down to it, he ain't no danger," Todd said. "Second, I just heard of this Teddy Gunderson last week. Seems he's trackin' bounties, now, and it looks to me like he's got the idea he's hit the big time, and now he's gonna pick up Lynch's bounty. California's got 'bout $13,000 on Lynch last I heard, dead or alive. Imagine Teddy's thinkin' to take him back west, over the border, then shoot him. Teddy's too careful to do it any other way."

Deputy Marshal Todd's speech was having a soothing effect on Jason, who, of the three men, was by far the most in need of it. He was, after all, responsible for everything that happened in his town. And everything out of it, according to Matt MacDonald, he thought angrily. Well, Matt had got his wish, after all. Jason had called in the U.S. Marshal's Office. But Rafe was no threat, which relieved him greatly, and Gunderson wasn't likely to shoot up the town or anything else in Arizona. But as for Davis . . .

As if reading his mind, Todd said, "Now, I don't know much of anythin' about this Sampson Davis character, save that he served two years in California for the 'accidental' death of a man named Silvers, in a dispute over a mining claim."

Jason said, "All I know is what Rafe told me— and I already told you—and that Davis scares the bejesus outta me."

Ward nodded, as if to say he was scared, too, but Todd remarked, "Y'know, I think you fellers are holdin' up damned well, considerin'. Glad you contacted us, though. And please call me Abe, boys."

Jason nodded and smiled. "All right, Abe. We like to keep things casual out here, too."

"Like our prisoner, here," said Ward, poking a thumb over his shoulder at Wash, who was flopped out on a cot, arms and legs everywhere, snoring blissfully.

Marshal Todd—no, Abe—leaned out a little, smiled and said, "I'll be dogged. That Wash Keogh, for real?"

Amazed at the marshal's handle on the situation, Jason nodded.

"He's some older than the last time I run into him, but I'd'a knowed him anywhere. You two ever need a third man to back you up on short notice, call on Wash. Good at fightin' Indians, too."

Jason nodded. "We know. Ward, here, just brought him in this mornin'."

Abe hoisted bushy brows. "For drinkin'?"

Jason let out a laugh. "No, to help with the gunfighters. But now we've got you. You got a place to stay, yet?"

"Naw. Was gonna get a recommendation from you."

"Well, Wash is already set to camp on Ward's spare mattress, so I reckon you can come along home with me for tonight, anyhow. Got a sister who's a whiz-bang cook," he urged.

"I'll take you up on that," Abe said with a smile. And then he said, "Sister? You folks ain't ol' Jedediah Fury's kids by any chance, is you?"

Jason nodded. "That we are. The town's named for him."

"Why's that?"

Ward spoke up. He knew Jason didn't like talking about his father over and over. "Jason's pa was the wagon master on the train that left Kansas City five or six years back. Jason came along as ramrod, and I was sorta a roustabout. Comanche got him when we was most'a the way through Texas. Folks here was real attached to him, real attached." Ward stopped and shook his head. "So Jason took his place and shepherded us this far, and then we decided we didn't want to go no farther. And that's how it was," he finished.

Jason was relieved. Ward was getting better and better at getting him out of tricky situations. Well, that was Ward's specialty, wasn't it? His father had relied on Ward for a thousand little details, and after Jason took over the wagon train, he had, too.

Abe was shaking his head. "I'm awful sorry to hear that," he said, "awful sorry. I knew Jedediah for years, when he was ferrying folks back and forth from west to east and back again. He was quite a man, God rest him. I'm real sorry for you and your sister, Jason."

Jason mumbled his thanks, and they set out for Jason's home.

12

After the introductions were made and they ate a good dinner, Jason and Abe retired to the front porch for a smoke.

Abe rubbed at his belly. "That was the finest spread I've seen for a long time," he said, referring to the amazing meal Jenny had created on short notice. "Lip-smackin' good!"

Jason nodded, exhaling a cloud of smoke. "She's turnin' into a fine cook, all right. Our mother was class A in the kitchen, too. Guess it runs in the family."

Abe, who was rolling his second smoke, said, "Yup. You come from a strong line, Jason. How old are you, anyway?"

Jason blinked. Nobody had asked his age in years and years. He hesitated a moment, then said, "Twenty-five. Give or take." He felt downright stupid. He could never remember if you counted from the year you were born, or the next year, when you were one. *Look at you*, he thought. *Some college material!*

"That's awful young to have to run a whole town," Abe said. He struck a match and lit his smoke.

"Tell me about it," Jason replied. "I been doin' it since we got here. All I wanted to do was go back East, to college, but they wouldn't have it."

"Who? The citizens?"

"Yeah."

Abe chuckled softly. "Was that after the first Apache attack?"

Jason felt his brow wrinkle. "How'd you know about that?"

"Word gets 'round, usually without much care for the details. But I heard stories about some little town where they held off Apache by makin' a moat outta fire."

Without enthusiasm—having told the story or listened to somebody else retell it on countless occasions—Jason said, "That was us, all right. We still keep a supply of tar handy, just in case. Get it regular, shipped out from those tar pits in California. The ones outside Los Angeles."

"Your idea?"

"Yeah." Jason dug into his pocket for his fixings bag. As he took it out and fiddled with the drawstring, he said, "You can still see some'a the scorch marks out south of town, right along where the wagon train's parked. We filled the moat back in after a while, but the ground . . ."

"That was a damn fine idea, Jason."

"Thanks." He lit his smoke, took a puff, and said, "Desperate times call for desperate measures. Or words to that effect."

He heard the door opening, and swiveled toward it. It was Jenny, carrying a tray. He stood up to help her, because the tray looked heavy.

"Thank you, Jason," she said, smiling. "Thought you gents might be thirsty, so I brought you some limeade."

Jason set the tray down on the small table they kept on the porch. "Limes? Where'd you get limes?" He'd got his hands on a sapling last year and planted it out back, in the corral, but it wasn't yet big enough to bear fruit.

"The wagon train, silly." She lifted the pitcher and poured out the first glass, which she handed to Abe. As she poured the second, then the third, she added, "I don't know where we'd be without the wagon trains that come through. They bring us all sorts of wonderful things!" She handed a glass to Jason, then picked one up herself. "Mind if I join you?"

"Not at all!" said Abe, and motioned her toward the spare chair. Jason sat down after she did. Abe took a long drink. "Right good, Miss Jenny, right good!"

"Thank you, Marshal Todd," she said off-handedly. And then, "Jason, will Rafe be all right? Don't you need to go get him or something?"

Jason slowly shook his head. "He knows about Davis, and I sent a note up about Gunderson. If he's smart, he'll just stick to that room of his. And Sam said he'd take meals up. Don't worry, he's well looked after."

"That's right, Miss Jenny. He stays in that room, he's dead safe."

Jenny turned toward Abe. "That's what I'm worried about. The dead part, that is."

"Sorry. Guess I put it the wrong way."

"No, you didn't, Abe," Jason said from his chair. "Rafe is gonna be fine. We just have to figure out how to get rid of Davis and Gunderson."

Jenny pursed her lips and made a face. "Well, Jason, can't you just throw them out of town? I mean, you're the marshal!"

"That's another thing I been meanin' to talk to you about," Abe began. "You ain't a marshal, you know. Technical-like, you're the sheriff of Fury. Technical speakin', that is."

"Only the U.S. Marshals can be marshals?" asked Jason. He'd been suspecting it for years. He took a drag on his smoke and said, hopefully, "This mean I don't have a job anymore?" before he exhaled a cloud of smoke.

"Oh, don't be a fool!" snapped Jenny. She stood up abruptly and announced, "I'm going to bed. Miss Electa Morton wants me in early." And with that, she simply took her glass of limeade and went into the house.

"Is it just me, or is she getting' snippy?" Jason muttered, mostly to himself.

But Abraham Todd had sharp ears, it seemed. He said, "She ain't that bad. Who's Miss Electa Morton, anyhow?"

Jason turned toward him again. "She's our schoolmarm. Jenny's her assistant."

"Interestin'."

It is? thought Jason, but made no comment. They sat there for a little while longer, Jason finishing his smoke and limeade while Abe finished off the rest of the pitcher, and then Jason led him into the house and down the back hall to the guest room.

It wasn't much of a guest room, he supposed, being only eight feet by ten and without a bureau, but there was a cot and a chamber pot, and nobody had complained yet about the marshal's hospitality.

Which reminded him: Was he now supposed to take on the title of sheriff, and repaint the sign and remold the badge?

The next morning, as he sat behind his desk, Jason was still considering this. Ward, who had gone on home after a quiet night, took a complaining Wash Keogh along with him. He'd decided not to chance the ten minutes he'd miss watching the saloon by simply walking Wash back to his lodgings, and so Wash had spent the night snoozing, as an unofficial prisoner.

It looked to Jason as if they weren't going to get much help out of Wash, if he was half as angry with Ward as he put on. Then again, you never could tell with him. Jason was a pretty fair hand at reading folks, and he could tell that Wash was withholding something or other from them, but he wasn't going to press him. Not right now, anyway.

He had left the house before Abe was up, figuring that the man had spent a long day on a hot and dusty trail the day before, and could probably use the extra sleep. But later today, when Abe came into the office, they were going to have a serious discussion about their plans for Davis and Gunderson.

He slid a quick glance across the street, but saw nothing, as usual: a fact which should have comforted him, but which only filled him with additional dread. He knew they had to be dealt with—and the sooner the better—but he wasn't looking forward to it in the slightest. He had a feeling that whatever action they decided on, the reaction to it was going to end up messy. And that was an understatement. He worried about Ward and he worried about Wash and now Abe, too. And mostly, he worried about himself—not whether he'd die, that being a distinct possibility, but whether he would acquit himself in a manner that would do honor to his father's name.

Oh, all right, and whether he'd be forever done with the chance to go to school, back East. That chance was slipping further away every day.

Halfway through the morning, before Abe had checked in at the marshal's office, Teddy Gunderson was waiting in the alley next to the Milchers' church, practicing his fast draw.

That was pretty damned fast, he told himself when he outdrew the shaggy dog that crossed the alley's mouth. *And I ain't bein' cocky about that, neither.*

A man in his profession had to be both fast and accurate, if he wanted to survive. And he had a lot to survive for. That great big bounty on Lynch was going to be the end of his career as a gun, and the beginning of his career as . . . *Theodore* Gunderson, San Francisco Brahmin. He had started to think about it yesterday, and at first, it had been just in fun. But then he got to kind of liking the idea.

He could picture himself groomed up slick in a silk suit, real fancy, smoking an expensive cigar in one of those big mansions, at one of those big, high-tone parties up on Nob Hill. He figured he had everything but the money. And it was just down the street, at the saloon.

He'd known that lousy bartender was lying to him. He'd figured all along that Lynch was upstairs. But he was too smart to go barging up there and banging on doors, especially with what looked like the town lawman sitting right there at one of the barroom tables.

No, he'd decided to wait for Lynch to cross his path, and then he'd just wing him, put him a little bit out of commission. And then they'd ride back over the Colorado River, to California.

Teddy Gunderson had it all figured out, all right. A desert sparrow suddenly fluttered down from the roof, and he drew on it, too.

Damn fast, he thought smugly. If he had pulled the trigger this morning, he'd have killed four sparrows, two doves, one pack rat, three quails, and the ugliest dog he'd ever seen. It would have been a high body count.

Inside the church, the Reverend Milcher saw the flutter of wings and glanced up at the movement.

He glimpsed the man he would later learn was Teddy as he pulled his gun on the bird, and wondered who in creation was out there, pretending to shoot sparrows.

He walked closer to the window for a better look.

Outside, Teddy holstered his sidearm once again. He was keenly attuned to the rustles and stirs which might be made by a potential target. A daring strike made by a finch, perhaps. Or maybe that really ugly dog would come by again.

Deputy U. S. Marshal Abe Todd had left Jason's house, and was walking up the street toward the Cohens' Mercantile. He was in a good mood, having been left to sleep in, and having partaken of some of the best of Jenny's kitchen—in unexpectedly large quantities.

He was just turning the corner to walk down the main street when it happened, he later said. He heard the hum of men conversing coming from across the street, and turned to see a Catholic priest talking with a man carrying a doctor's bag as they walked up toward his direction.

It was then that he saw the movement in the alley: He saw a man fitting Teddy Gunderson's description, saw him quick-draw his rig and aim it toward the men, and he shouted, "Down, Father!" in that gruff voice turned up to a full roar volume.

He got the Father's attention immediately, and

the man took in the situation. With remarkable speed, he threw out his arm and pushed his companion clear of the alley's mouth and followed him down as Marshal Todd fired upon the gunman back in the alley.

The man fell as suddenly and surely as the two living targets had thrown themselves on the ground, and Todd made his way across the street. When he got to the two men, he said, "You fellas all right?"

The priest, who introduced himself as Father Micah Clayton, helped the other man—a Dr. Morelli—to his feet. Both agreed they were all right, but rattled.

"Who was it?" asked Dr. Morelli, picking up his bag. "Is he wounded?" He followed Marshall Todd into the alley and quickly hunched down to the body.

"Dunno. Hope he's dead," Marshal Todd said in a voice divorced from emotion.

While Morelli fussed over the body, the priest reminded Todd that he was there. He asked, "Was he . . . is he Catholic?"

Todd said, "Don't think it matters much now, Father," and finally holstered his gun. Even the doctor's ministrations weren't going to perform a miracle, and he doubted that the priest was going to cause Teddy to rise from the dead.

Morelli said, "I'm afraid he's gone." Slowly, he got to his feet, and then looked up at Todd. "Who in tarnation was he, anyhow? And come to think of it, who are you?"

Abe Todd was on the verge of saying, "The man who just saved your necks," when Jason came running up the street toward them. He parted a gathering crowd of spectators.

"What is it? What happened?" he shouted, his gun in his hand. And then he saw the body, sheltered by the bodies of the doc and Father Clayton. He turned his attention toward Abe. "Is it Gunderson?"

"Yup. Don't know what the hell he was doin', drawin' down on these fellers, but there wasn't a lotta time to ask him."

A new voice spoke up. "Why, I don't believe that was his intention at all! I've been watching him for several minutes, and it looked to me as if he was only practicing with his firearm."

Jason looked at him. "And you saw this from where, Reverend Milcher?"

The reverend walked forward, then pointed down the alley to a window roughly ten feet beyond where Gunderson's body lay.

Jason said, "So you couldn't see the street?"

"I'm afraid not."

If you were to ask Abe, he thought the sheriff looked pretty damned relieved to have Gunderson off his plate. And he wondered why they were taking so long just standing around when they could be carting the body off and getting on down to the jail.

And then Jason said, "Doc, you wanta help us haul him to the undertakers? C'mon, Abe." He stepped through the alley, where he picked up an arm. Abe took the other one, and the two of them dragged Gunderson out into the street.

Abigail Krimp had come out to see what had caused the commotion, and stood in the street, arms folded, head shaking. "That's a true and certain shame," she said, "killin' a pretty boy like that. Don't he look just like one'a them angels in an Eye-talian paintin'?"

"He was drawing on Doctor Morelli and a member of the priesthood, Abigail," Jason said through clenched teeth. Dragging bodies through the streets didn't appear to be one of his favorite chores.

"He's purty, though," Abigail said with a sigh before she turned and walked back up toward her bar.

Abe, Jason, and now Dr. Morelli walked in the opposite direction, bearing Teddy Gunderson's corpse between them.

And Abe was thinking, *Hell, and it ain't even close to noon, yet!*

It was the beginning of a very active day in Fury.

13

Once they had Teddy at the undertakers, Doctor Morelli set to work on him, and discovered that Abe Todd's slug had taken him right through the heart. This explained the lack of blood flow to Jason, anyway. Abe didn't seem as if he much cared, one way or another, because all he said after Morelli made his announcement was, "So now we only got Davis to fret about."

He didn't even bother to turn around. He just stood by the window, amid stacks of chairs and tables and other things (the undertaker also being the town's furniture maker), and stared out into the street.

"We need to get back over to the office," Jason said, lifting his eyes from the corpse. *It really was a shame,* he was thinking. *Teddy Gunderson had his whole life ahead of him, but he'd chosen to throw it away.* He shook his head. He turned to Doc Morelli, who was washing his hands in the basin. "You'll wait for the undertaker, Doc?"

Morelli shook water droplets from his hands,

then picked up a towel. "That I will, but he'd best hurry. I need to get up to see Solomon and Rachael's baby."

"How is she, anyway?"

"Not good, the last time I saw her."

"Whole town's prayin' for her, Doc." Well, most of it was, anyway.

Morelli nodded. "Let's hope it helps."

Jason and Abe crossed the street, went into the office, and took seats on either side of the desk before they realized they had company. Rafe Lynch sat on a bunk in the first cell. His head was hanging down, and Jason said, "Rafe?"

Rafe looked up. "'Fraid so. Heard the shot and figured it might be a good idea to get my butt over here. Was I right?"

"You were."

"Who's your friend?"

"Oh, I'm sorry. Rafe Lynch, meet—"

Rafe stood up and Abe turned toward him. "Abe Todd!" He broke out into a big grin. "Spiders and snakes, it's been a coon's age!" He walked toward them. Abe stood up and met him in the middle of the floor, and they pounded each other's backs like long-lost friends instead of a marshal and an outlaw, Jason thought. He found himself on his feet, too.

"Hold your horses!" he said, breaking up the gabfest. "What's goin' on?"

Rafe, still grinning, said, "Why, me and Abe, here, are old buddies!"

"Knowed him since he was in diddies," Abe said.

"Thanks for admittin' how much older'n me you are."

"You better watch your step, you punk kid!" Abe joked.

Rafe gave him a friendly punch in the arm.

I don't need this, Jason was thinking. He was becoming more confused by the hour about where the line between good and evil lay. And he was beginning to think that Jenny was right. Maybe he *should* just go across the street to the boarding-house and put a slug between Davis's eyes. It'd sure make things easier. Maybe the citizens should vote in a new marshal, too. Like, for instance, Rafe. That'd be about their speed.

Abe said, "Grab a chair, Rafe. Let's all sit down and take a load off. All right, Jason?"

Jason lowered himself back down without replying.

Seated across from him, Abe said, "Jason, you look like somebody just stole your boat."

The analogy was lost on Jason, who'd never lived on the water in his life, but he let it pass. "You two just boggle my mind, that's all. I mean, you just killed a man, Abe, and when we got him to the undertaker's, you didn't pay him a bit of attention. And then when we came across Rafe, here—an outlaw of the first order—you treat him like your long-lost kin!"

"He prob'ly wasn't much help at the undertaker's 'cause he can't stand the sight of blood," said Rafe. "And where the hell's the third chair?"

Jason poked a thumb over his shoulder toward the place where he'd shoved his chair's remains.

"Hell, that ain't no chair," said Rafe with a grunt of disgust. "That's kindlin'!"

Dr. Morelli finally left the undertaker's and headed up the street to the mercantile, this time taking care to switch to the other side of the street before he came to the alley. *Once bitten, twice shy,* he told himself, and stopped to take a long look into the mouth of it before he dared pass.

He'd been fretting about Solomon and Rachael's baby all night and all day yesterday, too. He'd gotten down his old textbooks and read everything he could on heart problems, and on the very young, but he still couldn't make heads or tails of it. He just knew that there was something wrong, something wrong inside, something that made a "whoosh" when it should have made a solid "thump." She was too thin, and acted listless. And Rachael had told him that the baby hardly cried at all.

All of which was the wrong kind of news to hear about a newborn. He didn't like it, didn't like it at all. And the poor Cohens! If this baby died, he didn't know that Solomon would retain his sanity. Rachael was the stronger of the two. She would suffer, but she'd be all right. But Morelli didn't know that Solomon could stand to bury another child. He had changed his name mere months after the last boy died. What would he change it to this time?

Morelli shook his head and opened the mercantile's door to that damned little jingling bell. It sounded far too happy for the home upstairs. Solomon was there to greet him.

"Morning, Solomon," he said. "Just dropped by to check on little Sarah."

Solomon looked relieved. "Glad you could make it, Doctor. We heard a lot of hubbub on the street, earlier." He began leading Morelli back toward the stairs.

"Yes. It was all rather strange. Some man— someone I've never heard of—tried to gun down Father Clayton and myself from that alley, over by Milcher's church. A U.S. Marshal came from out of nowhere and shot him before he could shoot us. All very odd, very odd. And rather sad, too."

As they began to climb the stairs, Solomon said, "It's a day for odd things, my friend."

Morelli was confused until he heard the sounds of a baby. Crying! "Is that Sarah?!" he asked, amazed.

"It is, indeed," replied Solomon, who had arrived on the landing. He waited for the stupefied Morelli to catch up to him, and then pointed to Rachael, who was sitting in their rocking chair, trying to calm the infant.

"Hello," she said to Morelli with tears in her big brown eyes—but they were happy tears, not tears of heartbreak. "I'm thinking she's better."

Back at the marshal's office, Abe and Rafe had just left to go have a drink or two at the saloon and catch up on old times, when Salmon Kendall came through the door. Before Jason had a chance to greet him, Salmon said, "Jason, I believe we've solved our water problem!"

Jason blinked. "What water problem?"

Salmon cocked his head and said, "Oh, c'mon. You remember last summer, don't you?"

Jason did indeed. The whole town had suffered for weeks when both the creek and the well had run dry. They lost livestock and nearly lost some citizens, too, before a wagon train came through and saved their (by then, quite smelly) carcasses. He nodded, and said, "So what's your solution?"

"We're going to build a water tower."

Now, neither Fury nor its citizens had the cash or wood or labor it would take to erect such a structure, and he warily told the same to Salmon.

"That's why we need to use your office," came the reply.

"You're going to turn my office into a water tower?"

"No, no!" Salmon laughed. "We're going to have a meeting to pick the men who'll go up into the Bradshaws to cut down and mill the wood. We've got plenty of tar, don't we? And more on the way?"

Jason nodded. "There's always more on the way." Had Salmon lost his mind?

As if reading Jason's thoughts, Salmon said, "Don't go thinkin' I've got bats crowdin' into my belfry, Jason. We know what we're doin'."

And so Jason came to be thrown out of his office on that morning while he watched the town elders slowly file in.

"You're the jokers who made me marshal," he said under his breath as he turned on his heel and crossed the street, headed for the saloon. Muttering, "I might's well have a drink with Abe and Rafe while I'm in here," he pushed through the doors, figuring he deserved one after what he'd been through this morning.

"Please, Doctor, say again that you aren't fooling with us," Rachael said.

She appeared both anxious and thunderstruck. Morelli didn't blame her, for he felt much the same way. "No, Rachael, I'm not fooling. I don't understand why, but she seems much improved from yesterday. We're not out of the woods yet, but I think we have a good chance of making it."

Rachael scooped the squalling infant up from the table where Morelli had been examining her, and hugged her to her breast.

"Thank you, Doctor, and you should pardon me, but thanks should be to God as well!" She snuggled the child closer and Morelli could hear her whisper, "Sarah, oh, my little Sarah, praise Jehovah for your life! Praise Him for all good things!" Slowly, with a huge grin on her face, she sank down into the rocking chair while she murmured to the baby.

Solomon shook Morelli's hand, and shook his hand until he thought it might drop off! "Easy there, Solomon," he said at last, and Solomon let his hand go free.

"Sorry, Doctor," he said, a little ashamedly.

Morelli clasped him by the shoulder. "Your wife's right. You shouldn't be thanking an old country doctor. You should be sending your thanks to God. He's the only explanation for this." He shook his head. "I've never seen anything like it in my life. Well," he added, "I'll stop by tomorrow to see how she's coming along, all right?"

Solomon walked him down the stairs, asking only three more times about the baby. Yes, Morelli was sure, and yes, she was better, and no, it wasn't his imagination.

Morelli finally left the mercantile, but he was walking a little taller. *Thank You, Lord,* he said in his mind. *Thank You for watching, for paying attention, and for harkening to their words. Amen and amen.*

He went not toward his home and his office, but out to the wagon train once more. And while he walked down the line of wagons, he said another little prayer, in his thoughts, for poor Frank Saulk, the man who had been hit by a saguaro arm before the wagons came to Fury. His wounds had been complicated by his wife's failure to get out all the spines, although he couldn't blame her. Most of what was left, peppering the back, was invisible to the eye and had to be felt for.

He didn't suppose a screaming husband was the best patient, either.

He screeched when Morelli did it, too, but Morelli hoped to get the last of them out today.

If he didn't, Frank Saulk would die.

When he got there, Frank was dozing fitfully in the back of the wagon, and his missus (who'd said, "Call me Eliza") was off to the side, tending to a fire which looked like it had just been kindled. He greeted her, and proceeded to stick his head in the back of the wagon.

"Frank? Frank, are you awake?" he said, even though he knew Frank was conscious. He didn't like surprising people, especially patients on their deathbeds.

Frank lifted his head and cranked it around. "Yeah," he said, as if from another dimension. "Mornin', Doc."

Morelli climbed up into the wagon and squatted beside Frank. He hadn't seen their children. Perhaps their mother had sent them off to play. He asked Frank how he was feeling, and Frank just made a face.

Morelli could see why. Frank's back was an angry red and purple thing, almost a monster apart from the rest of him, and as septic as anything Morelli had ever seen, aside from some amputees during the War—some amputees who had later died. He smelled of death, too. Not a good sign.

"All right, Frank. I'm going to try to dig out the last few spines today, and then we're going to see if we can't clean up some of the pus. All right?"

"Whatever," Frank muttered, and said no more.

Morelli began to go to work.

Meanwhile, Salmon Kendall was closing the meeting of the town elders, officially known as the Town Council. The men were on their feet and a few of them had already left when Salmon said, "Somebody should tell Solomon, up at the mercantile. You want me to do it?"

The other men (having heard and in some cases, whispered) about the Cohens' sick newborn, were leery of setting foot in a house of sorrow, and all agreed. They would have Salmon do what they were afraid to.

When they had all filed out, he walked up the street and pushed open the jangling mercantile door. Surprisingly, he found Solomon in good spirits—very good, in fact.

"Solomon?" he said. "The baby's better?"

"Oy, my friend Salmon!" Solomon effused, arms held wide as if to engulf the entire town—or possibly the entire world. Salmon couldn't be sure, but he backed up a step. Solomon didn't seem to notice.

"She is much improved!" he went on. "The doctor was here, and said she has a good chance now, but I know better. God will *not* allow her to die. She is beyond harm, a blessed child!"

Salmon hoisted his brows. "And you know this because . . . ?"

"Because I know, that is why," Solomon said, and that was that. Or at least, Salmon took it that way. Sometimes, he had learned, Solomon was intractable once he got the bit in his teeth, which he seemed to have achieved now.

He moved on to more pressing things. He said, "The council just held a meeting. Sorry we didn't call for you, but things have been pretty rough up here, and . . ."

"You didn't wish to bother me?"

"Exactly. Anyway, we're going ahead with the water tower. I've got volunteers to go up north into the Bradshaws to get the wood, and I'll start making a list today of men to do the building and the tarring of it."

Solomon considered this. "It will have to be very strong indeed if we have another storm like we had the other night. Can we make it that solid? And where did you decide to put it?"

"Yes, it'll be strong, Solomon. We have plans to use reinforced crossbars on the legs and tie-downs. And I believe the weight of the water will hold it in place."

"God willing."

"Exactly. And you know that empty lot a couple door downs from the marshal's office? The plan is to put in there. It's centrally located so that everybody will have equal access to the water."

Solomon's brow wrinkled. "No one owns this lot?"

"Not a soul. Like most of Fury, it's a land grab." Salmon laughed at his own joke, but Solomon remained thoughtful.

"And the council members agree to all of this?"

Salmon nodded.

Hunching his shoulders, Solomon raised his palms into the air. "So be it, then."

"Drink to it?"

Solomon smiled. He felt like having a drink just to celebrate the good news about Sarah, anyway. "So be it," he announced, and marched over to the drawer where he kept a decanter of red wine, and also a whiskey bottle. He picked up the latter and held it out. Smiling, Salmon smacked his lips.

Solomon poured out two whiskeys. "To all good things which come from God," he said.

"Imagine the fellers who go up to get the wood'll have a little problem with that. You know, thinkin' it'll all come from courage and muscle and dumb luck. And later, they'll attribute it to wisdom and foresight and a staggering knowledge of lumbering skills. Perspective's funny that way. But I'll drink to the Lord's help, by God. May He bless this endeavor!"

Solomon raised his glass. *"L'chaim!"*

They clinked their glasses together, tossed back their drinks, and grinned.

About a quarter mile outside of town, Ezra Welk crouched on the brushy desert beside his grazing horse and slowly shook his head while absently scratching at his neck. What the hell had happened here, anyway? There hadn't been a blessed living thing here, aside from the usual snakes and bug-critters, the last time he was through! But now, it seemed like somebody had not only built a good-sized stockade—and chopped down practically every single tree that had once lined the bank of the creek—but had sent to California for a wagon train.

At least, that was what was parked along the stockade's southern wall. He assumed it was the same wagon train whose path he'd been following for the past few days.

At long last, he stood up and mounted his horse, having decided, after a long internal debate, to go ahead and ride in, to see what the hell was really going on. Just as well, because just as he settled down into the saddle and got his reins adjusted, a big, ugly dog near the wagons spotted him and began to bark. He would have just shot the damned thing, but it was on the end of a rope or something, and the other end looked to be held by a lanky kid.

"Get you later, dawg," he muttered, and moved his hand away from his holster. For the time being, anyhow.

Ezra Welk didn't make promises he didn't keep.

He moved his horse ahead, down the gentle slope, and toward the stockade.

14

Father Clayton got to Jason's office at roughly the same time Jason did. Fortunately, Jason thought, he'd held it to one beer across the street, and so he was a sober man when the father announced he wished to talk.

"'Bout what?" Jason asked as he ushered the father into the chair opposite his, then sat down himself.

The father smiled. "Your fine neighbors across the street, Dr. and Mrs. Morelli, have seen fit to let me stay under their roof while I peruse your town."

"And how do we read out?" Jason asked, while he wondered if someone had changed the definition of "perused" while he'd been away.

"Oh," said the father. He chuckled. "I see. Oh, dear, I just did it again, didn't I?"

Jason smiled. "Sort of sideways. What'd you want to talk about, Father?"

"The church I intend to build in Fury." He folded his arms and leaned back in his chair smugly.

Jason thought, *Well, aren't we full of ourselves?* but he

said, "You intend to build a parish? Here? Does Fury have enough Catholics to make that worthwhile?"

"Oh, my, yes, indeed it does!" said the father. "By my count it's over seventy souls, with a number of others with no place to worship."

If that was a sideways slam at Milcher, Jason supposed it was well-placed. But he figured the town needed something besides a Catholic mission to keep it morally "proper." Whatever that was. Actually, in his opinion, the town was pretty moral just as it was.

"Gee," he said flatly. "That many."

There hadn't been any question in the way he'd said it, but the father took it as one. He said, "Do you doubt my count, son?"

"Not at all," Jason said. "And if you don't mind, I'm not your 'son.' And please, just call me Jason." It made him uncomfortable, plus which, he felt as if it was an insult to his late father. As mixed as his feelings were toward Jedediah's memory, he wouldn't stand for that from anyone.

"Very well, then," said the priest, suddenly mild. It was as if he'd forgotten for a moment that anyone existed outside the Church's realm, and now he was humbled. Idly, Jason wondered if he was going to perform an act of contrition on the spot. But if he was expecting one, he was disappointed.

"I've chosen the best location for the mission—it will be more mission than church, I believe—and I need to discover who owns the lot. I'm told that you know everyone, and are therefore the person to ask."

Jason leaned forward and crossed his arms on the desk. "And which parcel has appealed to you, Father?"

"The lot just down the street from your office, Marshal. Just two doors away."

Jason lifted a brow. He didn't mind the Church being so close to his office, but wondered that the father would want his mission that nearby. He said, "Nobody owns it."

The father tilted his head. "No one?"

"Nobody's claimed it yet." Jason shrugged. There hadn't been anybody proposing interest in that lot for a very long time, either.

"Can I claim it? In the Church's name, of course," the priest added quickly, with a wave of his hands.

"You're as welcome to it as anyone, I suppose," Jason said.

"Do I need to sign something?"

"Nope. Just build on it and it's yours."

Father Clayton beamed at him and clapped his hands together. "Marvelous! Just *marvelous!* You don't know how welcome this news is, Marshal!" He nearly leapt to his feet.

Jason expected him to dance to the door if this was any indication, but he said, "And welcome to Fury, Father Clayton."

"Please, call me Father Micah!" the effusive priest said. "That's Micah with an 'H' on the end."

"All right, Father Micah. Good luck!"

"No, thank you, Marshal. I mean, Jason!" He stopped stock-still, and Jason could practically see the wheels in his mind turning rapidly round and round. He asked, "*Marshal* Jason, or just Jason?"

"Just Jason, Father," Jason said, standing. Nobody had been this tickled to grab land in town since they first built the place! He guessed he didn't mind the Catholics moving in with an official presence down the street from him.

The father—Father Micah, he reminded himself—made his exit, and Jason sat back down. So the Holy Roman Empire now had a stake in Fury. Idly, he wondered if they'd be of any help with the Indians or Sampson Davis.

He snorted out a laugh, and then went back to work.

Jason didn't discover until later that afternoon, where the town fathers planned to build their water tower.

"But you can't!" he sputtered. "There's a Catholic mission going in there!"

Salmon Kendall, who had given him the news, and who now stood across his desk, handing him the weekly newspaper, said, "But we've already decided, Jason."

Boiling but trying not to show it, Jason came back with, "Salmon, all buildings to be erected have to be cleared through this office, and that means me."

"You were drinking at the time."

Jason just stared at him. Why couldn't he back down, like a normal person? And where the hell was Marshal Todd? He'd been going to go up to the boardinghouse to have a word or two with Sampson Davis, and Jason had been waiting to hear something from him for several hours, but nothing, not a blessed peep.

"So anyhow," Salmon went on, "we're sendin' a contingent up into the Bradshaws first thing in the morning. The Slade brothers have spent the entire afternoon getting the wagons ready, I've been to the mercantile and bought saws and awls and dried beans and such, as well as rope, from Solomon, and my wife's been cooking all day so they don't starve to death on their own grub. Just thought you'd want to know." He dropped the paper on Jason's desk.

The headline read, MARSHAL SHOOTS KILLER LURKING IN ALLEY! but Jason just glanced at it. He said, "Find another place to put up your water tower, Salmon."

"'Fraid not. The site's centrally located, it's level, and that's where we picked. The Catholics can put their mission anyplace. That end lot, by the saloon, for instance. Or on the next street over," he added, poking a thumb over his shoulder, toward the office's back door. "There's plenty of room back there."

Jason now found himself championing a cause he had no stake in, either way, but he said, "Dammit, Salmon! I gave my word—the word of the town—to the Father when I said he could have the lot. And I will not go back on it!"

That was the whole point, he realized. His *word*. Well, tough.

Salmon, who was beginning to look a tad

peeved, grudgingly let out air between pursed lips, then said, "I'll have a word with the father, then?"

"Do what you want." Jason picked up the paper.

Salmon left, and when he was gone, Jason just sat there, shaking his head. The paper dropped from his hand, and he asked the air, "What do you people want from me, anyway?"

But he already knew the answer. They wanted somebody to do the dirty jobs they couldn't be troubled with, like handle the likes of Teddy Gunderson, or the perennially hysterical Matt Mac-Donald, or organizing them when they really *were* under attack. And the rest of the time, he guessed he could just go hang.

"Well, maybe I will," he muttered to himself. "Maybe I'll just ride on out of here and get myself back East, where I belong."

But first, he had to check on Abe Todd. He hoped he wouldn't find him shot dead, and chockful of Sampson Davis's bullets. On the other hand, he mused as he stood up and walked to take his hat off the rack, it'd solve a plethora of problems for him. . . .

He didn't find Abe across the street, in the saloon, nor did he find him (or any trace of Davis, for that matter) at the boardinghouse or the café. Where the hell had they disappeared to? He walked over to the stable, found nothing, then stuck his head into Abigail's place. Still nothing, not even a lousy card cheat. Scratching his head, he leaned against a post outside the mercantile and stared down the street.

A few moments later, he was rewarded by the

sight of Abe Todd, coming out of the barber shop looking slicked up and shiny as a new penny.

"What is this?" he muttered to himself. "Some kind of marshal's ritual, like 'Slick up before you shoot'? Or maybe I should say 'afterwards' . . . ?"

Todd spotted him, and waving, began to walk toward him. Jason moved forward, too, and met him in the center of the single, long block that made up Main Street.

"Been waitin' on you," Jason said, in place of a greeting. "What's goin' on with Davis?"

"Got me," replied the newly shorn Todd, who smelled too strongly of witch hazel. "I couldn't find 'im, so I went to the barber instead."

"Well, his horse is still at the stable."

Todd scratched the back of his neck, probably at some stray hairs. "Well, I guess he's disappeared, then." He looked up the street, past Jason. "Where else is there?"

Jason thought for a second, then said, "The wagon train?"

"Worth a little hunt," said Todd.

But when they got up by the gate, Todd didn't turn to go outside. Instead, he said, "Hang on a second," and walked forward, toward the schoolhouse. Or at least, what passed for a schoolhouse in Fury.

"You're not goin' to find him in there!" Jason yelled at his back.

"Not lookin' for him," Abe Todd bellowed, then stepped inside the little schoolhouse. The door closed behind him.

"You want somethin' done right, I guess you gotta do it yourself," Jason muttered with a frown, and strode on through the gates, out to where the wagons lined the wall.

Ezra Welk hadn't wasted any time once he rode into Fury. He found the livery and put up his horse, then grabbed a beer at Abigail's, which he found was practically deserted. But she gave him directions to the boardinghouse, where he was presently ensconced. Sitting in a chair beside the window, he looked out over the street below.

There was a marshal's office—no way to tell if it was federal or local from here, anyway—and while he watched, a Catholic priest went in for a few minutes, then came out smiling and practically jigging his way up the street. And then the law came out. Local, by the looks of him. Young, too, probably green as grass.

Ezra snorted. He didn't have anything to worry about here in Fury.

Fury. Now, that was a funny name for a town. Maybe there'd been some kind of battle here, some big whoop-up. It had to have been fought furiously, though, to earn the name, and you would've thought he'd have heard about it, even over in California.

Well, it was just another question to ask over at the saloon. There was one right at the end of the street, and it looked (and sounded) quite a bit more lively than Abigail's place had been. He watched while the so-called marshal made his way out of the saloon and ambled up the street, and only then did he stand up, light himself a new smoke, and make his way downstairs and outside, to the street.

Not a third of the way down the line, Jason ran into Doctor Morelli, who looked sour and pale.

"What's wrong?" Jason asked.

Morelli shook his head. "It's a day for death, Jason. I have a feeling that Frank Saulk will be dead before the sun sets."

Jason hadn't a clue whom he was speaking about, so Morelli added, "The fellow who was hit by the saguaro?"

Now he remembered. He nodded. "Yeah. He gone septic?"

Morelli nodded. "And he's getting worse as fast as I've ever seen. He'll leave that wife and those children behind to fend for themselves. It's a shame, a real shame."

Solemnly, Jason nodded. "Sure is. You seen Sampson Davis today, Doc?"

The physician said, "No, I haven't. Why?"

"No reason." He looked down the line. "Well, got to move. See you later."

Morelli waving him on, he set off. But by the time he reached the last wagon, there was still no Davis in evidence. Where the hell had he got to, Jason wondered as, frowning, he made his way back up to the gate. A man didn't just disappear like that. Especially such a big man as Sampson Davis.

By the time he'd walked clear back to the office, checking in every public building along the way, he still hadn't turned anything up. He was angry with Marshal Todd, mad at Sampson Davis, incensed by the town fathers and their damned water tower, and pretty much fit to be tied with the whole town and its situation.

"I should've just gone," he muttered as he shoved his desk to one side in passing. "I should have just left 'em to take care of the Indians by themselves. They didn't need me. They never did." He slumped down into his chair. "I never should have turned Cleo around and come back."

He closed his eyes and images flooded into his head, images of what should have been: him having a laugh with some boys outside the school library, him checking the grade sheets and finding nothing but "A's" beside his name, him applying for a position and shaking hands with the president of the company, him getting married. But the girl he pictured, the woman who became his wife, was Megan MacDonald. And when they rode home after the wedding, it was to Fury and the little house on Second Street, where he lived now.

He gave up. Fury had taken root in his fantasies, and there was no killing it, no stopping it now.

Thoroughly cowed by himself, he put his head down on the desk and tried to will himself dead, but it didn't work. Instead, he suddenly sat bolt upright.

He knew where Sampson Davis was.

He'd thought Davis would be back at the boardinghouse, shut up in his room with no one the wiser, but he was wrong. Not only did Mrs. Kendall say she hadn't seen him, but when she let him up to check the room, it was so empty of Davis that the place practically echoed.

He had run into the final wall, and hard.

But when he went back outside after that humiliating little hunt, Abe Todd practically ran smack into him on the sidewalk.

"Where've you been?" he asked, a little more huffily than he would have liked.

"Out lookin' for you," Abe replied. "Where *you* been?"

"Outside, siftin' through the wagons, lookin' for Davis."

"No luck?"

"Nope."

Abe shifted his weight from one leg to the other. "Well, come with me, then."

He started on down the walk, with Jason tagging at his heels like a pet dog.

He reminded himself of the dog, Hannibal, who, most of the time, had been given free rein of the town these past few days. He didn't like it, and he made himself catch up with Abe, then matched him, stride for stride.

"Where we goin'?" he asked.

"Saloon."

Jason put on the brakes and Abe stopped, too, looking curiously at him. He said, "What?"

"I'm not off duty, yet."

Abe laughed. "Hell, Jason, I ain't askin' you there for a drink! We're just takin' a look-see."

"I was in there earlier. He's not there," Jason insisted.

"People move around."

"Oh, all right," Jason said in disgust, and started walking again.

Davis was in the saloon, all right, sitting at a back corner table all alone, and slogging down whiskeys like they were sarsaparillas. A glance up to the second-floor balcony showed Rafe's door was closed, which Jason profoundly hoped meant that Rafe was locked up inside it.

"Don't worry," said Abe when he followed Jason's line of vision. "I told him to stay put in there."

"Like you think he'll listen."

"He listened." And then he steered Jason back to an empty table. "I'm gonna go have a few words with your friend, Davis." He quirked his mouth while he checked Jason's position. "You got a clear line'a fire from that chair?"

Jason checked, and nodded.

"Keep an eye peeled." Abe took off for Davis's table.

Jason watched while Abe approached and pulled out a chair across from Davis, his back to the room, as if he owned the place in general and Davis's table in particular. He couldn't make out Davis's face, but something told him that Davis wasn't too happy with the situation.

Abe leaned forward and started to talk, and the words, while Jason couldn't hear them, appeared to be delivered in a sharp, no-nonsense manner.

Davis said something, then Abe, then Davis again, and then Abe pushed back from the table and stood up. He said a few more words to Davis, then turned his back on him and made his way back over to Jason.

"Wish I could've heard that," Jason said.

"No, you don't." Abe pulled out a chair. "The man's bulldog-stubborn and bear-nasty. He's gonna stay if he has to move here, permanent."

Jason sighed. "Not quite what I wanted to hear."

"Didn't thrill me none, either." Abe waved a hand, and a pretty girl showed up, as if by magic.

"Order, sir?" she said.

"Couple shots of bourbon."

"Got you." She left.

Jason started to tell him again. "Look, I'm still on the—"

"No, you ain't. Look at your pocket watch."

Jason did. It was five past the hour. "Oh," he said, annoyed, and put it away. "So, now what?"

Abe shrugged. "I guess we wait." He shoved some change toward the serving girl who'd just brought the drinks. "Same thing again."

Jason scowled. "Must'a been thirsty work, talkin' to him."

Abe picked up his drink and tossed it back in one gulp. Jason hadn't touched his yet, and he'd only taken a sip when the girl showed up with the second round.

"I got me an idea," Abe said after he polished off his second bourbon. "How'd you like to be a U.S. Marshal?"

The query caught Jason completely off guard.

"Me?" he asked, then shook his head. "No way, Abe. Not in a million years."

"Why not?"

"Because then I'd be responsible for Matt Mac-Donald's Indians, and shepherding the wagons over to the next man and, well, a whole load of stuff that I'm not prepared to take on."

Abe cocked his brows. "You chicken?"

"No, I'm not. Jesus! I don't even want to be the town's marshal, never aimed for it. I belong back east taking exams, not out here in the middle of nowhere, riding shepherd over folks who don't give a good goddamn."

Abe snorted. "Just thought I'd ask. Don't get your knickers in a knot over it."

From his table at the opposite end of the room, Ezra Welk watched the whole scene play out. He sat alone, but there were enough bodies between him and the lawmen to prevent his discovery. That was, if anybody was even looking for him.

These boys seemed to have somebody else on their mind, entirely: a big hulking number he didn't recognize, who was sitting at another table, about halfway between himself and the batwing doors. One of the marshals—a middle-aged one he hadn't spied before—walked over and had himself some stern words with the big galoot, who looked just as nasty as he was barrel-chested. If it had been up to Ezra, he would have shot the bastard, just for being ugly.

But it wasn't up to him, especially with the two lawman present. They were currently sitting at a table up toward the front of the bar, talking.

Ezra wasn't worried, though. He ordered a new whiskey and sat back to watch the show.

15

Before he walked home, Jason checked into the office just to make certain that Ward was on the job. He was, but so was an angry Wash Keogh, waving the newspaper.

"Blast you, Jason!" he shouted. "What's wrong with you, takin' out one'a your guns afore I had me a chance at him?"

Jason held up his hands. "I didn't take him, Wash! Abe Todd did, and it was kind'a a surprise for everybody."

"And while we're not on the subject, how's come you talk different accordin' to who you're doin' the talkin' to? Droppin' g's and sayin' 'ain't' and stuff you don't do otherwise? Huh?"

Wash had a point, and it took Jason back a step or two. He *did* do that, he realized. He shrugged his shoulders. "Don't know, Wash." He really didn't. "Sorry if it bothers you."

Wash pulled himself up. "Well, it don't, really. But this Gunderson deal does. And just when I was gonna strike it rich!" He dug into his pocket.

"Yeah, sure," Ward muttered from behind the desk.

Wash made a growly face at Ward, then produced his nugget.

Jason let out a long breath and said, "Jesus, Wash! You been carryin' that thing around in your pocket this whole time?" He'd never in his life seen such a rich nugget, or such a gigantic one, and he was certain that he'd told Wash to put it in the bank for safekeeping!

Ward was still intent on the papers before him, and Jason said, "Ward. I thought you were gonna take him up to the bank."

Ward lifted his head and his focus fell on the gargantuan nugget in Wash's hand. He dropped his pen and his mouth hung open. Then, "Mother of God! Wash, you said you were goin'!"

"What'd I tell you?" said the old prospector. "You brung me into town without no sleep and then you turn around and shoot the feller I was here to take care of! You beat everything, you know that?" And then he stomped past Jason, pocketing the gold again, his pants listing with its weight, and walked out onto the street and toward the saloon.

"You think that thing's *real*?" Ward asked.

"Looked like it was." It hadn't even qualified as a nugget. If it'd been much bigger, Jenny could have used it in her rock garden, out back of the house.

"I need a smoke." Ward fumbled in his pocket.

"I'll join you."

The two men sat in the office smoking for a while before Ward said, "You ever seen anything like that in your whole cotton-pickin' life?"

Jason just shook his head. As yesterday, he told himself that it could have been pyrite, but he figured himself a good enough judge to tell the difference. If he knew where Wash had been digging, he would have been out of town like a shot.

No, he wouldn't. It was Wash's gold. And he kept on repeating that to himself. "It's Wash's, it's Wash's."

"Key-rist," said Ward. "Now I know what they mean by having larceny in your heart. How much you suppose a thing like that's worth?"

Jason shook his head. "Have to have it assayed. But I'd say somewhere in the thousands. Maybe tens of thousands."

"Key-rist," Ward repeated.

"First thing in the morning, you make him go over to the bank and have Megan put it in the vault. I mean it this time, all right? I don't like him walkin' around town with it on him. Liable to fall through a hole in his britches."

Ward stared out the front window. "Check, boss."

Jason stubbed out his smoke and stood up. "I'm goin' home."

Later that same evening, while Jason was at home having one of those good "Jenny dinners" and Wash was still at the saloon, Ward Wanamaker was making his evening rounds, checking that everything that was supposed to be locked up *was* locked up, and that everything was pretty much in its place. He paused, halfway through, when he got up to the gate. It was being left open at night

these days, in case something should happen—
Heaven forfend—and the wagon train members
needed to get inside in a hurry.

He leaned against one of the posts and rolled,
then lit a smoke, breathing out a hazy plume into
the crisp night air. The sun had barely set, but
nights on the desert were cold, and this looked
like it was going to be a real toe-and-finger freezer.

He was almost finished with his smoke and
about to stamp it out and get on with his rounds,
when he spied movement out there, in the expanse to the south. He waited a moment, which
was just enough time for the movement to turn
into a horse and rider, a rider who was moving like
a bat out of hell.

He was yelling something, too, but Ward
couldn't make it out. All he could hear was somebody shouting something, and all he could see
was that same somebody flapping his arms and
fanning his horse and riding like sixty.

"Who the heck's that?" a voice, much closer,
asked. Ward looked toward it and saw Riley, the
wagon master, strolling over toward him.

"Dunno," Ward replied with a shrug. "Mighty
odd. Guess we'll have to wait till he gets close
enough that we can hear what he's—"

"Indians! Apache! Help!" came the cry, finally
clear.

"Sayin'," Ward finished. "And don't go gettin'
yourself in an uproar. I reckon it's just one of
MacDonald's men. Apache don't attack at night,
but MacDonald sees Indians like other men see
tumbleweeds."

Riley folded his arms and stared out toward the rider galloping toward them. "He's gonna ruin that horse."

"Probably." Ward ground out his smoke. "Reckon I'd best go round up the marshal. The U.S. Marshal, that is. Me and Jason, we ain't got no jurisdiction out at MacDonald's ranch."

Riley said, "Well, good luck, then," and wandered back toward his wagon while Ward started down the street, to the saloon.

That dang Matt MacDonald sure had a way of messing up his evenings.

Abe Todd was minding his own business, getting smashed at the saloon and keeping an eye on Sampson Davis, when the batwing doors burst in and two men shouldered through. Ward was one of them, and he raised a hand to acknowledge him. He didn't expect Ward to come over to his table, though, but that's what he did next, followed by the shorter man who'd come through the door with him.

The shorter man stared at the badge on Abe's chest just long enough for Ward to say, "Sorry, Abe," and shrug before the other man—a boy, really—started in.

He elbowed Ward aside and said, "I'm Steven McCord, sir, and I work for Mr. Matt MacDonald down south at the Double M, and we got Indians, a passel of Indians, the Apache kind, and he sent me to come get help right away and the town law ain't never any help, so I come straight to you." His long sentence finished at last, he leaned forward, catching himself on the tabletop as if he were exhausted.

Abe didn't move, except to tilt his elbow and take another slug of bourbon. "At night?" he finally said. "You got Apache attacking you at night?"

McCord nodded his head frantically.

"Anybody actually shoot an arrow at you?"

McCord's features bunched up. "What? No, but they're comin'! Mr. MacDonald, he seen their dust cloud on the horizon."

Abe studied his glass. "He did, did he?"

"Yessir! C'mon! Time's wastin'!"

Abe leaned back in his chair and Ward sat down, probably to watch the show. Abe let the edification begin.

"Son, the Apache aren't attackin' your boss's ranch. They don't attack at night, for one thing. And for another, if they wanted to attack you, you wouldn't see 'em comin'. They'd just be there, and you'd be dead—or wishin' you were."

"But—"

"No 'buts' about it," Abe cut in, and lifted his glass again. He polished off the last of his bourbon. "Now, go on back home. Or sit down and have a drink. Your choice. But I ain't runnin' out there like some dumb cluck with my head cut off."

"But—"

"Sorry, Steve, but that's all she wrote," Ward said, standing up, putting a hand on both of the young man's shoulders, and turning him back toward the door. "Your boss's imagination is runnin' off

with him again. That's all there is to it, and this
time, we ain't gonna play, all right?"

Steve McCord, a nice kid who had come in with
the wagon train before last, walked out the door,
dejected. Ward called, "And you walk that horse
for at least a mile, McCord."

A muffled, "I know, I know," came from the direction into which he'd disappeared, and then he
was gone. Ward pulled out a chair again, wondering if Jason'd shoot him if he had a beer.

But then, he figured Jason'd be so tickled that
he'd got rid of MacDonald's rider that he wouldn't
mind, and so he signaled the serving gal and indicated a beer.

"That was right masterful," he said to Abe.

"Nothin' but the truth." Abe leaned farther back
in his chair, and for a second, Ward thought he
was going to go to sleep. But when the barmaid
brought Ward's beer, Abe sat up and said, "One
more round, honey."

"That kid's gonna be in a peck'a trouble when
he gets back to the ranch alone," Ward said, sipping his beer gratefully. It tasted good. "Matt Mac-
Donald ain't somebody you want to cross."

Abe picked up his shot glass. "Not my problem,"
he said, and drank half of it down. "The U.S. Marshal's office ain't for babysittin'."

Ward nodded. *The marshal's office must be for
getting drunk instead,* he thought, then wiped the
idea from his mind. He wasn't there to judge
Abe Todd. He was there to have a beer. He took
another sip.

He wondered what Jason would have done, though.

Jason, relieved to be off-duty, finished a good dinner, then went out to the porch to smoke. He was halfway through his cigarette when Jenny came out.

"What's wrong?" she asked, sitting down in the chair beside him like a bag of bricks.

"Nothing." He turned toward her. "Why?"

"Because you didn't say two words during dinner, or when you came into the house. Something's eating at you, Jason. Anybody could see that."

"It's just . . . sometimes I wish I wasn't marshal. Sometimes I wish we hadn't come west at all."

"Why? I like it here!"

"I know you do, Jenny. And to tell you the truth, that's the only reason I'm still here." And it *was* the truth, he just realized. Epiphanies could be curious things, and this one fell on him like a keg filled with nails. He wanted to weep.

"For me? Jason, you don't need to stay for me. I'm fine!"

He took a drag on his smoke, then stubbed it out. "You wouldn't be so fine if the Apache attacked again. Or if you married that jerk, Mac-Donald. Or if you—"

"Stop it!" She slouched back in her chair, hard. "You can stop listing things."

Jason pulled out his fixings bag again and muttered, "That's what you think."

She stared at him through the darkness. He wasn't going to find any comfort here tonight. He stood up.

"Where you going?"

Fixings bag dangling from his fingers, he said, "To the saloon. I feel like a drink."

Jason didn't know how he felt, truth be told.

He guessed it all had to do with the people and the situation concerned. But he was shaken up, no doubt about it. He wished he could just wave his hand and permanently get rid of Davis and Lynch and Todd and the town fathers and the whole world, and go happily back East. He'd force Jenny to go with him, that's what he'd do. He'd bind and gag her until they got east of the Missouri or maybe even the Mississippi! Maybe by then she wouldn't want to yell at him so much. Maybe she'd feel home calling to her, too.

He realized he'd stopped walking, and was leaning against the rail out front of Solomon's Mercantile, and suddenly, he wondered about the baby. The lights were on in an upstairs window, and he heard, just faintly, the sound of Solomon laughing. Jason allowed himself a small smile. The baby must be some better, then.

But even that implied good news couldn't cheer him up. He just felt . . . itchy. Like something bad was going to happen, something he didn't have any control over, and he didn't like it. He was used to having control over most things that mattered, but not the thing that was coming. Whatever it was.

He rolled himself a smoke and started on down the street, lighting his cigarette as he walked. The smoke tasted more brittle than usual, oddly dirty, and he almost put it out, but by then he was on the walk outside the saloon. "Aw, screw it," he muttered, and pushed his way inside.

The first thing he did was check the place that Davis had staked out earlier, and sure enough, he was still there, still tossing back his rotgut like there wasn't enough in the world to get him drunk, wasn't enough to even make him stagger a little. And then from his right, he heard, "Jason!" and looked over to see Ward and Abe slouched at a table quite near him. He walked on over.

Abe was there, looking a little drunk, and Ward was with him, nursing a beer and not impaired in the slightest, his hand still raised in a wave. He guessed he couldn't ride Ward about the beer. He'd had one himself today, and intended to have a few more tonight. "Wash go on home?"

Ward said, "To my house, yeah. And I guess you heard, though I can't figure how. Did you come on down to celebrate with us?"

Jason wended his way over to the table, pulled out a chair, and sat down. "Heard what?"

"About MacDonald, of course!" said Ward.

"What about him?"

Ward went on to explain the evening's excitement in great detail, and finished up by including Abe's response to the situation. Abe, on the other hand, spent the entire time staring over toward Davis's table.

For a moment, Jason aped him. Davis was still sitting there, drinking, and not much else. Jason glanced up toward the second floor, saw that Rafe's door was still closed, and quickly looked away in case Davis had seen him.

His attention returned to the table before him, where Ward was nearly collapsed in laughter. Jason said, "Well, I guess whatever works, works."

"Amen," said Abe, and ordered another bourbon. Then he turned toward Jason. "This Miss Electa your sister works for: What's her story?"

"She's one of the Morton girls," Jason answered, a bit surprised by the question. "The unmarried one. She teaches our school. Why?"

"Just wonderin', that's all. No warrants or anything?"

Jason was shocked. He said, "On Miss Electa? Certainly not!"

Abe had turned to stare at Davis. "Sorry," he said. "Had to ask."

But why? Was he asking because Jenny worked for her, or did he have some kind of personal designs on Electa? Jason didn't ask. He was too embarrassed to pursue it.

"Don't ya think that's a riot, Jason?" Ward, to his left, elbowed him in the ribs.

"What?"

"Key-rist! About what Abe said to young Steve McCord! MacDonald's man?"

"Oh, yeah. Pretty slick."

"Well, you don't need to sound so all-fired excited 'bout it." Ward drummed the table with his fingertips.

"Sorry, Ward. I've got a lot on my mind."

Barely audibly, Abe muttered, "Don't we all."

16

Sampson Davis finally gave up and went home, leaving Jason, Ward, and Abe in the saloon with nobody to keep an eye on. But Matt MacDonald's worries were beginning to trouble Jason. What if this time there actually *were* Apache lurking out around his place? It would be about Matt's speed to have something like that happen, and just when he'd worn out the local law. Which, actually, he'd done a long time ago, but Jason just kept on humoring him.

He wasn't tired, not nearly ready for bed, and he announced, "Guess I'll ride out to the Double M. Just to make certain."

Ward stared at him as he rose. He looked like he was wavering between riding along, just to make sure that his boss didn't do something stupid—like go the rest of the way crazy—or just slugging him in the jaw to keep him in town. But in the end, he stood up, too. "All right. Count me in." He didn't look too happy, though.

Abe Todd seemed annoyed, but sighed and said,

"Well, if you boys're gonna ride out there for nothin', I reckon I might's well tag along and get the lay of the land." He knocked back the last of his drink and stood up.

They readied their horses and left town within a half hour. It was dark, but the moon was bright and there were plenty of stars shedding their light, so Jason set the pace at a slow lope. The path they traveled was safe, having been worn bare by various riders coming and going, usually in a hurry. It was too chilly for snakes, and so they traveled fairly carelessly, taking their time. Until they heard the shots, that was.

Jason automatically fanned Cleo into a hard gallop, and Ward and Abe were close behind. They came over the ridge just before they hit Matt's ranch. They saw the backfire from shots inside the ranch windows, and heard the whoosh of arrows hitting the sides of the ranch house.

"Well, I'll be double damned and deep fried," Abe muttered as he slid off Boy and sent him back down to the shelter of the ridge behind them. Ward and Jason followed suit with their horses.

"Why they attackin' at night?" Ward asked, skirting a barrel cactus. "They ain't supposed to do that!"

"Search me," said Jason, and got a shot off at the nearest brave just before he could fire his arrow.

The three of them were down in the brush, now, hidden from observers, and sighting carefully through the weeds and cactus. There weren't many Indians, Jason was sure of that. Just a handful, really. He made out three more over in the weeds where he'd shot the first brave, and one shadowy figure over by the barn. He figured if he could see three in the brush, there were at least three more he couldn't see. That still, however, didn't make a raiding party. He thought that these few had probably broken off from a larger group and were operating on their own.

Anyway, he hoped so. He'd hate to run this crew off and have the main force show up in their wake.

Abe muttered something that told Jason he was thinking the same thing, and heartened, Jason let fly another shot. It missed, but he felt better.

Ward took down a second brave, and Abe, who had thought to grab his rifle, knocked off the one trying to break into the barn. The few left in the brush slithered off, and Jason didn't see them again until they'd mounted their ponies and were making a getaway into the distance.

"Hello the house!" Jason called, deciding he didn't want to get himself shot by Matt MacDonald, who'd probably take him for an Apache.

After a moment, somebody—probably Matt, himself—yelled back, "Who's out there?"

Jason called out, "The law, Matthew! We ran your Indians off, and we're lookin' for a drink. You wanna thank us, don't you?" He knew full well that Matt didn't want to thank him, but he got a kick out of asking, anyway.

"Come on down." The reply was grudging, but at least there was an implied drink in there somewhere.

"Sounds friendly enough," said Abe.

"Optimist. Ward, you all right?"

"Yeah. I'm gonna get the horses."

Jason nodded. "All right. See you in a few." Ward traipsed back through the weeds and over the rise, while Abe and Jason walked down the slope toward the ranch house. More lights went on in the house as somebody lit lanterns, and soon they were on the porch and Jason's knuckles were raised to rap on the wood.

When it opened, he didn't see Matt. Two ranch hands came out past them before Matt stepped to the fore. He looked as worn out as Jason felt. Jason nodded. "Matt, I'd like you to meet Deputy U.S. Marshal Abe Todd. Abe, this is Matt Mac-Donald."

Abe stuck out his hand and Matt took it and shook it enthusiastically. "Finally. Some *helpful* law!" He ushered them into the house.

"Tell me, Mr. MacDonald, what—"

"It's Matt, just Matt," the young rancher broke in.

"All right, then. Matt, just what did you do to those Apache to make 'em mad enough to try stormin' the ranch at night?"

"What, me?" Red-faced, Matt nearly exploded with anger. "Nothing! They've been thieving my cattle! They've been threatening us with their presence! I haven't done one single thing to aggravate them!"

Jason had already stretched out in an easy chair, and now Abe joined him, making himself comfortable on a settee across the room. "All right, you ain't done a single thing. Somebody say somethin' 'bout a drink?"

Matt left the room, headed for the kitchen, and

Jason checked his pocket watch. It was still early. He heard Ward rap at the door and hollered, "I'll get it!"

Ward entered, looking as thirsty as Jason thought he would. All three horses were hitched to the rail outside. Ward had once worked for Matt for a few months, and was no stranger to his wrath. "He pitchin' a fit?" he asked quietly as Jason let him in.

"Near to it."

"How near?"

"'Bout an inch and a half."

"Great," Ward muttered, and walked on into the parlor, shouting, "And one for me, Matthew!" Over his shoulder, he hissed, "That oughta push him the rest'a the way over." Smiling, he sat on the other end of the settee and nodded his hello to Abe.

Back in town, the lawmen had not left unnoticed. In his front room on the second story of the boarding house, Sampson Davis had seen the three lawmen walk past when they went to get their horses, then ride out of Fury at a slow lope.

It didn't take him long to figure out what he wanted to do. Well, not wanted, exactly. But if he was to get what he came for, he'd have to do it. He'd walked up to the livery and saddled his horse, then ridden out after them.

He was halfway there when he heard the sound of faint gunshots drifting toward him, and thought better of it. They were shooting it out with someone or other up ahead, and that should keep them busy long enough. Long enough for what he needed, anyway.

He turned around and rode back. But when he got there, he didn't put his horse away. Instead, he tied him to the rail outside the boarding house, gave him a pat on the neck, and walked the rest of the way down the street to the saloon. He figured Lynch would be downstairs by this time, having figured he'd gone to bed.

He paused outside the window, back from the glass, and looked over the tables. There was a different bartender on duty now, replacing that nosy one who always swore up and down that Lynch wasn't there when Davis knew damn well that he was hiding upstairs, in one of those rooms. And there was Lynch, sitting at a table with four other fellows toward the back of the main floor, playing poker and having himself a high old time.

Well, not for long, if Sampson Davis had his way. He ran his hand over his back trouser pocket, feeling the bulge of the manacles he'd secreted there. He planned to clap them on Lynch's wrists first thing, then get him out of Fury. Kicking and screaming, if he had to. Just as long as he got him out of that town marshal's reach.

Why did everyone have to like Lynch so much? He couldn't see the good in liking anybody with Lynch's reputation. It just didn't make sense. But it wouldn't be long before Lynch stopped charming anybody. He was going to get him out of town, then shoot him deader than the proverbial doornail.

He let out a sigh, then started for the batwing doors, shoving them open and walking through. He glanced at the barkeep, who apparently had been coached by the fellow that worked days, because he brought a shotgun up from behind the bar and stood stock-still, staring straight at Davis.

Flies, Davis was thinking. Nothing but flies to be brushed away.

Nodding at the barkeep, he began to slowly make his way toward Lynch's table—Lynch, who hadn't seen him yet, had just won the pot and was raking in the money. A big pot, too. Well, lucky at cards tonight or not, he was going to get a surprise, now wasn't he?

He rubbed again at his back pocket just before he got to Lynch's table. He stood quietly on Lynch's left for a moment—this was as close to Lynch as he'd been in two years—and took it in.

Then he said, "Rafe Lynch?"

Two of the other players looked up, and Lynch twisted toward him, saying, "Yeah?"

When he saw it was Sampson Davis, he uncontrollably jumped a little. A slow grin started to creep across Davis's mouth. He said, "Your buddy, the marshal, rode out of town to the south a little while back. Seems to me he's got his hands full and won't be back for a spell."

Lynch stood up and faced him. Davis hadn't expected that, but he didn't give any ground, either.

Lynch's eyes narrowed. "Get outta here. Get outta here and leave off pesterin' me, Davis."

Davis shook his head. "I got as much right to be in here as anybody. More'n you, I reckon. Now, don't you make a fuss. C'mon with me."

"No."

Davis was ready. He dug out the handcuffs and snagged Lynch's right wrist—his gun hand—with one ring, snapping it closed and held Lynch's hand high, well away from his gun.

But Lynch made no attempt to retrieve it. In a loud voice, he said, "Are you tryin' to kidnap me, Davis?"

"Maybe."

"Well, kidnappin's against the law, even in Arizona Territory."

"Just shut up and come with me!" came the growl of a reply. He heard the bartender's shotgun cock behind him. The saloon had grown very quiet.

"No. You're keepin' me from my poker game, Davis."

Davis heard boot steps approach from behind him, then felt the unmistakable imprint of a sawed-off shotgun press into his back. Then a voice said, "Leave go'a him, mister. I won't say it again."

The shotgun's barrel nudging him in the back, Davis slowly let Lynch's hand down, then let go of the other handcuff ring. "You're makin' a big mistake," he said to his unseen gunman. He thought it was probably the bartender. "This man's a murderer. He's wanted in California."

"Well, he ain't so much as spoke harsh to a dog in Arizona, far's I know." The gun's barrel jabbed Davis again. "Now back off."

At the very back of the bar, unnoticed and unrecognized, Ezra Welk watched all this with great interest. It seemed there was a lot more to Fury than a body would think.

Welk watched as, the tables turned, the man called Lynch slapped the big man's own cuffs on him, then marched him out of the saloon and across the street, to the marshal's office.

"Crazy little wide spot in the road," he muttered to himself before he snagged a barmaid again and ordered himself another beer.

Jason sat, sipping at the good whiskey which came from MacDonald's stash and getting madder by the second. Matt had been complaining to Abe for the past ten minutes, maybe more, and non-stop. He'd been protesting his mistreatment by the Apache, and mostly by the local sheriff's office—meaning Jason.

Abe had already very patiently explained several times just why Matt's spread wasn't in Jason's juris-diction, and every explanation was either ignored or talked around by Matt.

Finally, Abe took his feet, signaling the other men to rise, too.

"You know what, MacDonald?" he said, staring Matt straight in the eye. "You just don't listen. And you really are a jackass." And he punched him in the jaw, just like that.

Matt crumpled, a surprised look on his face, and he was out cold by the time he hit the floor.

Abe looked up from the body and shrugged.

"You gotta let folks know where you stand. Some folks take more convincin' than others."

Abe led the way to the front door with Jason and a chuckling Ward bringing up the rear, and by the time they got outside and mounted their horses, Ward was laughing right out loud.

Jason, who couldn't help but grin, said, "Ward, can you hold it down till we get out of earshot of the house, anyway?"

Ward clamped a hand over his own mouth, and reined sharply away and toward the north, toward Fury. He dug his heels into his horse, and this time he was leading the way, with Abe and Jason trying to keep pace with the cackling deputy.

When they finally slowed down to an easy jog trot, all three men were laughing. "Man, you sure told him, Abe!" said Jason. He was fast growing to like the marshal more and more. "I should'a done that a long time ago."

"Yeah, you should'a!" said the laughing Ward. Then he turned serious. "How come you didn't?"

Jason shrugged. Actually, it was because he thought it might be a misuse of his power as marshal. He certainly wasn't afraid of Matt, or what he could do physically. Jason had it on him in spades, and they both knew it. They'd both known it for years, even before the original wagon train had departed from Kansas City.

Jason said, "I did, once. And once was enough. 'Fraid that if I hit him again, I might kill him."

"He's sure a tender one," said Abe, "if that glass jaw'a his is any indication." He started to roll a smoke, and Jason and Ward followed suit. It was a good time for a smoke.

After Jason took his first drag and blew out the smoke in a long plume, he said, "You got any idea why in the hell those Apache attacked at night?"

Ward shook his head, but Abe said, "He's done somethin', somethin' to piss 'em off big time. Don't know what yet, but I'll find out. I'd like to ride back down there tomorrow and talk to his men."

Jason nodded. "Fine by me."

Ward asked, "You want company? Be glad to tag along."

"Nope." Abe shook his head. "Town needs you to get some sleep so's you can keep an eye on Davis tomorrow night. But thankee kindly for the offer."

Ward tilted his head, then nodded.

But Abe had done the damage already—he'd reminded Jason that he'd left the town with no one to watch it, and Sampson Davis on the loose.

17

Back in Fury, Rafe Lynch was having himself a high old time. The bartender, being inexperienced in such things but knowing that the jail was the place for people who tried to kidnap other people, had relieved Davis of all his firearms, poked through his pockets until he found the key to the handcuffs (which Rafe promptly let himself out of), then handed him over to Rafe for incarceration.

Rafe had walked Davis—wearing his own manacles—across the street, then locked him in a cell. He was currently sitting behind Jason's desk with his feet propped up and a cigarette smoldering between his fingers.

"You know, Sampson, I oughta be real mad at you, trailin' me here and tryin' to grab me outta the saloon. But I guess I can forgive you. After all, you're wrong about me killin' your brother-in-law. You oughta be goin' after the doc for that. But I reckon you got your mind all righteous and set, 'bout like a dog after a jackrabbit. You know, a man's gotta do what a man's gotta do and all that crud."

He noticed that his smoke had almost gone out, and took a long drag off it before he stamped it out in Jason's ashtray.

Sampson wasn't listening as far as he could tell. Wasn't even looking at him, and he hadn't since he set foot in the cell. He just sat on the edge of his cot, staring at the floor.

"In fact," Rafe went on, "I figure you owe me. Your brother-in-law stole my daddy's gold shares in one'a them shady poker games of his. Either that, or he held a gun on him 'til he signed. And then he killed him, shot him right through the head. Now, that weren't very nice, was it?"

No reply from the cell.

Rafe hadn't expected one.

"And on top'a that, now you're keepin' me from a good poker game. I figured to win big tonight."

Surprisingly, a mutter came from the cell. "I ain't keepin' you, Lynch."

"Yeah, you are. Somebody has to be here when the marshal comes back, and that somebody is me." He paused to lick a fresh cigarette paper. "I don't like you much, Davis. Come to think of it, I reckon I don't like you at all. But if you keep on houndin' me, looks like somebody's gonna end up dead. Smart money's on you."

He lit the new cigarette and leaned back in the chair to smoke it. It tasted damn good.

* * *

Jason was suddenly in a big toot to get back to town, and Ward quizzed him on it. "Why we pushin' these horses? What's so important that we gotta get back to it?"

"Sampson Davis. Rafe Lynch."

Ward couldn't see why so little time made so much difference. "Aw, they can take care'a themselves, Jason," he called over the galloping hoof beats. "And Wash is in town!"

"Don't count on him." And with that, Jason pulled ahead a full length.

Abe, now riding beside Ward, lifted his brows. "Ours ain't to reason why," he called.

"What?" Ward called, but Abe just shook his head, then lifted a hand and pointed forward. The town's lights, from a bonfire here and a window or two there, were coming into sight.

Abe pulled ahead and hollered something at Jason that Ward couldn't make out. And Jason slowed clear down to a soft jog trot. Ward could tell Jason's mare was grateful by the way she dipped her head over and over. The horses were all plumb tuckered out, if you asked him. Which, of course, no one did.

They soon reached the town gates and the wagon train, and rode on through. Jason didn't take Cleo home as usual, though. He rode on down to the office and dismounted. "Can you walk her out for me, Ward?"

"Guess so."

Ward had dismounted as well as Abe, and he gathered the reins of all three horses and started up the street, leading them and muttering under his breath.

The office lights were on, and when they walked a little closer, Jason saw Rafe Lynch sitting behind his desk, big as life and smoking a cigarette.

He frowned a little and paused, wondering what the hell was going on, when Abe poked him in the back and said, "Ain't nobody gonna go see if you don't."

"Yeah, yeah," Jason muttered, and stepped up on the boardwalk, with Abe right behind him.

Rafe didn't move an inch when Jason shoved in the door. Instead he said, "Howdy, boys! I brung you a prisoner." He pointed to the cell, and it took Jason a moment to figure out who it was.

He said, "Well, I'll be double damned! Rafe, you amaze me!"

Abe shifted his weight and shook his head. "Ditto. What the hell happened?"

"You'd best ask the bartender cross the street. He saw more'a the deal than I did, and he's the one what turned Davis in to me." Rafe shrugged and attempted to look pious. "I am only a vessel."

Abe went across the street while Jason stayed at the office, booting Rafe out of his chair and lighting a smoke of his own. This kept up, he thought, and he was going to smoke himself like a ham, only inside out.

Ward walked in, much earlier than Jason had expected. "Horses all right?"

"Yup. They weren't as used up as we thought. Left Cleo over in your barn. Stripped her tack."

"Thanks, Ward."

Ward suddenly realized that they were not alone. He nodded at Rafe, then looked toward the cell for a moment before he said, "Davis?"

Jason nodded.

"Well, big chief? What we gonna do now?"

"Wait for Abe." He noticed that somebody, probably Ward, had tidied up the pieces of his old chair and put them into the wood bin next to the stove. They weren't fit for anything but fuel anymore, anyway.

Twenty minutes later Abe came back, bringing the story of Rafe's near-kidnapping and the barkeeper's bravery in a time of crisis.

Ward said, "Well, I'll be damned."

Jason said, "Lew's playin' it up for all it's worth, isn't he?"

Abe nodded. "A regular John Wilkes Booth. Far as the actin' goes, anyhow. I seen him once, in Baltimore, y'know."

Rafe leaned forward at that. "For real? You get any indication of what was to come?"

Abe shook his head. "Damn good performance, though. Can't recollect the name'a the play just now. . . ."

Jason waved a hand. "Can we get back to the business at hand, gentlemen?"

They all stared toward Davis's cell. He was nothing but a dark shadow, sitting in profile to them on the edge of the bunk, hat pulled low, face down, seemingly fascinated with the floor between his boots.

Abe, who had been sitting on the edge of Jason's desk, stood up. "Gotta think on it, but it may be a case for the U.S. Marshal's Office. Attempted kidnapping, that is. You boys be up for an answer come the mornin'?"

Jason nodded, and Abe let himself out and soberly walked across the street to Kendalls' Boarding House.

Jenny was asleep by the time Jason finally got home and settled Cleo in, and he quietly got ready for bed and slid his body between the covers. And the whole time, all he was thinking about was "what next?" He supposed most of it would hang on Abe's decision, but that would entail Abe having to haul Davis up to Prescott. No matter how you looked at it, that wasn't a happy plan. There were too many mountains to climb and too many streams to cross, and just plain too many opportunities for Davis to break free.

It wasn't that Jason mistrusted Abe's abilities. But he didn't know what Davis was capable of, and he didn't like the idea of Abe going out there alone with him.

Finally, after some fitful tossing and turning, he decided to send Ward along. Ward would enjoy the outing, he figured, and Abe would enjoy the company. All this hinged, of course, on Abe's decision. Taking into account his friendship with Rafe and his swift reaction to Matt, earlier this evening,

Jason wouldn't be surprised if he just dragged Davis up into the mountains and shot him.

He shook his head. No, Abe wouldn't do that. But then again, he might. It was impossible to tell.

At last, slumber's beckoning became insistent, and Jason fell fitfully asleep. He didn't rouse until Jenny woke him the next morning.

But when Jason finally sat down in his office, Abe was nowhere to be found. According to Ward, he hadn't been by the office, and nobody'd seen him. Sampson Davis, at least, was still in his cell, and silently ate the breakfast that Jenny had made for him—careful to keep it kosher, of course.

Abe finally stuck his head in the door at about lunchtime and apprised Jason that he'd come to no decision as yet.

Jason was both relieved and disappointed, but if anybody had asked him, he couldn't have said why.

He walked over to the saloon with Abe and rounded up Rafe (prying him loose from a game of blackjack, which he'd been winning all morning), and they all hiked up to the café to grab some lunch. Jenny had sent him off to work with a chicken sandwich, but he figured to eat that later on. Talking was more important now.

And Rafe and Abe were both full of talk. Unfortunately, mostly stories about Rafe's daddy and Rafe's childhood and Rafe's growing up, and no speculation about just what the hell they were going to do with Sampson Davis.

Abe seemed in a particularly good mood. Had

Jason been so inclined, he might have even referred to him as "high-spirited." Quite a departure from his usual demeanor. Odd, Jason thought. Very odd.

He finally asked. "Where you been this morning, Abe? Couldn't turn you up, and I about turned over every stone in town."

"Reckon you didn't think to look where I was," Abe said cryptically.

"Where was that?"

"In the schoolhouse." Abe grinned. It was a silly grin, almost like a smitten youngster.

"What the heck were you doin' in school? Hey, you weren't romancin' my baby sister, were you?"

Abe held up both hands, palms forward. "Don't go gettin' yourself in an uproar, Jason. That Jenny's a good kid. She took over classes for Electa while we went out back and talked."

Now Jason was really confused. Even Rafe looked a little taken aback. Jason said, "You went outside with Miss Morton?"

"Ain't gonna be 'Miss Morton' for long," Abe remarked with a grin that tried to be cryptic, but failed.

Rafe slugged him in the arm. "You old dog!"

It took Jason a little longer, but he finally said, "But you haven't even met her yet!"

"I was up there yesterday for a spell, and I seen her the day I rode in. Damned handsome woman."

"But still, that's hardly a basis for—"

"Jason," Abe said, "my pa knew my ma for about twelve hours afore they got hitched, and they're still hitched to this very day. Sometimes, lastin' love happens fast."

"Maybe, but—"

"No buts about it." Abe signaled the waiter. "Three pieces of apple pie—with cheddar. We're celebratin'!"

"But did she say yes?" Jenny asked again. "My gosh, I sure couldn't tell anything from the way she acted. I mean, not that she'd just been proposed to!"

"Yes, she said 'yes'," Jason replied. He didn't really understand it himself, yet. "Except she wants him to go ask her father, first."

Jenny's hand were suddenly planted firmly on her hips. "Why? I mean, she's got to be like, forty years old or something!"

"Thirty," Jason corrected. "And thirty's not that old if you're still somebody's kid. You got any more'a that cake?"

She sliced off another piece and practically threw it at him. "How can you eat cake at a time like this?"

"It's good cake. And what do you mean, 'a time like this'?"

"When your only sister is about to have to take on teaching the whole school—by herself! They'll move to Prescott, you know. They'll be gone and I'll be left with Cyrano Jones and Junior Krebbs and that whole crowd. 'Course, they'll be graduating in June and out on the town and they'll be yours to deal with, but there are others coming up that are going to be just as difficult if not worse, and—"

She put her hands up to her eyes, covering them, and he saw a single tear trickle through her fingers. "What am I gonna do, Jason?"

"You'll go on like we all do, Jenny." He knew it wasn't comforting, but it was the best he could come up with, considering the circumstances.

"You're no help at all!" she shouted and ran from the room.

As her bedroom door slammed behind her, he muttered, "Yeah, I know," and then he pulled his cake toward him and dug in. It really was good cake.

Later, on the porch, he considered that Jenny was just being selfish, or perhaps jealous. Or maybe she was really, truly scared of teaching the class on her own. In the end, he supposed it didn't matter. If Miss Morton left town, Jenny was stuck.

To tell the truth, Jason wasn't crazy about the idea, either. Some of those boys that they taught were big galoots, sullen and brutish, and far beyond the normal age for school, having been held back a few times. And Jenny was small, almost tiny. If one of them got her cornered . . .

He stubbed out his cigarette to take his mind off of it, but it didn't work. He was still brooding when he went into the house. He stopped in the kitchen to eat yet another piece of cake, and it was while he was thus occupied that his sister came down the hall.

"Jason?" she said. "I'm sorry. I don't mean to act like a baby or a sore loser. I wish Miss Morton all the best, I really do. This is a silly time for me to be thinking about myself." She turned to go back down the hall, then suddenly spun back. "Are you eating *another* piece of cake?"

Jason swallowed, then said, "But it's good!"

She shook her finger at him. "Nobody likes a fat marshal." And then she turned again and went back to her room.

Jason watched her retreat, then stared down at the cake, and gave a thoughtful gaze at his belly. Muttering, "I've got a *long* way to go before I'm fat!" he picked up his fork and happily went back to work.

That night, long after Ward had made his final rounds and Jason was fast asleep, Deputy U.S. Marshal Abraham Todd sat in the far corner of his room, smoking. He'd given up counting them a long time ago, but he knew he was almost out of papers.

He wished he could get Jason interested in taking the position of Deputy U.S. Marshal. It would surely solve a passel of problems for him. 'Course, that meant they'd get dumped on Jason, but Jason was better at this than he thought, and he had himself a mighty good deputy in Ward Wanamaker. Good enough that he'd considered asking Ward to join up if he couldn't convince Jason.

When he got married—oh, Electa, his lovely Electa!—he was thinking about resigning. The job wasn't fair to a wife. He'd have to spend so much time away from home, and there was always the chance that he could be killed. . . .

But then, the job had been his life up until now. Maybe he couldn't just drop it that easily, for thinking about it and actually doing it were two different things.

He took a final drag off his smoke and stubbed it out in the ashtray, then methodically began to roll another. It was the next to the last paper, he noticed.

He began to daydream about Electa again, about having someone to come home to, someone to cook for him and darn his socks, and most of all, to bear his children. He was nearing forty-five, and felt like he was pushing his luck, for someone in his line of work. Electa was smart and Electa was pretty. A right handsome woman, his pa would have said.

And Electa had the bearing and the air of authority. He'd seen her with those kids. Hell, some of them were big enough and mean enough that they spooked him! But she had them in her hip pocket. A person didn't learn that, they had to come by it naturally.

Just that air of hers, that command, had convinced him that she was the woman for him.

He decided that he'd ride out to her father's ranch in the morning and ask his permission to marry his daughter, just like Electa had requested. It never crossed his mind that Mr. Morton would say no. Electa was so ripe she was going to burst if somebody didn't marry her, and quick.

There were two Morton families, she'd told him, and her parents lived in the first house he'd come to, if he followed the trail. It seemed simple enough.

He stubbed out the smoke and, rising, hauled his carcass over to the bed and lay down, a silly smile plastered over his weary face. *Oh, Electa,* he thought as he drifted off to sleep. *My Electa.*

18

At about four-thirty in the morning, Jason was awakened by a spate of gunshots coming from the east. Down by the jail, he thought, and muttered, "Crap!"

He sprang up from the bed, tugged on his clothes, and ran from the house and up the street to the sound of hoofbeats fading into the distance, headed south.

"Ward!" he called as he kept running, down toward the office. "Ward!"

There was no answer except from Mrs. Kendall, who was out on the street in her nightclothes and shouted, "What happened?!" as he ran past.

"Don't know!" Jason shouted over his shoulder, and shoved open the jailhouse doors. The lamp on his desk was lit and there were signs of a struggle, and Sampson Davis's cell was empty.

Muttering, "Damn it," and then shouting, "Ward!" again, he heard a soft moan coming from in front of the other cell. Rushing toward the source, he nearly tripped over Ward's body. He knelt to it, saw that he was still breathing, but that he had one bullet hole, bleeding profusely, in his chest, and another in his shoulder.

"Dear God," he said, and went back to the door, throwing it wide. "Call Dr. Morelli!" he shouted to Mrs. Kendall, still where he'd left her. "Ward's been shot!"

He scurried back inside again, and knelt beside Ward. His deputy's breathing was shallow, but steady, he thought. He said a silent prayer that Ward would make it—what would they do without him?—and waited for the doctor to show up.

Morelli was there faster than he could have hoped, dressed in his nightclothes but carrying his black bag. "What happened?" he asked.

"Don't know. The shots woke me. But somebody was galloping hell-bent for leather out of town when I was running up here, and Davis is gone."

"I heard the shots, too. There were four of them, altogether."

"So Ward fired back. He's a dead shot, Doc. At least one'a those slugs of his had to connect."

"We'll hope. Right now, help me get him across the street. He needs surgery, right away."

The door burst open again just as Jason and Morelli managed to get Ward halfway up.

It was Abe, who had his gun out, ready for anything. But he stuck it back in its holster once he took in the situation and said, "Oh, Christ. Not Ward! Is he . . ."

"Not yet," said Jason. "Give us a hand with him, all right?"

Abe grabbed Ward around the middle, and the

three of them managed to get the deputy across the street and into Morelli's surgery. Once Morelli had ushered them back out into the waiting room and closed the drape between them, Abe asked, "Davis did it, didn't he?"

Jason, on the verge of tears, nodded. "Morelli said he heard four shots, and only two of 'em are in Ward. One's in the wall beside the clock, which means that Davis has got one of 'em in him."

"How the hell'd he get a gun?"

"Good question."

"Where'd he go?"

"Outta town, riding south."

"What're we waitin' for, then?"

Abe's eagerness fired up Jason rather than sinking him down into deeper despair, and he jumped up and headed out the door and home to saddle up Cleo.

Once Cleo was tacked up—and in record time— Jason rode up to the livery to find not only Abe, but Rafe waiting for him. Jason eyed Rafe. "You sure you wanna come?"

"'Course I'm sure."

"But—"

Rafe waved him off. "Let's go!" He wheeled his mount and took off through the gates, heading due south.

"How's he know where to go?" Jason shouted to Abe.

"I told him!"

They followed Rafe nearly all the way to the

Double M, where he slowed and searched, in the dawning light, for a hint in the brush. He finally found one, and held up his hand. "This way!" he said, pointing to the west, and then took off again.

Jason and Abe followed, although it was obvious that Abe had more confidence in Rafe's tracking skills than Jason had. As for Jason, he was busy being torn up by Ward's near death, and praying that he'd survive. This would kill Jenny, he knew. It was already killing him.

Damn the West, anyway! It was nothing but a place where men went to die when they could have stayed back East and lived long, productive lives.

He was continuing this train of thought when Rafe suddenly reined up. He and Abe did, too.

"What?" he asked.

"He's up ahead."

"Of course, he's up ahead! We're followin' him!"

"No," said Rafe. "Right up ahead. Behind those rocks, on the right." He indicated a tumble of large boulders, each as tall as a man if not taller.

Jason considered this possibility. "Then why doesn't he shoot us right now?"

"Sun's in his eyes," Abe said quietly. "He's waitin' for us to get closer or the sun to rise a little higher, whichever comes first."

"I say we don't give him time for either one," Jason said. "Can we sneak around the far side of those rocks? Way back up there, on the north?"

"Better'n waitin' to get shot like Ward. C'mon, Rafe," Abe said.

Rafe turned toward them, skirted a bed of manzanita, and began to follow them back to the north.

They took a wide, circuitous route that Jason hoped would keep them out of range—pistol range, anyway—and at last came to the northern-most point of the rock pile. Jason signaled the men to be quiet and on their guard. He couldn't be certain that Davis hadn't figured out their plan. Davis could easily be waiting for them, his guns drawn, ready and willing to commit triple homicide.

Jason dismounted, ground-tied Cleo, and tentatively walked to the edge of the last boulder. He peeked around the back side of it.

He saw nothing. Not a man, not a horse, nothing.

But there were plenty of nooks and crannies in those boulders for Davis to hide in, and hide his horse in, too. He beckoned to Abe, who ground-tied Boy, too, and joined him.

"Crud," Abe said quietly, after a moment. "You think he took off the other way while we was bein' all sneaky?"

Jason shook his head and whispered, "No. We would have heard him. Sound carries like crazy out here."

Abe nodded. "I know. Well, who goes first?"

"I do. It was my deputy that he gunned down."

"Yeah," said Abe, "but that was back in your jurisdiction."

Rafe suddenly appeared between them and asked, "What're you two cookin' up over here?"

"Shhh!" hissed both Jason and Abe.

Rafe rolled his eyes. "You want Davis, he's out here."

Jason beat Abe to the edge of the rocks and sure

enough, saw the silhouette of a rider jogging further south.

"You any good with that rifle of yours?" he asked Abe.

"Yeah. But Rafe's a mite better."

"Rafe! Consider yourself temporarily deputized."

"But I—"

Abe cut him off. "He wants you to shoot Davis. He's makin' like he's no good with a rifle."

"Well, I'm not. Hurry up, he's getting away!"

Rafe said, "Okay, okay!" and pulled his rifle from the saddle's boot. Jason watched nervously as he sighted on Davis, then slowly—it seemed like a lifetime!—squeezed the trigger.

The blast took them all by surprise, Rafe included. But it took no one more off guard than Sampson Davis. He continued on a few steps, then slid awkwardly from his horse, disappearing into the tall weeds with a slump.

Abe clapped Rafe on the shoulder. "Helluva shot, kid, helluva shot! Your daddy'd be spit-polish proud!"

Rafe was staring at his rifle and didn't look up. "I 'bout forgot how loud it was."

"Well, let's go pick him and his horse up." Abe was already mounting his roan.

Jason hadn't yet moved. "What if he's not dead?" he asked, his voice flat. "What if he's just lying there in the weeds, waiting for us to get close enough for him to pick us off?"

Abe tilted his head. "Good thinkin', Jason. But if he is, there ain't nothin' we can do about it, 'cept get shot. C'mon, you two! Let's move!"

* * *

Davis proved not to be dead, but he wasn't far from it.

They loaded him on his horse, tied him down (after they relieved him of his firearms), and Jason found the gun he'd used to shoot Ward. It was a snub-nosed handgun, stuck down inside his boot—the one place Jason supposed Rafe and Lew hadn't patted down when Davis was arrested the first time. When Rafe saw the gun, he at least had the good grace to look sheepish.

They started back. At a walk this time, not a gallop. Davis remained out cold, though Jason checked on him from time to time. His breathing was shallow but regular, so far as he could tell, and his color looked good. But he wasn't taking any chances. He watched Davis like the proverbial hawk.

They were riding along when Abe said, out of the blue, "Y'know that creek we crossed on the way out?"

Jason looked over. "What of it?"

"It seem to you like it was some deeper than back in town, and quite a bit slower?"

Jason scratched the back of his head. "Come to think of it, yeah."

"Somebody's got 'er dammed up farther down the line, I reckon."

Jason froze. Of course! What else would cause the Apache to attack at night? And it sure explained why Matt was so nervous! He spat, "Crap! MacDonald's got it dammed up for his cattle so that it's not reaching the Apache camp!"

He figured he'd go shoot a few arrows into Mac-Donald, too, if he cut off the water supply to Fury!

Abe nodded and said, "Thought so."

Rafe jogged up from behind. "What you boys jabberin' about up here?"

Jason filled him in, and he repeated Abe's sentiment almost word for word. Then he said, "Don't s'pose we could go check it out, could we?"

"Gotta get Davis back. Gotta check on Ward. After that . . ."

Rafe nodded. "Gotcha, Marshal. Me, I'm wantin' to look in on ol' Ward myself." Then he brightened. "Did you see? He got Davis in the side, shot him right through the meat. Served the rat bastard right!" He spat into the weeds, as if to underscore what he'd just said.

"Only thing that would have served him better," Abe said, "was if Ward had got him straight through the heart."

Jason tended to agree with Abe, but said nothing, except, "Well, he's sure shot now."

"Think we can move this up into a jog, Jason?" Rafe asked. "I'm growin' weary of ploddin' along, and I wanna get back and see how ol' Ward's doin'."

Jason goosed Cleo into a soft jog and the others followed suit, with Rafe muttering, "Thank God."

Davis survived the trip back to town (more's the pity), and Ward was still breathing, although Morelli wasn't any too hopeful about his recovery. "The one in his shoulder isn't too bad," he told Jason, "but that other one went right through his lung. Patched him up the best I could, but . . ." He shook his head.

Ward lay there on Morelli's table, with tubes coming out of him, tubes that drained pinkish fluid into glass jars. He looked like a ghost, he was so pale, and Jason said a silent prayer over him in the hope that somebody, somewhere, was listening.

They left Davis on a bench outside the surgery, and Morelli, after a cursory examination, said he didn't look good at all, not with that slug in his side, and not with Rafe's bullet having just missed his heart. He said he'd try, though.

It was all Jason could ask.

He wanted somebody left alive to hang.

And every one of them, to a man, got so wrapped up in Ward's situation, dangling between life and death, that all thoughts of MacDonald and the dammed creek flew clean out of their heads.

For the time being, anyway.

19

The next morning, Jason woke to horrible news: Ward was dead. He had passed during the night, Morelli had told Jenny, who was up and awake to answer the door when he dropped by. Morelli seemed upset, as did Jenny, but Jason, while he shed a silent tear or two, thanked God that at least Ward hadn't suffered at the end. He thanked Him for Ward's life, and he thanked Him for Ward's friendship, and for Ward's company, even though it had been short-lived.

And then he prayed that God would let Davis live, so that he might have the pleasure of executing him.

He had never felt like this before, not even when his father passed, and while he couldn't change the way he felt, he wondered that he, in fact, did feel that way.

When he got to the office, Morelli and Abe had already moved Davis over to the jail, and locked the patient safely in a cell. Abe, after saying how sorry he was about Ward's demise, said the doc had warned him that Davis wouldn't regain consciousness for at least two hours or so, which was fine with Jason. The less time he had to spend in the presence of Davis's conscious mind, the better.

He had come to the conclusion that the man—if he was a man at all—was evil incarnate.

After Abe left, Jason went to the back room and wept again, crying for Ward, for himself, for Jenny, and for the town, but mostly for Ward. And then he pulled himself back together, and vowed this would be the last time he would ever cry for Ward. The very last time.

But Davis was going to pay, all right, and pay with his own life if Jason had any say in it. Briefly, he wished he could make him suffer, then booted the thought from his mind. Vengeance wasn't his to parcel out. That belonged to a higher power.

One whom he fervently hoped was keeping His eye on the situation.

Morelli's second stop of the morning was at the mercantile, where he found the whole family in good spirits. Baby Sarah was doing wondrously well, and Solomon and Rachael were well aware of it. Morelli was pleased that what he'd wished for had come to pass. Time *had* healed the infant, time and faith and love all mixed together. He knew he certainly hadn't had anything to do with it.

He prayed with the Cohens (although he refrained from crossing himself until he got outside, in deference to their beliefs), and while he told them their daughter wasn't out of the woods yet, she was well on her way.

The Cohens were delighted, naturally, and offered Morelli a glass of the sweet wine they favored, which he accepted. They weren't aware of it, but he wasn't looking forward to his next call. He'd be going out to the wagons to check on Frank Saulk's poor, spine-peppered back. He didn't have much hope for a positive outcome.

At last, he bid good-bye to the Cohens, went outside, crossed himself, and set out at a brisk clip, through the gates.

He found the Saulks' wagon surrounded by weeping women and dry-eyed men, doing their best to comfort their wives. The Saulks' children were beneath the wagon, comforting each other, and he found Eliza Saulk in the wagon, sitting quiet and pale beside her husband's body.

"Eliza?" he said softly, leaning into the back of the wagon to get a better look at Frank. Even from this distance, he could tell Saulk was dead. For one thing there was the odor, but Frank had smelt of death long before he died. No, it was the pallor of the body, the utter and compete stillness of it. "May I come in?"

She nodded in the affirmative.

He climbed up and officially made certain that Frank had passed—during the night, he thought—then covered the head with a sheet and turned toward the new widow.

"Eliza?" he said again. When she didn't reply, he ploughed ahead. "Would you like him to be buried here in Fury, or out along the trail?"

"Here." The word was no louder than a mouse's squeak.

"Shall I take care of the details for you?"

She nodded.

He sighed. "All right. Shortly, there'll be someone along to take his body to the undertakers, all right?"

She nodded again.

"You think you'll be all right, or would you like me to send one of the town women out to sit with you and help with the children?"

"I'll be fine." She said it without inflection or emotion or any kind, as if the living soul of her had died along with her husband, and all that was left was a blankly animated husk. Morelli had seen grief before, and many kinds, but nothing like this.

He excused himself and crawled down out of the Conestoga, telling Riley Havens (who had just joined the crowd) of his plans.

"Thanks, Doctor Morelli," Riley said. They had moved a little way off from the others. "I know you done the best you could for ol' Frank."

"Yes," said Morelli, shaking his head. "I just wish it could have been more. Enough to save him, at least."

Riley put a comforting hand on his shoulder. It was something that the doctor wasn't accustomed to, especially from anyone except his wife, and it startled him. Reflexively, he moved away.

"Didn't mean to . . . Well, I'm sorry, too," Riley said.

"Thank you. Well, I'd best be getting on with

my errands for the morning." He tipped his hat. "Good morning, sir."

He walked off, toward the city gate.

Riley watched him go around the corner of the gate and disappear, and then he walked back toward the Saulks' wagon. He said his "sorries" to Eliza and told her that he'd talked to the doctor, and then he left her. He doubted that she'd heard a word he'd said, anyway. Grief had a way of making people deaf, dumb, and blind, he'd learned, and Eliza was surely stricken. He sure felt bad for those kids, too, having to grow up without a pa. Or maybe not. Eliza was not a great beauty, but she was comely enough. Maybe she could attract another man who wouldn't mind raising a dead man's children.

Oh, well. It wasn't his place to worry about that. His job, he reminded himself, his *only* job, was to get these people back to Kansas City and civilization. If some of them decided to drop out (as had Judith Strong, the dressmaker, and Father Micah), that was none of his nevermind.

Actually, he was about to lose more folks than he had counted on. The Reverend Fletcher Bean had come to the decision that he was leaving the West in haste, and that the people of Fury needed him. The Grimms, owner of the dog Hannibal and parents of three children, had also decided to stay, provided they could find a place to set up their bakery. And if they couldn't, they were surely going to leave Hannibal behind. He was proving too costly to feed with their limited means. And

Bill Crachit had come to the decision that at sixteen, he wasn't up to making the full journey by himself. He'd rather stay on in Fury for a year or two, maybe find work on a farm or a ranch, and then go on back East once he'd saved up some cash and could grow a full beard.

Riley wasn't aware of any of this yet. In fact, only some of the people had made up their minds completely. But chances were that he would lose a good part of his wagon train before he left the little settlement of Fury behind.

Oblivious, Riley walked up ahead to his wagon, then past it and the gates to check his team. They were eating well and seemed content, as did his saddle horse. Fury had been good to the wagon train, and they were about to be good to Fury.

Once again, Ezra Welk started his day at the saloon. The town's beer and whiskey drinkers had him pretty much up to date on the town's recent goings-on (whether they knew it or not), leaving him continually surprised at the activity level in Fury.

Especially when he had nothing to do with it.

Usually, he was the one responsible for any ruckus, and this was a change of pace for him. He was actually finding it . . . pleasant. He kept one eye peeled in the direction of the marshal's office. The boy marshal had ridden out before the dawn broke to the eastern horizon the day before, theoretically chasing after Sampson Davis. At least, in theory. Davis had supposedly shot up the deputy during the night, probably killing him. Anyway, that's what the woman who ran the boarding-house had blathered on and on about during an otherwise decent breakfast. Hell. They should have done what had first come to Welk's mind—just taken Davis out and plugged him, the ugly bastard.

But then, nobody had asked him, had they?

He sniffed derisively. Well, at least it was entertaining. Davis had already killed that lanky deputy, taking him off Welk's "possibilities" list. But to look on the bright side—as his mother always used to say before sending him out to the woodshed to wait for another one of his father's beatings—they'd probably all end up killing each other, anyway.

He'd already decided to stick around for the finish.

The Reverend Milcher picked up his order from Salmon Kendall's print shop, carried it home, unwrapped it, and spread the flyers out on one of the pew benches. The blue paper was just as fine as Salmon had promised it would be, and the printing, urging people to visit his church on Sunday, was perfect. Not one word misspelled! It had taken all the change he could scrape to-gether, but he looked on it as an investment—an investment in himself, and an investment in the good people of Fury.

After scraping the papers back together, he first stood right outside the church's front door, handing out flyers and shaking hands with everyone who passed. He kept his face and demeanor affable, and found it was true—you *did* get more flies with honey than with vinegar!

After a bit, he moved on down the street and stood in front of the café, where he glad-handed every passerby, handing out fliers and inviting them to Sunday's service. Everyone was so nice! Why, it was positively refreshing! He reminded himself to pay more attention to the cat. After all, she had given him the idea, bless her!

It was at about the time that he handed out the last flier that he noticed the sky. It was darker than it should have been, filled with black and dark grey clouds where before there had been only white wisps. A storm was coming, and coming soon.

The wind was already whipping papers and bits of detritus along the street. Several of his own fliers passed him by. He put a hand atop his head to hold down his hat, then strode back up the street on his long, thin, black-panted legs, to the church.

"Lavinia?" he called as he climbed the stairs. "Storm's coming in again!"

Before the weather turned bad, Deputy U.S. Marshall Abraham Todd had set out to the north, to visit the Mortons and make his plea. He was as slicked up as it was possible to get in Fury, and he had even taken the time to groom his blue roan to a spit shine. He imagined, as he followed the path that his Electa had made going to and from the school five days a week, that he fairly glittered in the sun. At least he hoped he did. He wanted all the help he could get with Electa's folks.

He reached the ranch in under an hour. It lay spread out before him, cupped in a wide valley, with two big houses and one slightly smaller, three barns, plenty of corrals, and the sounds and smells of cattle and hogs and horses and freshly mown hay.

He instantly felt right at home.

He dismounted in front of the house Electa had told him belonged to her folks, tied his horse to the rail, and climbed up the steps. He stood there a moment, shifting from boot to boot, tugging at his vest, and nervously clearing his throat before he raised his knuckles to rap at the door.

It was immediately answered by a small, attractive, grey-haired woman, who smiled at him and said, "Yes?"

"Would you be the Mrs. Morton who's Electa Morton's mother?" he asked. He could barely get the words out, and for a second, he thought he was going to choke on his own tongue.

But she seemed not to notice his discomfort, and replied, "I am, indeed. And you must be Marshal Abraham Todd, from Prescott."

He felt his head nod. "Yes'm, that's me. I wonder, could I speak to you and Mr. Morton? About Electa?"

She opened the door wider and stepped back. "Do come inside, son."

Nobody had called him "son" since Hector was a pup, and he sort of liked it. He went inside and followed her down a wide hallway, then turned to the right, into a large parlor. There sat (he supposed, at any rate) Mr. Morton, reading a newspaper.

Mrs. Morton said, "He's here, dear."

The paper lowered, and he got his first glimpse of Electa's father: a rugged man, serious in spirit and probably honest as the day was long, with grey-white hair and a long beard to match. He was dressed in a farmer's togs, overalls and a plaid shirt, and wore the farmer's badge—a tan line straight across his forehead, where his hatband stopped.

The hat itself hung neatly on a peg beside the doorway he'd just come through. Which served to remind Abe that he was still wearing his. Belatedly, he swept it off his head, then ran his fingers through his hair to put it back into order.

Mr. Morton had apparently been sizing him up, too, because in lieu of "hello," he said, "Well, you look the part anyway, young man."

Young man? Nobody had called him that, either, not in a *year* of Sundays! He said, "Sir?"

Morton swept his hand toward a side chair. "Rest your bones, boy. I understand that you want to talk to me about Electa."

Abe collapsed into the chair more than he sat in it, and said, "Yessir. First off, I want you to know that I'm a deputy U.S. marshal, and I make good money, enough to support us both and then some. Got some money saved, too, up in the Prescott Bank. Got near about four thousand dollars, by my reckoning. My folks came from Massachusetts and their folks came from England, and they moved to California when it was still under Spanish control. That's when they had me. I grew up on stories about Zorro and Joaquin Murrieta and the like, cause my pa worked as a manager on a big hacienda for several years."

He stopped to catch his breath, and when he did, Morton asked the big question: "And how do you feel about Electa? Do you love her? Promise to take care of her come drought or famine, hell or high water?"

Abe swallowed hard. He said, "Mr. Morton, I love your daughter with all my heart, and the rest of me, too. I'd die for her, but I'd rather live with her as man and wife. With your permission, of course, sir."

There. He'd said it. Filled with relief as well as a sickening sense of dread, he leaned back in the chair, and let out a light-headed sigh.

For the first time, Morton smiled. He leaned forward in his chair and said, "You'll do fine, son."

Abe passed out.

When he came to, it was to Mrs. Morton pressing a damp cloth to his head and soothing him with her voice. He couldn't make out what she was saying, yet, but it sounded nice. And then, remembering why he'd ridden out here in the first place, he sat bolt upright, startling Mrs. Morton as well as himself.

"Did he say yes?" he said, not sure what was dream and what was reality.

Mrs. Morton smiled softly. "Yes, Abraham, he said yes. Would you like a glass of water?"

Abe nodded. "Yes ma'am, please."

She disappeared in the direction of what he

assumed was the kitchen, and returned with a tall glass of water, complete with—ice?

He stared at it. The glass was cold.

"We bring it down from the high mountains," she explained, as if anyone could do it. "And we store it in a cellar under the house. I understand that Miss Krimp, in town, has much the same arrangement."

Abe wouldn't know, but he nodded and muttered, "If you say so, ma'am." He seemed to have lost all his sense of authority the second he stepped over the Mortons' threshold. This was no way for a Deputy U.S. Marshal—one with twenty years of experience and over seventy-five arrests to his credit, no less—to behave!

He stood up, his hat still in his hands. "I'd best be getting back to town, if that's all right with you, ma'am."

She laughed. "Don't call me ma'am, son. You can call me Mother Morton if your mother is still living, or just Mother if she's passed."

Abe managed a smile. "Mother Morton, then."

"Excellent! Now, that wasn't so hard, was it?"

Grinning, he shook his head. "No, ma'am, not hard at all. A real pleasure, in fact."

She put her hand on his arm. "Come along with me, then, Abraham," she said, ushering him away from the front door and deeper into the house, toward the cellar steps. "I want to send a little something along to Electa with you."

20

Abe rode back to Fury during the beginning of the storm, galloping for the final third in hopes of beating the worst of it. He cantered into town and to the livery in time to see the sky gone black and feel the wind whipping his clothes. His hat had blown clean off somewhere outside of town, but he hadn't had the heart or the time to look for it. It was likely sailing over the Colorado River by this time.

The wagon train was still and silent, and folks had tied themselves inside their Conestogas to avoid the worst of the coming damage.

He passed through the gates and pulled into the livery, and walked his horse up and down the aisle countless times until he was satisfied that it was cooled off sufficiently, and then he put the gelding in its stall and grained and watered it. "Some storm, huh, Boy?" he asked, stroking the horse's dark-blue roan neck. "Well, guess I'd best get over and tell Electa the good news!" he added, brightening.

He gave his horse a final pat, turned up his collar, put his shoulder to the door, and shoved his way outside into what had become a raging torrent.

He immediately wished he was back inside with his horse. The air was full of flying, stinging pebbles and bits of plants, and he couldn't even tell which direction it was coming from, it whirled so quickly! He felt, more than saw, his way up the street to the schoolhouse, then struggled a bit with the door.

Once in the cloakroom, where Electa kept spare books and school supplies and the cleaning equipment, he slumped on a bench and shook detritus from his hair. At least he'd just had it cut the other day, so the damage to the floor wasn't too bad. But enough twigs and grit went flying that he took a quick look in the mirror to make sure he didn't look like the ghost of Pecos Pete—or worse—before he went in to see his beloved Electa.

When he had himself brushed off the best he could, he cracked open the door to the schoolhouse proper, and took a peek inside. Electa and Jenny were at opposite ends of the blackboard, Electa writing out complicated mathematical problems at her end, and Jenny writing out simpler problems on the other, probably for the younger children.

He quietly stepped inside and took a seat along the back wall, behind the students. There weren't many kids, probably twelve or fourteen, but there were enough of them to keep two women on their toes. The two biggest boys passed something between them, and he immediately stood and took a step forward.

He held out his hand and stared the boy in the eyes. The boy, who appeared to have been kept back a couple of years somewhere along the way, made a face, hissed, "Shit!" and handed over a pocketknife.

"Don't swear," Abe said, momentarily forgetting where he was.

"Marshal Todd!"

He looked up to find Electa smiling at him. "Miss Morton," he said. "I wonder if I might have a word with you?"

"Certainly," she replied, and added, "Children, will those of you to the left of the center aisle begin working on these problems, and those to the right start work on those that Miss Fury has just written out? I'll be right outside, Miss Fury."

"Certainly, Miss Morton," Jenny replied, as a beaming Electa walked back toward Abe.

He couldn't help himself. He was beaming, too.

Jason was in his office, and all he could think was, "Lord, not again!" He hadn't even caulked the doors or windows or floor yet!

It was three in the afternoon but it was nearly as dark as midnight, and this time the rain had come in with the wind, both of them hurrying and flurrying in rapid, nonsensical, lopsided circles that could be as big as a house or as small as his thumb, and all of it carrying the desert into Fury with it.

The mild winters and the pleasant year-round evenings aside, he sometimes hated Arizona. It was a tricky place. Every which way you turned, the weather was out to make a jackass out of you, to make you look foolish. Or worse, to kill you just as surely as it had killed that fellow out in the wagon train, the one with the cactus in his back. What was his name? Frank something. Frank . . . Saulk, that was it, Frank Saulk. They'd been planning to bury him today, along with poor Ward. Practically the entire town was planning on turning out for the funerals. Well, practically the entire town would have to stay home, now.

Until tomorrow, anyway.

Jason couldn't say that he was looking forward to it. Tomorrow or its proceedings, either one.

He'd had the bad luck to be standing out on the walk, talking to Father Micah, when Abe came riding into town and tucked himself up in the livery, and he was surprised that he hadn't shown up at the office by now. He wondered if Abe had stopped off at the schoolhouse again. Was he paying court to Miss Electa? It certainly wasn't to Jenny, that he knew. Jenny wouldn't have—and couldn't have—kept that a secret for more than two seconds. But a fellow didn't get all shaved and barbered and doused in witch hazel to go see a bunch of kids, though, that was for sure.

No, it was Miss Electa, he remembered with a scowl and hit upside his own head. How could he have forgotten something like that? All he could hope for was that Abe wouldn't move Electa out of Fury. Better, he'd move her inside it, so she wouldn't have that long ride in and out of town every day, and so the town could keep its school-marm and Matt MacDonald could have his own private goddamn police force.

This last bit, he thought with some degree of violence, and kicked his desk leg, hard.

"Easy, boy," he told himself when his toe instantly began to throb and sting. "You don't want to see your desk go the way of your old chair." He glanced at the stove's wood bin, still piled high with broken spindles and chunks of varnished wood. And then he glanced at Davis, still sacked out in his cell.

Sighing, he leaned back in the new chair, crossed his arms over his chest, and stared out the window at the storm. It had come up quite a bit since he'd last looked. Where there had been minute chunks of flora whirling in the wind before, he now saw a whole branch off a cottonwood, complete with leaves, being blown up Main Street, roughly three feet off the ground.

He sure hoped the Milchers had their cat indoors for this one. A wind like this could carry little Dusty off to San Diego in a half hour!

He watched several fellows try to leave the saloon.

Not a one made it past the overhang, and to a man, they all gave up and went back inside.

Well, that was one thing in a dust storm's favor. About all you could do during one was drink and play cards. Or pray.

He didn't reckon he'd be seeing Rafe today, either.

He rolled himself a cigarette, lit it, and leaned back to watch the storm.

The time came to let school out for the day, and Jenny tapped on the anteroom door before she threw it open so that the children could run out. Abe had risen at the sound of her knock, and so all the students and Jenny saw was Miss Morton, primly seated on the bench, and Marshal Todd, leaning against the wall, facing her. The children wouldn't recognize it, of course, but Miss Morton had a "well and freshly kissed" look on her face and color rising in her cheeks.

"If it's too far for you to go in one stretch, take temporary shelter in the Milchers' church," Jenny shouted after the kids. They'd be a little the worse for wear when they got home, but they'd make it. The town of Fury raised tough kids.

It was taking most all of her fortitude to keep holding off her knowledge of their engagement. But she turned to Miss Morton and said, "You're not riding home in this. You'd never make the distance! Please, come and spend the night with Jason and me. Marshal, you're invited for supper, too, of course!"

Marshal Todd, who certainly had nothing better to do, said, "Electa?"

"It's fine with me, Abraham."

They were already letting on that they were on a first-name basis? It was a surprise to Jenny, and it must have shown on her face, for Electa said,

"Jenny, my dear, we'd like you to be among the first to know. Abraham and I are betrothed."

"Oh, Miss Morton!" Jenny exclaimed at last, and threw her arms about her employer, hugging her tight. She was as relieved at finally being told as she was delighted for the news, itself. "Oh, I'm so excited for you!"

Miss Morton extricated herself as kindly as she could, and then she stood up. "Thank you, child. We both accept your congratulations."

But Jenny couldn't stop herself. She was all over the marshal, then Miss Morton, then the marshal again before she regained what little was left of her composure. "Please, please do forgive me," she said before a giggle bubbled up. "It's just that this is so . . . *wonderful!*"

They scurried out into the whirling wind and rain, and ran all the way to Jenny's house, where they arrived streaked with muddy rain, but laughing.

When Jason locked up the office—and Davis with it—for the night, it was still storming, but not so angrily as earlier. The wind buffeted him as he made his way up Main Street, and he made a side trip to stick his head out the gate and look down the line of wagons. Not that he could see all of them, but what he saw led him to believe they were all buttoned up tight.

He stopped at the school to see if Jenny or Miss Morton had tried to wait it out, but found the door locked.

He took the rest of the way home at a half-run, half-jog, and vaulted up onto the porch, clearing all three steps in handsome style. "Let's see you beat that, Matt MacDonald!" he said happily. He was home, and nothing had exploded or burnt down or been ripped to shreds by a grizzly all day long!

But when Jason walked into the house, there was Abe Todd, sitting in *his* chair beside *his* fire, reading *his* copy of *Outriders of the Lonesome Spread*, the book he'd been parceling out to himself in little literary squirts so that it would last. It wasn't exactly timeless literature, but it surely beat the alternative, which was nothing. Unless a wagon train came through carrying lots of books for sale—and they hardly ever did—he was stuck with wanted posters or the Bible. And he'd already read the Bible, cover to cover, five times.

Finally, Abe looked up from the book and said, "Well, how-do, Jason! The wind's been bangin' at the shutters so hard I didn't even hear you come in!"

"No problem," lied Jason, and forced a smile. "How you likin' our weather?"

Abe arched a brow along with his own smile. "You're a funny kid, Jason, I'll give you that." And then belatedly, he added, "Say, your sister asked me and Electa to dinner. Hope that's okay with you."

Jason's sigh was audible. "Well, welcome, then! Blowin' too hard for Miss Morton to ride home, I suppose?"

"That it was. Sounds like it still is, too." Outside, the storm threw hailstones mixed with gravel and cactus bits at the house. Jason thought it was a miracle that it hadn't upended the rainwater barrel. Then again, maybe it had. . . .

During supper, Jenny couldn't stand to hold the news in any longer and announced Abe and Electa's upcoming nuptials. Jason seemed taken aback, but in a good—and convincing—way, she thought. He was likely thinking that if they stayed on in Fury, he wouldn't have to put up with Matt MacDonald any longer. She couldn't have known how right she was.

Jenny was hoping they'd stay, too, but for reasons all her own. First, she in no way wanted the responsibility that would come with being the schoolmarm. And second, she really liked Miss Morton, and would miss her terribly if she were to leave.

Abe spoke up. "Well, now that we're officially announced, I reckon I can give you this, Electa." Smiling, he dug into his pocket and pulled out a small black-and-gold box, worn at the corners.

"Your ma, she gave it to me to give to you. For the engagement." He faced the box toward her and opened the lid.

Electa clapped both hands over her mouth and Jenny heard her say, "Oh, my word!"

Jenny couldn't wait. She was up and out of her chair almost before Electa had finished her sentence. And when Jenny saw what was in the box, she, too, clapped her hands to her mouth. It was like nothing she'd ever seen before, and it was incredibly beautiful!

"Is somebody gonna tell me?" Jason asked.

Since both women were temporarily speechless, Abe said, "It's Electa's grandma's wedding ring. They tell me it's an honest-to-God emerald."

"Ringed by little diamonds," whispered Electa, "and set in the purest gold. Grandfather had it made for her when they were still in London."

Jason had to look, and what he saw set even him back a few notches. The emerald was huge and a clear, clean green. He'd seen a few emeralds before, but they had all been cloudy or hazy, or what Shem Klein, the son of the town jeweler back home, had called "included." As Jason recalled, Shem had told him that a good-sized, "clean" emerald was worth more than a diamond!

Well, this one was clean as a whistle.

"By Christ!" he whispered. "Electa, are you rich?"

He didn't mean it to sound so crass, and he immediately joined the covered-mouth crowd, except that he was blushing, too. After a moment, he said, "I'm so sorry! I didn't mean to be rude."

Electa grinned. "I believe I had much the same reaction when Mama showed it to me for the first time. I was twenty, and out running errands with her—we were living in Baltimore, then—and she said she had to stop by the bank. When we got there, she brought out a little key and told the clerk she needed to open her safety deposit box. Of course, I had no idea what that was, back then. But I learned that day. Oh, goodness!" She raised her eyes and put a hand to her heart. "The wondrous things my parents kept there!"

"Like this?" Jenny said, her eyes still glued to the ring.

"Yes, like this," Electa said. "Mama gave a beautiful ruby ring to my sister when she was wed, too."

Jenny cocked her head. She hadn't seen any such ring, and couldn't imagine not wearing it if it were hers.

But Electa finished by saying, "The poor dear. They sold it, to outfit themselves for the trip to the West. And to pay off some old debts."

"I'm so sorry," said Jenny.

"A real shame," said Jason.

"Hadn't you best try it on? You know, see if it fits?" said Abe, who seemed not the least bit impressed by any of this ring lore.

"Oh, I know it fits," Electa said. "It fits me perfectly and will do so forever, just like you're going to, Abraham."

With an audible sigh of delight, Jenny sank back into her own chair.

Jason was loathe to admit it, but he knew just how she felt.

21

"Look, Father Micah," Jason said for practically the hundredth time, "I'm sorry, but I can't have you erecting a church underneath a water tower, especially one that's probably going to fall down or blow down if we have another storm like we did last night."

"But you promised!"

"I know. But Salmon Kendall and the town fathers had already picked that spot for their tower." Jason shook his head sadly. "I'm sorry. I know it's a blow."

It had been a blow to him, as well. That damned Salmon! He already had his men clearing the site and laying out markers for the footings, which was why Father Micah had shown up this morning, mad as the proverbial hell. That was, if a Catholic priest could get that mad. Jason figured he probably could, but wouldn't admit it in a million years.

Father Micah was staring at him.

"Would it be helpful if I were to find you another spot?"

Father Micah didn't say, "It's the least you can do, you bum," but he looked like he was thinking it when at last he said, "Yes, thank you."

At the moment, Davis was safely locked in his cell, sleeping, although Jason had to run and fetch the doc for him first thing. Well, he didn't actually *have* to, but Davis's moaning was distracting him from his work. So Morelli came and got him to take some kind of powder, and that knocked him out again. On his way out the door, Morelli said that Davis must have the constitution of an ox, for any other man with his wounds would be long dead.

Jason said, "C'mon with me, Father," and locked the office door behind them. He was taking no chances with Davis again.

They walked down to the lot, then through it to the alley, then back up a few yards. Jason pointed to the two empty lots to his right. "Did you take a look at these?"

Father Micah nodded. "Yes, but I thought you said this would be the place for my living quarters and so on."

"Well, it's the place for both the mission and you, now, Father." Jason said it flatly, as if this were the only possibility. "You can take both lots. Run 'em together, if you want."

Actually, there were three vacant lots up by his house, but he didn't let on. He knew that Jenny wouldn't be too happy living in the Church's back yard, so to speak, and neither would he.

Finally, after a long moment seemingly lost in thought, the Father said, "All right. All I need is a cell off to the side, anyway," he admitted. "Will this site be saved for the Church?"

"Yes, it will."

"Although it's not within my personal better judgment, I must have faith in God, and that the He will work through you, my son."

Jason didn't really like being an "instrument of God," but if it would shut the father up, he'd be Satan's fiddle.

He said, "All right, then," shook hands with Father Micah, and turned to go back to his office. He had work to do.

Ward Wanamaker's funeral was scheduled for eleven in the morning, and practically the whole town showed up for it. Folks were packed six and seven deep in the little cemetery, and even those who had been at Frank Saulk's funeral stayed on for Ward's. Jason stood at the graveside, his arm around Jenny, who was already crying and sniffling into her hankie.

The Reverend Milcher, who had been called upon to perform the service, started in, and Jason was amazed—and pleased—to notice a new, lighter tone to his ministering. He spoke of the founding of Fury, and of Ward's services in getting them there. He spoke of Ward's kindness, his warmth with children, and his good heart with animals, including his rescue of the kittens the night of the first storm, and how well he always treated his horse.

He spoke of things even Jason hadn't been

aware of, such as Ward's boyhood in Arkansas and teen years in Alabama, and his joining up with Jedediah Fury later in life, illustrating how former enemies—the North and the South, in this case— could make strong alliances.

In the end, Milcher spoke of Ward's dedication to duty, and how he had died in the service of it at the hands of a prisoner, and talked about his leaving his friends and comrades far too soon.

Even crusty old Wash Keogh was sobbing at this point, along with the rest of the town.

"And so," Reverend Milcher said in conclusion, "we say our final good-byes to our friend and our public servant, Ward Wanamaker. I know that many of you have personal stories of your own about Ward, but these are things best shared and enjoyed in private, and I leave you to it. Here lies Ward Wanamaker, Lord. Let his face and his badge shimmer long in our hearts and memories. Amen and amen."

Milcher closed his Bible and stepped back, as did the rest of the mourners, but Jenny stepped closer, dropping a handful of desert roses down into the grave, and then a handful of dirt. Jason, who had squired her forward, heard her whisper, "Good-bye, Ward."

His throat thick, Jason said, "I'll be seeing you, buddy."

"Just not right away," said Jenny, and began to cry all over again.

She clung tightly to Jason's side all the way home.

* * *

Despite the sadness of the day's proceedings, the Reverend Milcher had done very well for himself—financially, that was. He had netted better than sixty-five dollars from Ward's funeral, between the marshal's office paying the basic fee, and different parishioners stuffing a dollar or two into his pocket as they came up to thank him for the sermon. He thanked each one, kindly saying, "We'll be seeing you on Sunday, I hope?" and receiving nothing but yesses or teary nods in reply.

Something good had come out of this tragedy, then. Ward Wanamaker had been murdered, but the Milcher family would survive.

Rafe Lynch dropped by the office at around three that afternoon. Surprisingly, he'd been at Ward's funeral, but Jason hadn't had a chance to speak to him.

"How you doin'?" he asked as he came through the door.

"About how you'd think," Jason replied. He shuffled his papers together and indicated the chair opposite his.

Nodding, Rafe sat down and propped his elbows on the desk, aping Jason's posture. "Thought Abe might be around."

"Haven't seen him since breakfast."

Rafe didn't say anything for a moment, but then he said, "Wonder if he ever got back out to the MacDonald ranch. Said he was gonna."

Jason shook his head. "Don't think so." Abe's

time was pretty much taken up by Miss Morton, of late. "Why?"

"Thinkin' of goin' out there myself."

This was a surprise to Jason. He hadn't thought that Rafe had any interest in Matt MacDonald, other than as the butt of an occasional joke. He again said, "Why?"

"'Cause I think he's got somethin' fishy goin' on out there. Somethin' fishy enough to make those Apache raid him at night. You notice the creek this mornin'?"

Shocked at the sudden change of subject, Jason said, "Nope. Haven't looked at it in a couple days."

"It's full up to its banks."

"'Course it is. It rained last night, y'know."

Rafe smiled. "Yeah, I know. But it's hardly movin'."

Jason's brows narrowed, and he cocked his head, recalling his conversation with Rafe and Abe a few days earlier. "You think—"

Rafe's grin broadened. "Yeah, I do."

Jason shook his head. "Well, that sonofabitch!"

"My feelings exactly. He did that to me, I'd raid his place, too! So, you comin'?"

"Not without Abe. He's in charge once we leave town."

"Well, let's go find him!" Rafe stood up.

"Not till I check my prisoner." Jason pushed back his chair, walked around his desk, and strode across the room. "Wake up, Davis!" he hollered. The man on the cot didn't stir. Jason turned around to face Rafe. "All right. Let's go find Abe."

* * *

Abe turned out to be at the café, having a "late lunch"—which, in his case, meant a large serving of apple pie with extra cheese, coffee, and fritters—and once he polished off his meal, the three of them set off to get the horses. Jason had seen Abe at the funeral as well, but, again, hadn't had a chance to speak with him. Once they were ready to ride south, he asked the questions that had been nagging at him.

"Abe?" he began, as the three men rode out the gates of Fury, heading south, "I don't know if you've given any thought to staying on in town once you're married, but—"

"Already wrote the marshal's office 'bout that," Abe said as he rolled himself a smoke. "Doubt he'll gimme much of a fight over it. They been looking to have a man down here, full-time, for quite a spell."

Jason grinned. "Well, you'd sure be welcome. Hell, you can share my office if you want!"

Abe nodded. "Thanks. I'll think it over. Outside'a MacDonald, you ever have Apache troubles?" He finished building the quirlie and stuck it between his lips while he fished in his pocket for a match.

"Once, right after we got here and had maybe a quarter of the town built up, we had it in a big way," Jason said, and went on to explain the Indian attack, and how they had at last driven off the Apache by building a moat filled with burning tar and grease around the town.

Abe nodded. "Yup. You told me about that. Heard tell about a couple other little skirmishes, too. But there ain't been no big to-do's since that one, have there?"

Jason shook his head, but Rafe couldn't keep his mouth shut. "I heard about that, too! I mean, clean over in California, I heard about it! Wish I'd been here to see it!"

Jason wished he had, too. Maybe they would have made Rafe the marshal, then. That would've kept them *both* out of trouble.

"So, you're thinkin' that MacDonald's got the water dammed up so the Indians ain't gettin' any?"

That was about the size of it, and Abe had succeeded once again not only in hitting the nail on the head, but in abruptly changing the subject, as well. Jason nodded. "That's about it."

"Well, hell," said Abe. "Who in tarnation figured that little puzzle out?"

Rafe said, "Wasn't much of a puzzle. And I think you did, didn't you?"

Jason's brow furrowed. There were only three of them, and God knew how many Apache. He piped up, "You think we need more men?"

Matt MacDonald wasn't expecting company. He was expecting simply that in about an hour or so, Cookie would send him up a plated dinner of beef stew and hot biscuits, and in anticipation, he'd already set the coffeepot on the stove to start perking.

So when he heard the hubbub outside, and one of the men yelling, "Riders! Riders coming in!" he was on his feet like a shot and out the door, scanning the southern horizon, looking for the cloud that would signal an Apache presence.

But there was nothing, no sign at all. And then

he saw Curly, down by the barn, pointing to the north. The north?

He spun around, and then he saw them, too. Three riders, taking their time, were riding in from the direction of Fury. Three riders who he quickly realized, by the palomino ridden by one, were the so-called law.

Under his breath, he growled, "I didn't send for you, Fury!" and then lifted his arm in a wave. If they were riding this way, they must have a damned good reason. He might as well act friendly, anyway: He wasn't as big a dolt as most people thought.

And whose fault is that? asked a tiny voice in his head, which he promptly ignored.

The riders neared the ranch house, and now he could see that they were Jason and that Rafe person who'd been out here the other night, and that damned U.S. Marshal. The one who'd slugged him so hard that he was still nursing a loose tooth.

He made himself smile anyway.

But when the riders stopped their mounts before the house, they didn't dismount. Instead, Jason said, "Afternoon, MacDonald. Wonder if we could have the use of six or eight of your hands."

Matt's smile disappeared. "What for? It's almost suppertime."

"I want 'em to ride on down the creek with us for a spell. I think you know why."

Matt tried to look innocent. "Don't know what you're talkin' about, Fury."

"Figured you'd say as much." He signaled to Rafe, who rode on down to the barn, toward Curly.

Marshal Todd spoke up. "If you've done what we

think you did, I just might not come the next time you have Apache trouble. I *know* the town marshal ain't comin'."

Jason just sat that damned palomino of his, staring down toward the barn and ignoring him completely.

Dad-blast it, anyway! For the millionth time, Matt asked himself why the hell he'd stayed on in Fury, why he hadn't just crossed over into California where there were some civilized people, at least, and decent food and even an ocean! Why in God's name had he stayed here?

Megan. His sister was why he'd stayed. And Jenny Fury. He'd been quite taken with her. He wasn't anymore. He hadn't even spoken to her—outside of an emergency situation, that was—in, what was it now? Two years? No, that little dalliance, even though they'd never got around to any actual dallying, was over.

It was hard to keep on liking the sister of a man who hated your guts.

And whose guts you hated even more.

Matt wouldn't be outdone on anything, even detestation.

"You listenin', MacDonald?" asked the marshal.

Matt came out of his stupor long enough to say, "Help yourself, Marshal Todd. Looks like you're already doin' it, anyway."

"Good. Keep me from filin' obstruction charges, anyhow." He turned to Jason. "Rafe look about ready?"

Jason nodded. "Yeah."

"I'll be back, MacDonald," said Marshal Todd before he signaled to Jason and they both rode off toward the barn.

22

They rode out from the Double M with not five or six but seven hands, all of whom seemed eager to go—once they were out of sight of the ranch house, anyway. Marshal Todd led the way in stony, assured silence, and Rafe gabbed and joked with the hands, but Jason was lost in thought.

What would they do if they found what he suspected? Rafe had the ranch hands equip themselves with shovels as well as a couple of axes, but still, what would keep Matt from pulling the same jackass stunt again, with nobody to keep an eye on him twenty-four hours a day?

Marshal Todd, Jason suspected, but he was only one man, and this part of the territory went west to the Colorado River and south to Yuma, if not the Mexican border. Lord only knew where the other boundaries lay, and frankly, Jason didn't want to think about it. He figured that the less he knew about the business of the U.S. Marshal's office, the better.

He was more than likely right.

The farther they followed the stream, the deeper, wider, and muddier it grew. The water, formerly so sparkling and clear, was filled with storm debris: Chunks of cactus floated in the water, along with partially submerged tree limbs and smaller branches. Jason spotted a few items that proved civilization was moving in—a piece of paper, floating limply near the bank, its ink washed away and illegible; an empty tin that had once contained peaches; and a ripped and battered lady's bonnet.

Near the location of the bonnet, they also found some frayed ropes and a silver concho, the kind Jason had seen Apache either wear themselves, or use to decorate their bridles. Or, at least, what he supposed they would call a bridle. Most of them used contraptions made out of rope or leather thongs, and some used no bridles at all, relying on breast bands or simply their hands and legs to signal and control the horse.

Soon they entered a canyon—narrow at first, then widening out into a broad space which was mostly filled with water. Abe gestured to Jason to follow, then cantered around the water to what had been the creek bed.

"Damn that Matthew!" Jason breathed when he saw the contraption that Megan's brother had built—or caused to have built. He sure couldn't see Matt out here, shoving some of these logs around with his own dainty hands.

Abe set the men to work, marshaling teams according to who had which tool, shovel, or axe, and within two hours, they had taken apart the most of it and the sky was growing dark.

Jason said, "Abe? I think the water's already got down to the Apache camp."

"Why?"

Jason gestured up toward the western rim of the canyon. There, silhouetted by the setting sun, stood a lone brave, just watching them. His bow was in his hand, but it wasn't strung.

Abe raised his hand in a greeting and shouted something in guttural Apache that Jason didn't understand. *Hello*, he supposed.

Showing no expression, the brave responded by raising his unstrung bow, and then walking back out of sight.

"We'd best be goin'," Abe said, once the brave had disappeared.

It was past dark when they got back up to the Double M, and the hands cut out right away, heading for the barn or the bunkhouse. Jason wasn't looking forward to meeting up with Matt again, but found he was disappointed when Abe decided not to stop at the house.

"I thought you were gonna talk to him!" he complained.

Abe turned in his saddle and said, simply, "Better to let him sit and stew for a spell."

Rafe, riding behind him, said, "Makes him more tender to the tooth that'a'way," and laughed.

Abe snorted out a laugh, and that was the end of the subject. At least, as far as everybody else was concerned. Jason wasn't of the same mind, but decided to let it rest for the time being, reminding himself that Abe was in charge out here, not him.

The bright moon showed them the way back to town, and they were home before Jason knew it. He left the other men to put their horses up at the livery, and rode on home, to bed down Cleo in her own stall. Once there, he fed her a fair ration of grain and hay, and refreshed the water in her bucket.

When he gained the house and went in the back door, he found Jenny waiting with a stern expression blocking her otherwise sunny countenance. Jason said, "Sorry I'm late?"

She crossed her arms over her bosom. "And just where have you been?"

"The Double M. Matt had built a dam across the creek, so the Apache were running dry. Which was why they were sending raiding parties up to his place, the dirtbag." Jason practically fell into a kitchen chair and propped his elbows on the table.

"Well, I'm glad you didn't come around the front," she replied.

"Huh?"

The door to the parlor burst open, and in poured people. And not just people, but friends! Solomon and Rachael, the Kendalls, Megan Mac-Donald, and on and on, and bringing up the rear, Abe Todd and Rafe Lynch!

"What are you all—?" Jason began.

But he was cut off by the group's shouted, "Happy birthday!"

He had forgotten completely, but they were

right. If he looked half as stunned as he felt, then Jenny and her cohorts had got their money's worth.

Sometime, while everybody was busy pounding his back and congratulating him, Jenny produced a gigantic layer cake with the words *Happy Birthday* piped on top of the frosting, along with cartoonish frosting pictures of Cleo and his lawman's badge.

He would have rather they'd cooked him a steak, but he was more than grateful for the cake. That must have been a real job, and he pulled his sister close and whispered, "Thanks, Jen," in her ear, then kissed her cheek.

In response, she clapped her hands together and giggled, then said, "Blow out the candles, Jason! Be sure to get them all!"

He puckered up and blew as hard as he could, and managed to get them all out, at which point everybody cheered.

As he cut the cake, he was thinking that life wasn't so bad, after all.

But he sure wished that Ward could be here.

The wagon train pulled out in the morning, leaving behind Father Micah and Mrs. Judith Strong, along with Bill Crachit, who had found work in Solomon's stockroom, and a dog in the form of Hannibal, the Grimms' dog (who was fast becoming a fixture around town), and Frank Saulk's widow, Eliza, and their kids. Judith Strong had taken pity on Eliza Saulk and offered her not only lodging, but work in her dress shop as well, which would be opening in a few days.

The town, Jason thought, was taking on a little more shape with every wagon train that passed through. Of course, they were getting yet another preacher, Fletcher Bean, in the bargain, but Jason supposed it was none of his business. He just hoped that it wouldn't pull trade from the Reverend Milcher. Not that he was a big fan, but they were the "grandparents" of his kitten—rather, Jenny's kitten—and he figured it was only the nice thing.

Then again, Milcher had done fine at Ward's funeral. No talk of fire and brimstone, just praise for a good man.

And sorrow at the loss of him.

Milcher's tone was a satisfying change of pace, and more than that: The eulogy had actually done Ward justice. He had to give Milcher credit for that.

But he had other fish to fry today. First off, he had to find another desk somewhere, for he doubted that a Deputy U.S. Marshal would be happy doing business out of his lap. They'd need another file cabinet, too, to keep the town papers separated from the federal.

And besides that, he had to figure out what to do for a deputy. He'd considered not replacing Ward at all—after all, he was, in a lot of ways, irreplaceable. But he didn't like leaving the office locked for the night—especially not with a prisoner (even a drugged one, like Davis) in the cell. He'd considered asking Wash Keogh for assistance, but then he remembered the gold. Wash wouldn't want to walk away from that!

No, it had to be somebody else. Somebody who could handle himself with confidence in most any circumstance, and who he could stand to be around. It came down to one man, and he was sure, right from the start, that he'd made the wrong choice: Rafe Lynch.

Rafe was affable, a crack shot, and hadn't put a foot wrong in the whole territory. So far. That he knew of, at any rate.

He could see no way around it: Nobody else could fit the bill. But wasn't it highly unusual for a man, worth so much in bounties in a bordering state, to *be* the law in another?

In the cell across the room, Sampson Davis muttered something through his dark haze of laudanum, and then took his final breath.

Jason didn't notice. He just sighed deeply and stared out the window.

Solomon Cohen was a happy man. He had a beautiful wife, three robust sons, and a new daughter who was growing stronger with each passing hour. He had a fine business with a new employee, as well.

In fact, he only had one problem: the dog. How could he hire Bill Crachit with one breath, then with the next tell him he couldn't keep the dog there? He couldn't. He didn't have it in him. But he had to dig deep and find it somehow, before the dog ate him out of stock and out of business!

The first day that Bill had worked there, the dog had eaten three pounds of raw, smoked bacon, two dozen fresh eggs, and a jar of pickled eggs, and at least a pound of hard candy. Solomon didn't know exactly how much, but the voracious beast had drooled over another three or four pounds, which had to be thrown out. All this in the slim space of less than ten minutes, while he was upstairs and Bill was out, running an errand for him.

They had tried keeping the dog outside—where he normally was, anyway, roaming the town—but he kept finding always new and more inventive ways to let himself in when nobody was looking. This day alone, he had already cleaned out the canned meats shelf (Solomon was at a loss to figure out just how he knew which cans had meat, and how he knew to open them without slicing his mouth up), hit the candy jars again, and chewed up a pair of men's dress shoes in the Osterman's display. Solomon was beginning to think he was lucky not to have left the baby alone downstairs!

But how to do it, and what to do? He didn't like the idea of separating the boy from his dog, but it was either that or fire Bill, who was proving to be of great help to him. He leaned his elbows on the counter and his head in his hands, and stared at the patent medicine poster on the wall across from him.

He was still staring when the bell above the door jangled, and he turned to find Jason entering the store.

Jason raised his hand in a greeting. "Howdy, Sol."

"How goes it, Jason?" Solomon came out from

behind the counter. "Rachael and I, we had a fine time at your party. *Mazel tov* once again!"

Jason laughed, then said, "Thanks, thanks. Those socks you folks gave me will be greatly appreciated come colder weather, I can tell you that! Say, have you got a minute?"

"For you, my friend? Hours and hours."

"Good. Let's talk."

Solomon led him to the front of the store, where they sat down in the two chairs usually reserved for ladies trying on shoes—and where Solomon could keep an eye on the canned meats section and the penny candy aisle.

"Sol, I've got a problem."

Solomon hiked a brow. "Which is?"

And Jason spilled his guts about Ward's death and his hunt for a deputy and his finally deciding— but not deciding—on Rafe Lynch, and begging for Solomon's opinion.

Sol carefully considered Jason's dilemma (which, on the face of it, was much simpler than his own), and said, "Why shouldn't you hire him? He has no strikes against him in this territory, and from what Marshal Todd and you, yourself, have told me, his 'murders' were not 'murders' at all. I like him."

"Then, you'd hire him?"

"How do they say it? In a New York minute!"

Before Solomon could stop him, Jason was on his feet and heading toward the door, saying, "Thanks, Solomon, you've been a real help."

Solomon shot to his feet. "Wait!"

Jason stopped stock-still. "What is it?"

"Jason, I have a small problem, as well."

Jason came back to the shoe section and sat back down beside him. "Tell me."

Solomon did, right down to the last horehound drop, then asked, "What should I do? I can't be asking young Bill to give away his dog, but I can't have him here. The only time I'm safe from his pillaging is at night, when he's locked up in the back room with Bill."

Jason pursed and relaxed his lips several times, a sure sign he was considering the matter. Suddenly, he looked up from the floor and said, "If you want to talk this over with Bill, I'd admire to take that dog, and Bill can see him any time he wants. I've got a strong liking for Hannibal. And I know that Hannibal would admire Jenny's cooking."

Jason grinned at him, and Solomon felt a weight lift from his shoulders. He still had to talk to Bill, but he felt he had his bases covered. He said, "Wonderful, wonderful!" and both men rose.

He walked Jason to the door, but halfway through it, Jason stopped and turned to face him. "I almost forgot to mention it, Solomon. Sampson Davis died this afternoon. We're gonna bury him tomorrow, I guess, barring any religious ceremony . . ."

Automatically, Solomon muttered beneath his breath, "Blessed are You, Lord our God, King of the Universe, the true Judge," then he held up a hand. "Wait. Someone should be sitting *shiva* for him, someone needs to—"

This time, Jason was the one with his hands in the air. "Hold on. None of this makes any sense to me, you know. Is this something only Jews can help with?"

Sadly, Solomon nodded his head. "Some is best with a rabbi, but only Jews, yes." And then he realized that there would be no need for them to sit *shiva*. That was to be left to his people in California.

When Jason didn't speak, Solomon asked, "Could we have the use of the jail? The body needs to be prepared for burial."

"Well, I already sent him over to the undertakers, but I reckon we can get him brought back. That be okay?"

Solomon nodded. "It's a start. And we'll need a coffin. Plain pine, with no metal, no nails. Only wooden pegs." He sighed, thinking, then looked up again. "I'll go get Rachael."

23

Over at the saloon, Ezra Welk was innocently gathering information as quickly as it came in. He had got to be on a first-name basis with Nicky, one of the few barmaids who worked the day shift, and Nicky was his new font of information.

Sampson Davis had perished sometime during the day, and had been moved from the jail to the undertaker's, then from the undertaker's back to the jail. Nicky wasn't certain why, but after she reported, a short time later, that Rachael Cohen (wife of Solomon Cohen, the mercantile owner) had entered the jail carrying packages and clothes, he managed to put two and two together.

They were all a bunch of Jews!

Which meant that Davis was one, too. Or had been.

It figured. He'd known there was something wrong with Davis right from the very start, hadn't he? He wasn't a religious man—far from it—but the term "Christ killer" rolled nicely on his tongue. And he'd never admit it, but he liked

having somebody around he could feel morally
superior to. He congratulated himself on his pre-
science, and ordered another beer. There was just
enough time to drink it before he needed to be
back at the boardinghouse. That was, if he wanted
a share of that big turkey that he'd seen Mrs.
Kendall put into the oven this morning.

His stomach rumbled at the thought of it!

That evening found Rachael in the jail, quietly
attending to Davis's body. It was dark and she
was alone, so when she heard the door open she
jumped.

"Solomon?" she said, scolding herself. But the
next voice she heard didn't belong to her husband.

"Mrs. Kendall told me you were preparing the
body for burial," said a female voice.

"Yes," said Rachael, then, "Who's there?"

"Sorry," said the voice before its owner stepped
into the feeble light of the solitary lantern Rachael
had lit. Judith Strong peeled the light gloves from
her hands and shrugged. *"Ich, auch, bin Juden,"* she
said, indicating that she, too, was of the Jewish
faith and heritage.

Rachael was so shocked and happy that she
nearly fell to her knees and kissed the woman's
hem! After all this time, all these years, another
Jewish woman!

Instead, she began sobbing. "Praise be to Jehovah!" she gasped through her tears.

"You mean it's just us?" the woman asked, and

when Rachael nodded, she shook her head. "No *chverah kadisha,* then?"

Rachael's head shook, to indicate there was no sacred Jewish burial society. How could there be, when she and her family were—or had been—the only Jews in town?

"America," the newcomer muttered, shaking her head as she went to the basin and began to wash her hands. "Small towns. My name's Judith, by the way. Judith Strong."

"R-Rachael Cohen."

"I know. I've seen you before. Your husband, he owns the mercantile?"

Rachael sniffed. "Yes."

"And you just had a baby, I hear?"

Rachael smiled, just a tad. "Yes. Little Sarah."

Toweling her hands, Judith Strong nodded. "I heard she was very sickly. She's better now?"

"Thank you, she's much improved, knock wood." Rachael had a grip on herself by this time, and wiped her eyes with her hankie. She accidentally glanced at Judith Strong's hands, and saw the many tiny scabs covering her fingertips. She said, "You're our new milliner and dressmaker?"

Judith smiled and said, "My hands give me away every time."

"I'm sorry," Rachael said self-consciously, and flushed. "I didn't mean to stare."

Judith's smile widened and she put a hand on Rachael's shoulder. "It's all right, my dear. Do you have *tachrichin*?"

Rachael nodded, and pointed to a paper-wrapped package on the desk. She only had the *tachrichin* left from the long ago journey west, because she had been afraid that either she or her husband would die during the journey. She had wanted to be sure there was enough of the plain, white shroud—this one was hand-loomed from cotton, not linen—to wrap the body and bury it. And now it was going to wrap the body of a killer, the man who had murdered their friend Ward Wanamaker.

"Very good, then. And I know the prayers for each part of the ritual, if you don't."

Rachael said, "Please. Yes, you preside, please." A small smile crossed her lips. Imagine, a woman knowing an "official" part of the preparation of the body! She added, "And then we will sit and be *shomerim*? Through the *aninut*?" she added, to make certain that she wouldn't be left alone with him again until he was in the ground.

"Yes," said Judith, curling her long arm about Rachael's shoulders and directing her back toward the cell, and the body. "We will both stay to guard him. *Sehr gut*?"

Rachael's head bobbed up and down. "*Ja*," she said in her pidgen Deutsch, which Judith seemed to be speaking more than pure Yiddish. "*Sehr gut.*"

Very good.

Outside the town walls, Father Micah was burning the midnight oil, quite literally. Just south of where the wagon train had been parked, he sat on the ground with his lantern beside him, forming a mixture of Arizona's plentiful caliche earth, plus straw, plus a mixture that Mr. Cohen had given him, into adobe bricks. He picked up another handful of mud and pressed it firmly into the wooden mold before him, then turned it out, upside down, besides the countless others he'd made during the day.

Well, he hadn't actually made them alone. Several of his future parishioners had helped during the day. Mrs. Morelli, the most. What a kind woman! But when night had fallen, they had all retreated within the walls. It was suppertime, after all. But Mrs. Morelli had sent a plate out to him, bless her. He could still taste the delicious lasagna she'd made, and wondered if the whole town ate this well every night.

He had used up the last of the mud and was wondering whether it was worth it, in his exhausted state, to make another, when he heard sounds to the south. Riders?

He pulled himself up to his feet and peered into the distance. Then, like a jackrabbit, he sprinted for the gate!

"Indians!" he shouted as he hurried inside and pushed the big gates shut behind him. "Apache! To arms! To arms!"

Jason was running the second he heard the alarm sounded, and quickly gained the top of the stockade wall to the south. There were Indians, all right, but they weren't stripped and greased for battle. At least, not that he could tell in the moonlight. He heard a rifle cock to his left, and shouted, "Hold your fire! Hold your fire!" loudly enough that the whole town, silent and holding its breath, could hear him.

He watched as the Apache drew closer, then halted and spread out in a long line that went from the creek on the west and out into the darkness in the east. Jason rubbed at the gooseflesh covering his arms.

He couldn't figure out why they were there! They weren't attacking, that was for certain. But what other reason would they have for riding all this way? And why the hell were they spread out like that?

One brave, the war chief it looked like, rode out from the line a few feet and stopped his pony. "Todd!" he cried, and it took Jason a second to realize that the savage was saying Abe Todd's name, not speaking Apache gibberish.

Beside him, Abe was just gaining the top of the wall.

Jason said, "They're askin' for you," as Abe peered over.

"I hope to kiss a pig, they are," he said, then raised his voice, shouting, *"Caballo Negro!"*—which Jason's lousy Spanish translated as "Black Horse"—followed by a string of guttural words and phrases that he didn't understand.

In fact, the exchange turned into quite a conversation. Every once in a while, Abe would stop and translate part of it for Jason, which put his mind at ease and stopped his quaking in his boots, but Abe was just a little too chummy with the redskins for his taste.

After about ten minutes of this, they must have

said good-bye, because the brave backed his horse into the line before they all regrouped, then turned and cantered off to the south again.

After they were gone from sight, Jason turned toward Abe. "Friends?" he asked, one brow arched.

"Reckon. 'Bout as close as you can get with an Apache without dyin' for him. Or marryin' his daughter." Abe cracked a smile. "Why? You plan on tryin' to cozy up?"

Jason started backing down the ladder. "Hell, no! How'd you get to be so friendly with 'em, anyway?"

"Well, about five years back I was down the Colorado—marshal business—when I sorta got tangled up with 'em," Abe said as he followed Jason down the ladder and joined him on the ground. "I ended up being took prisoner along with the man I was with. I was haulin' him up north for trial. Anyhow, the Apache killed him, but for some reason, not me. Never did understand the why of it, and I was too grateful to ask. Never thought I'd be good at it, but I picked up their tongue right off." Abe shook his head and chuckled. "Dangedest thing! Just come natural to me, I guess. Anyhow, they ended up lettin' me go, once they'd had some fun with me."

"I'm assuming this is the short version?" Jason said as they started down the street. It seemed the whole town was coming out to join them.

"Yup," replied Abe, and he remained silent until Salmon Kendall came running up to them.

"What happened? What did they say? Are they going to attack?" he asked all in a rush. Jason finally had to take him by the shoulders and give him a little shake to calm him down long enough so that he could listen.

"Tell him, Abe," he said. "Salmon's our newspaperman, so don't spare the details."

Abe obliged. "You're safe, there, Salmon. Everybody's safe. They just rode up from their camp to thank us, that's all."

Salmon's head tipped to the side. "Thank us for what?"

Abe turned to Jason. "You didn't tell nobody?"

Jason shrugged.

Abe shook his head and began from the beginning, telling Salmon that they had taken a ride down to Matt MacDonald's place the day before, and backtracked the creek. "MacDonald had built himself up a dam down south of his place. We figured as much, since the stream clear up here in town was sluggish and near topping its banks. So anyhow, we busted it down, us and six or seven of MacDonald's men. There was Indians watchin', but they didn't show any signs of tryin' to stop us or nothin'. Guess one of 'em recognized me, 'cause that was practically the whole dang tribe, coming to thank us for the water. See, MacDonald had cut off their water supply, which was why—"

"Cut off their water supply!" Salmon chirped, happily making notes. "Oh, this is grand, just grand!"

"You write down that this doesn't make us 'blood brothers' with the Apache," Jason piped up. "Just means there's a temporary truce, that's all."

"For which we're grateful," added Abe.

Jason nodded. Solomon Cohen was at his side, patiently waiting to talk to him, so he said, "Abe, why don't you take Salmon down to the saloon and fill him in? I'm gonna go on home."

"Right," said Abe. "See you tomorrow." He led an attentive Salmon on down the street.

Jason turned toward Solomon, saying, "Yes?"

Solomon said, "I was listening while Marshal Todd talked. I believe I have most of it, thank you. And I mean, thank you for everything!"

Curious, Jason cocked his head. "Huh?"

"For everything," Solomon repeated. "For breaking down the dam and getting rid of those Apache with no one getting hurt, for giving us the use of the jail tonight, for everything."

Jason's brain had to throw on the hand brake before he figured out the jailhouse business. He smiled. "No problem. To any of it." He wasn't lying. It could have been much, much worse. "It's Abe Todd we ought to be grateful to, for speaking such good Apache."

"Of course. But still, you have our thanks, Rachael's and mine. Along with the whole town, of course!"

Sol shifted the bundle in his arms, and it wasn't until that moment that Jason realized he was carrying baby Sarah. He reached over and gently pulled back the fold of swaddling covering part of the sleeping infant's face. "How's she doin'?"

She looked healthy enough, but it was only polite to ask.

Solomon broke out in a wide smile. "Fine, just fine! She is much better, and thank you for asking.

I was just goin' to the jail to see if Rachael was all right. She's there alone, you know."

Jason nodded.

"Well, then . . ."

Jason held back a little chuckle. "Go on with you, Sol. I'm sure she's fine. And you can fill her in on what just happened."

"She's probably scared silly. You know women." Solomon shifted the baby again and walked away.

Yeah, I know, Jason thought as he turned to go back to his house and avoid the crowd already gathering outside his office. And then he reconsidered.

No, he thought, shaking his head. *I don't know 'em at all.*

24

The town of Fury buried Sampson Davis the next day.

The only Jew serving as a pall bearer, Solomon, was aided by Jason, Salmon Kendall, Wash Keogh, Rafe Lynch, Marshal Todd and, of all people, the Reverend Milcher. Solomon had resisted Milcher's inclusion long and hard, but when no one else came forward, he had to give in. Neither the Reverend Bean nor Father Micah was anywhere in sight.

They carried his body in a casket made with no metal fittings, just pegs and wedges to hold it together, and before the casket left the jail, both Rachael and Judith performed the ritual *keriah*, or symbolic rending of their clothes. This entailed each of them making a small tear—made where Judith said she could fix it, of course—in her clothing, in lieu of Sampsom having no family present.

When the procession made its way up the street—stopping seven times for reasons Jason didn't completely understand—and into the cemetery, the "mourners" recited the 23rd Psalm, Solomon recited the memorial prayer *El Maleh Rakhamin*, the Mourner's Kaddish, and since they had no rabbi present, the eulogy. It was short but memorable, and during the first part of it Solomon was so nervous that he shook and stuttered a bit. But all in all, it went pretty smoothly, Jason thought, right through the part where they all had to shovel three scoops of earth onto the echoing coffin, say, "May he come to his place in peace," and then stick the shovel back in the pile of earth where he'd found it. This was to avoid the passing on of death, Solomon told them, as if it were catching.

They all had to wait until the grave was completely filled in, then the pall bearers were told to wash their hands before they left—Jason and Abe used the horse trough—and that was it. So far as Jason was concerned, anyhow.

While nearly the entire saloon had emptied to go and catch a peek at Davis's funeral, Ezra Welk sat nearly alone in the saloon, deciding if right now would be the best time to go and shoot that goofy excuse for a dog that seemed to be hanging around town. He finally decided against it.

But he was bored silly. This town was getting entirely too calm for him. He was pissed that he'd missed the whole Indian thing, pissed that he didn't get to see Davis hang, or at least watch them haul the marshal's body into town over his horse. Either marshal would have done. What was the danged West coming to, anyhow?

He thought again about the dog, and thought something that ugly surely didn't deserve to live. He'd decided not to shoot it, but now he reconsidered. After all, who the hell'd miss it?

He downed the rest of his beer, stood up, and started for the batwing doors.

Bill Crachit, having been left by Solomon to guard the mercantile against Hannibal, sat slouched in a chair beneath the overhang. There were no customers during the funeral, and he'd spent a peaceful half hour sitting out front, watching Hannibal drowse (and chase imaginary rabbits in his sleep) on the sidewalk outside the marshal's office.

But as he watched, he noticed a man come out of the saloon. He'd figured about everybody else was at the funeral, but he'd been wrong. He hadn't seen this fellow before, either.

The fellow started to walk across the street, toward the marshal's office, and as he walked, he pulled his gun.

Bill stood up, all the hairs on his neck standing on end.

The man stopped in the middle of the road and raised his pistol, pointing it at Hannibal.

"Stop! Don't!" Bill leapt off the porch and took two long strides before he heard the shot.

At first he thought Hannibal was dead, and then he realized that the gunshot had come from behind him. The man down the street had fallen, while the dog was just gaining his feet, yawning and stretching.

From behind him, a voice asked, "You okay, Bill?"

Tears pooling in his eyes, he whirled about and recognized the speaker, who was just shoving his Colt back in its holster.

Thickly, he replied, "Yessir, Marshal Fury. I mean, Jason." Then he got some of the stiff back in his spine. He shot an accusing finger toward the body lying down the street. "Did you see? He was gonna shoot Hannibal!"

Jason nodded. There was another man with him. The deputy U.S. marshal, Bill thought, and he was wearing a brand new hat, a heavy-duty Stetson. Mr. Cohen had sold it to him the first thing this morning.

Jason said, "I don't believe he's gonna try that again, for a while, anyway."

"Mebbe not never," said the U.S. Marshal, and started ahead, on down the street.

Bill heard Jason mutter, "Christ, no . . ." before he took off, running down the street after the older marshal.

Jason skidded to a halt next to Abe, just as he stopped beside the downed man. "Is he . . . is he still alive?" he asked hopefully, his voice shaking almost as hard as his knees. He'd shot men before, but never just for threatening a dog! What had he been thinking?

Abe didn't answer him, at least not yet. He had bent to the body, checked for a pulse, and was going through the pockets. He found a worn wallet, stood up, and started going through it.

After what seemed like hours (during which Jason imagined himself going through a trial, then being marched out to a scaffold and hanged, then being read over by the Reverend Milcher in a much less kindly tone than he'd used for Ward), Abe looked up and said, "Thought so."

"What does that mean?"

"Thought he looked familiar. He was Ezra Welk, wanted for a string'a killin's and robberies over the last ten, fifteen years or so." He looked over toward Jason. "Wanted in the Arizona Territory, too. Reckon there's a bunch'a folks who'll be tickled pink to close the books on him."

Jason felt his insides slowly begin to settle themselves again.

"C'mon, hero," Abe said, thumping Jason's arm. "Help me drag this dog turd over to the side'a the road."

They went back to the office when it was over, and Abe pulled out a chair, lit himself a smoke, and said, "Well, I'd best be makin' my way back up to Prescott."

"What?" asked Jason. It was the last thing he had expected.

"Gotta file my report. Gotta turn in ol' Ezra." He tipped his head toward the door. "Gotta talk to my boss 'bout gettin' hitched." He grinned self-consciously. "Gotta arrange a change in duty, too."

"Electa know about this?"

"Oh, yeah. We talked it all over yesterday. Sure gonna be nice to have her to come home to."

Abe was fast fading into a waking dreamland, and Jason tried to engage him in conversation. "So, when're you two tyin' the knot?"

"What? Oh, next Saturday. I already talked to the reverend."

"Milcher or Bean?"

"Milcher," Abe said with a shrug. "He's the only one what's got a church. Electa says he used to be pretty pushy, but somethin' must'a happened, cause he's got a lot softer lately."

Well, that was true. But Jason kept on talking. "You find a place to live yet?"

Abe blew out a long plume of smoke before he said, "Well, Electa said that her folks'd be tickled pink to have us move in with them for the time bein', but I told her that I think I really oughta stick around town. You know, keep in touch."

Jason nodded. He wholeheartedly agreed.

"So, I reckon we'll stay at the roomin' house. I've already got a room over there. And Mrs. Kendall says she can give the two of us a bigger one, iffen we want." He stopped and smiled. "I reckon we'll take her up on that. Till I can get us a house, that is. Why don't this town have a telegraph?"

The question caught Jason a little off guard, but he said, "'Cause nobody's strung the wires, I guess. Don't know that we've got anybody here who knows how to use the damn thing, even if we had one."

Abe snorted. "Oh, I reckon *somebody* knows. Just gotta get some wires strung up, that's all. I'll check on it while I'm in Prescott." He stubbed out his smoke and stood up, stretching slightly. "Oh. And I'll tell 'em about Lynch—don't you need a new

deputy? Been thinkin' he'd do better'n most—
and Teddy Gunderson and Davis and such. That
crazy MacDonald character and how he blocked
off the Apache water supply, too. Head marshal'll
get a kick outta that one," he said with a grin and
a shake of his head. "Well, I'll see you in three,
four days, Jason. Hold the fort."

"You're leaving now?"

"Good a time as any," Abe replied, already
halfway out the door. Jason figured he must be in
such a big toot on account of Electa and getting
married and all. It was none of his nevermind, but
he suddenly realized that in a very short span of
time, he'd come to depend on Abe more than
he'd wanted.

Well, stiff upper lip and all that, he supposed.
He stood up and said, "You have a safe trip, now,"
and watched the big man exit his office and head
up the street, toward the livery. Then he went back
to his desk and sat down with an audible thud—
and a heavy sigh.

Hannibal, who was now ensconced in the first
cell, echoed his sigh, then lay down on the cot.

Jason flicked a finger toward the cot. "Get down,
Hannibal."

No response.

"Off, Hannibal."

Nothing.

"What the hell. Stay up there and shed."

The dog immediately hopped down and stretched
out on the floor, leaving Jason to shake his head.

The door opened and Rafe walked in. "That was
sure somethin', wasn't it?" he asked, grabbing a

chair and swinging it around backwards before he plopped down. "And who's the dead guy on your sidewalk?" He reached for his fixings pouch.

"What was something?" Jason asked before the gears of his brain managed to engage. "Ezra Welk? Oh. You mean the funeral! Yeah, it sure was. I found Davis's address in his pocket, so I gave it to Solomon. He's gonna write to the family, let 'em know everything's handled."

"Good," said Rafe, then held forward his tobacco pouch. "Smoke?"

"Thanks." Jason patted his pocket. "Got my own."

Well, he'd been thinking it, and now Abe had said it. He supposed he should just do it and get it over with. He cleared his throat, then said, "Rafe, how'd you like a job?"

Rafe puffed on his smoke for a moment, then said, "Ain't like I need the money, but what you got in mind?"

"I'm needing a deputy, now that Ward's . . . now that he's gone. What'd you think?"

"Ain't comin' in in the mornings."

"I want you for night deputy."

Rafe stared at the cigarette twisting in his fingers, then looked up. "Sure. 'Bout time I spent some time on the right side of the law, don't'cha think?"

Jason nodded. "I do, indeed." He still had his doubts, but he figured he was pretty well stuck with it. And he was stubborn. Once committed, he'd hold his ground until hell froze over.

Rafe was shaking his head and grinning. "Boy, this is a heck of a turnaround, ain't it?" He turned toward Jason. "You realize I can't go to California, right? At least, not in an official what-ya-call."

"Capacity."

"Yeah, that."

"I realize it."

"Well then, yeah. I'd admire to, and thanks for askin'!"

Jason began to roll himself a smoke. "No problem," he lied, then paused and leaned forward. "I'm trustin' you, Rafe. Don't let me down."

Rafe just grinned at him.

Father Micah was back making his adobe bricks, and had been since breakfast. He had help from inside the walls, as yesterday, and today they were not only making new bricks, but transporting the dried and finished ones inside, as well. Father Micah had already staked out where he wanted the walls and doors to go, so the Morelli and Donovan kids knew where to pile the bricks once they were hauled inside.

In all, the Father had most of five families doing duty this morning, packing brick molds with the mud mixture, turning them out to bake in the Arizona sun, or loading cured bricks onto handcarts for the children to take inside the walls.

He pretty much had a handle on it, he thought to himself, always visualizing what the building would look like when it was finished, and praising God for this opportunity to serve.

And he wasn't alone in working. There was an entire crew at work in town, erecting the water tower, and Salmon Kendall was their foreman. Or he would be, once he got the type set for his headline story. He'd said he figured that young Sammy could crank the presses as well as anybody else, and he was needed across the street.

The men working on the water tower made so much noise, in fact, that they finally drove Jason from his office and over to the saloon.

"Beer," he said to Sam, the barkeep, once he arrived. He turned toward the doors and made a face. He could still hear them clear over here, hammering and yammering, but at least it wasn't so cotton-picking . . . immediate!

Sam slid the beer in front of him, and he gratefully took a long gulp. "How do you stand the noise?"

Sam shrugged. "A body can get used to 'bout anythin', I reckon. And well," he added, grinning and tugging a plug of cotton from one ear, "these help."

Jason cocked his head. "How'd you hear me when I ordered, then?"

"Read your lips," Sam replied. "You'd be surprised what a feller learns, tendin' bar."

Jason tipped his hat, then carried his beer to a table in the front corner of the place. Business was slow, it still being the forenoon, but he noticed a few other fellows coming through the doors and holding their ears, including two that had been working on the job site.

Jason waved one of them over to his table. It was Steve Jeffries, one of the newcomers from the wagon train several months back.

"Mornin'," Jason said.

"Mornin' yourself," Steve echoed. "We makin' enough noise for you?"

"More than enough. Say, when you fellers plan to finish up, anyhow?"

"Today? Mr. Kendall says we're workin' till dark." Jason waved his hands. "No, no. I mean the whole job."

"Oh. Well then, I don't know. When it's finished, I reckon." He snorted out a laugh. "Guess you'd have to ask Mr. Kendall. He's runnin' the show."

Jason sighed. "Okay, thanks, Steve. I'll do that."

But in his mind, he thought only one word: *Crap!*

Solomon Cohen finally finished up the letter he was going to send to California, to Sampson Davis's family. He had labored over it long and hard—a wastebasket filled with crumpled paper bore witness to that—but it was finally finished, and he set it aside more forcefully than one would normally lay down a piece of paper.

"Finished?" asked Rachael from the kitchen, where she was hard-boiling eggs.

Solomon sat back and sighed. "I suppose." He almost asked her if she'd heard the bell jingle before he remembered that he'd left Bill Crachit on duty downstairs. He relaxed again. "The service. It was all right?"

"How many times are you going to be asking? It was fine, Sol, just lovely. His family would have been pleased. Now, stop, already."

Solomon shook his head. "Such a burden to have a kvetching wife . . ."

Rachael stuck her head around the corner. "I heard that," she growled. But she was grinning. "You know, Solomon, that even a rabbi couldn't have done a better job than you did. I couldn't help but be proud."

Solomon felt himself color slightly at her words. "Thank you, my Rachael. But you shouldn't say such things. A rabbi would have been much better. Much better."

She was still smiling. "Yes, dear. You know best, dear."

Solomon felt the shroud of uncertainty lift from him like a cloak had been pulled from his shoulders, and barked out a laugh. He jumped from his chair and lunged for Rachael, who tried to duck back behind the shelving, but didn't make it. Solomon caught her in his arms, and the two of them laughed like maniacs until Rachael was in tears.

"Stop, Sol!" she cried. "Stop, already! You'll make me wet myself!"

He let her go, although he was loathe to, and she stepped back, still tittering, and moved the eggs from the burner to the sink, where she poured off the boiling water and replaced it with cool well water from a bucket.

"Why do you always do that?"

"Because you're greedy, and I don't want you to burn yourself."

"Always thoughtful."

"I try."

He took her in his arms again. "And you succeed, my Rachael. You succeed."

He kissed her, long and hard.

25

Jason was at home and halfway through his dinner—Jenny had made him pork chops and mashed potatoes—when the wind kicked up again. *You're off duty,* he told himself. *Don't worry about it. Just stay tucked up in here and let Rafe deal with it.*

He'd had a full day. There had been the killing, of course. He still wasn't quite over it. After Abe had come down from the livery and collected Welk's body for transport to Prescott, he had gone through his files and finally found some old paper on Ezra Welk. Welk had been quite a piece of work, having already been responsible for the deaths of seven people by the date of the poster, which was January, 1866. How many more had he killed since then? Jason hadn't touched his pistol since, though.

In addition to all the racket the boys were making putting up their damn water tank, there'd been the official swearing in of Rafe—he was still nervous about that—the divesting of Ward's house of his things, and all the normal stuff, plus bidding good-bye to Wash Keogh and being a pall bearer at a funeral, most of which he didn't understand.

Ward's place had been the worst of it. He'd been putting it off, but finally decided he couldn't delay any longer. All that Ward had to show for his life was currently contained in a small wooden crate, out in Jason's living room.

But no. A little piece of Ward still lived in his heart, and Jenny's, and in the core of practically everybody else in town. He would be sorely missed for a long time.

And he was glad that the Davis funeral had gone all right. At least, the Cohens seemed happy. Judith Strong as well. It was good that now there was another Jew in town. Rachael, at least, would have another Jewish woman to talk to. He knew that she'd been ostracized by most of the other women in town for a long time, and he'd felt awfully sorry for her.

The Reverend Bean: Now there was a whole different kettle of fish. He'd made no attempt to secure land for a church, as Father Micah had done right off the bat (even if it hadn't turned out too well), and had just about the same as disappeared. Jason hadn't seen hide nor hair of him in days.

He shrugged and took a piece of dried apple pie from Jenny. It looked pretty good, too. He barely registered the hunk of prickly pear cactus that flew past the kitchen window.

But Jenny said, "Jason, what's the matter? You've been mopin' ever since you set foot over the threshold."

The wind began to rattle the chairs and table outside.

He looked up from his pie. "Oh, nothin'. Just work, I guess. Well, that, and cleaning out Ward's house."

She slowly shook her head. "No, there's something else. Is that business with Ezra Welk troubling you?"

He shook his head.

"Then have you been thinkin' about leavin' again?"

The next gust had hail in it. A few pellets dinged the window. A lot more pelted the side of the house.

"I'm always thinkin' about it."

"More than usual, I'd venture," she said, crossing her arms over her bosom. "What's got you goin' this time?"

"Oh, all right." He set his fork down and leaned back in his chair. "Abe. The town's got Abe, now, or they'll have him in a few days. And he's a whole lot better at this than I am. And they've got Rafe. And I don't want to be here. I wanna be back East, back where there are books and schools, and I'm not in charge of who gets which land, or what's official in the newspaper, or what to do when a million Apache ride up on the town. Where they don't even have Apache and never heard of a dust storm!"

The wind was really howling, now.

Jenny huffed out a little sigh. "You don't wanna be where I am?"

"That's just it! Jen, you could come back East

with me! Think about the dress shops and the shoe stores and the grocery stores where you can just go in and buy food, and not have to raise it yourself. Think about all those boys and men who are out there, just hungry for wives! Think about—"

She held up her hand, silencing him. "That's just it, Jason." There was a crash as something glass collided with the back of the house. Probably the lantern he kept out back.

He glanced out the window, then back at Jenny again. "What's just it?"

"Rafe asked me to marry him." She just said it out and let it lay there.

"What?!"

"You heard me."

"When did this happen?" He was suddenly as mad as a rabid badger, and ready to beat the living tar out of something or someone, Deputy Rafe Lynch in particular.

"While you've been busy doing all your official marshal things," she said calmly, "he's been courtin' me. Took me to lunch at the café three times, sweet-talked me on the porch, showed me how to check when my mare needs shoeing, and went to visit my kitten with me at the Milchers."

"You're marryin' somebody because he went to visit your *cat*?!"

"Oh, for heaven's sake, calm down!"

"No!" He shoved back his chair with a scrape that would have been deafening, but for the storm raging outside. "I won't! Jennifer Fury, have you lost your mind? Have you forgotten that he's wanted for murder? For *murders? Plural?*"

"I don't care. Love doesn't read wanted posters, Jason."

"Well, I do. And I'm gonna put a stop to this right now." He ripped the napkin from his collar and started for the front door.

"Jason? Hadn't you better wait 'til the storm calms down some?"

Past the front window, out in the street, a small saguaro surrounded by swirling dust moved west, end over end, giving him pause. *My only sister, marrying a criminal!* he thought. *The world's coming to an end.*

Something on the front porch went *bang*, but he couldn't bring himself to look down. Sweet-talked her on the front porch! They probably kissed, too! Dear God, what would his father think?

What would his father think. Jason slumped into a chair. Was that what had him all het up? Worrying about the opinion of a dead man? He hadn't realized it until just then. He figured he'd better calm down and think this over rationally.

He sat there in the dark for a long time, listening to the storm's thuds and howls, until finally Jenny came in, bearing a fresh cup of coffee and his untouched desert. She placed them before him.

"Just in case you weren't full up," she said.

He muttered, "Thanks." Then he looked up at Jenny, really looked at her. She was no longer the fifteen-year-old kid who had started the journey west. She was a woman, fully grown, and able to make her own decisions.

"When you plan on making it official?" he asked her.

"Three weeks come Saturday," she said as calmly

as if he'd never objected. "Rafe wanted to ask you first. Isn't that cute? Anyway, guess I kinda jumped the gun. Pretend like you don't know, okay?"

Jason just looked at her. How could he feign ignorance? But then he reminded himself of the mental breakthrough he'd just had, and slowly nodded while he picked up his coffee. "'Kay."

"Just leave your dishes in the sink. I'm going to bed, all right?"

"Yeah. 'Night."

She smiled at him, then bent and kissed his forehead. "I knew you'd get used to it." And then she was gone.

Jason put down his coffee and rolled himself a cigarette. Lighting it and listening to the storm outside, he thought, *It was on purpose. She did it on purpose, just to keep me here. The bitch!* And then he scolded himself for calling his sister names. She was right. Love didn't read—or reason, either. It just happened. She couldn't help it, and likely, neither could Rafe.

He set the cigarette, half-smoked, in the ashtray and picked up his pie plate. Jenny had done it again—the pie was great. And then he started to think about his stomach. What would he eat with Jenny gone? At least, he assumed she'd be gone, with a home of her own.

Now, there was another good reason to be angry with Rafe: He was liable for starving the marshal to death!

He heaved a sigh, inaudible over the storm. His old life was over with, that was all there was to it. He couldn't go back East now. Leaving Jenny alone in Rafe's hands was out of the question, although leaving her with Matt MacDonald would have been far worse. Thank God she was over that!

He found himself smiling, imagining how Mac-Donald would react when he heard that Jenny was not only marrying another man, but his deputy! And then he wondered whether Abe had ever made it back to the Double M to talk to Matt.

None of his business, he told himself. That was county stuff, or territorial stuff, but not anything to do with Fury. He'd just wait and see, and that was all there was to it.

He felt himself relax and give in. He couldn't control everything any more than Solomon could stop being a Jew, or Jenny could stop being a girl. All he could do was go along and hope for the best.

Hope for the best, that was it. He set aside his pie plate and clasped his hands over his chest, slumping down in the chair. He suddenly felt too tired to make the short walk back to his room, and he let his lids drift closed.

Tomorrow would bring new problems and new surprises, but he was too tired to worry about them now. As he drifted off to sleep, he was thinking that tomorrow would be just another normal day in Fury.

Whatever that was.

EPILOGUE

Dear Carl,

Well, that's it. Sorry if I burst your balloon about the killing of the gunman, Ezra Welk, but sometimes the truth is, far and away, more interesting than anything you or I could make up. And certainly I couldn't have come up with anything more poetic than the real reason for his death.

Jason Fury has already read this, by the way, and given his go-ahead on the project. He lives alone now, in the same old house he built on Second Street, although the place has certainly grown some. Fury now has a real grade school, a junior high, and a high school, and there is talk of a junior college. They're well past Second Street these days and up to streets in the forty-somethings. They are, in fact, nearly halfway up to the Mac-Donalds' spread.

And since the Apache no longer pose a threat, the east wall (along with the northern one) has been taken down and the cactus that the wind planted beside the wall has been turned into a

pretty (if prickly) little park that separates the east
and west ends of Main Street.

Fury has also become a popular vacation spot for
Hollywood types, and several well-known names
(including Tom Mix and William S. Hart) own
property there, or at least come to stay over for a
week or two here and there. As you might guess,
this had led to the development of a number of
swank restaurants and so on, and added to the
townsfolk's bank accounts.

The marshal's office has been replaced, as have
several other buildings. Solomon Cohen's mercantile is still there, although now it is run by his
grandsons, Issac and David. Did I mention that
Solomon, in his later years, invented the valve for
the modern flush toilet, adding to the work already done by the original English inventor, Mr.
Crapper? It made him quite wealthy. And by the
way, there is now a good-sized Jewish community
in Fury, with its own synagogue and its own private cemetery. I noticed that they hadn't moved
Sampson Davis over there, though. Perhaps they
thought he wasn't worth the bother, and perhaps
you agree with them, as do I.

The Catholic church is booming, too. A new
structure was erected in 1900, and although Father
Micah is long gone, the new priest, Father Tim
McKay, seems a good fellow, and had no trouble
letting me peruse the church records and regaling
me with stories of Fury originally told to him by
Father Micah.

The Reverend Milcher's old church has been re-
furbished and now serves as the First Presbyterian.

Reverend Bean eventually opened a Baptist church, which only survived three years.

You'll be interested to know that the town of Fury has erected an enormous, heroic, bronze statue in the center of Main Street, where the community well once stood, of old Jedediah Fury, himself. Jason tells me it doesn't do Jedediah justice, but then, you'd expect any son to say that about any edifice erected in his father's image. (Water is now piped direct to the houses and so on, and there is a municipal sewer system in place, along with a small water treatment plant.)

Jason's sister, Jenny, is the widow of the late Rafe Lynch, who passed away in 1903 after being mortally wounded by a would-be bank robber. However, he is survived by not only his wife, but three children and six grandchildren, one of whom serves as the present marshal (or chief of police, as they now call the position) of Fury. He is called Jason, after his great-uncle, and frequently seeks his advice and counsel.

Jason, himself, married a few years after the time of our story, and it came as a surprise to nearly everybody in town. He is a widower now, but his sons have gone into the family businesses, as it were. The elder, Jeremy, is a U.S. Marshal, and the other, Jasper, sells real estate. Between them, they have given Jason three granddaughters and four grandsons.

Most of the others in the story have passed on, more's the pity. I would have greatly admired to have met old Salmon Kendall and Abe Todd.

I should probably say here, too, that old Wash Keogh never did strike it rich. Apparently, that enormous nugget he found was a one-of-a-kind relic (although he kept looking for some years), but he never cashed it in. It is presently under guard and on display at the Fury Historical Society and Museum, along with several souvenirs from the original wagon train, including the Milchers' original piano, a real Conestoga wagon, a great many wanted posters from back in the day, and so on.

I must cut this off, for I hear the train pulling in to the depot, and they usually don't stay over too long. I want to get this off to you as soon as possible, my friend, and I trust that you'll enjoy reading about what I trust was the most action-packed week (in non-fiction, at least) in Arizona, ever!

Best Wishes,
Bill

Turn the page for an exciting preview!

**In Utah the Loner finds religion—
behind the barrel of a gun . . .**

SHOWER THE BRIDE WITH LEAD . . .

The damsel is in distress, or so it seems to
Conrad Browning. On his way across the wide,
tall Utah Territory to California, the Loner
meets a beautiful Mormon girl on the run from a
forced polygamous wedding—and the gun-toting
faithful trying to hunt her down. But there are
two sides to every story. Sometimes, the one you
don't hear is the one that can get you killed.

The runaway bride has a little history of her own.
The Loner touches off a storm of unholy gunfire,
drawing blood from an outlaw and a death
sentence from a patriarch. Among murderers
and Mormons, Bibles and bullets, the Loner
finds himself riding to a wedding—a ceremony
he intends to crash with a vengeance. . . .

The Tenth in the Blazing New Series!

The Loner: The Blood of Renegades

by *USA Today* bestselling author J. A. Johnstone

On sale now, wherever Pinnacle Books are sold.

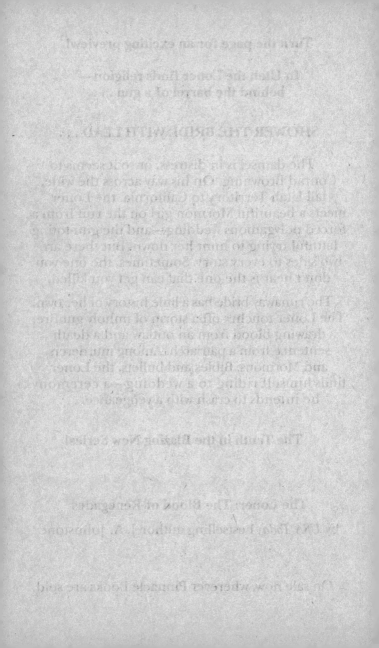

1

Rugged, snowcapped mountains rose in the distance, a majestic sight under a beautiful blue sky.

The same couldn't be said about the terrain over which Conrad Browning and Arturo Vincenzo traveled. There was nothing majestic about it. The landscape was mostly flat and semi-arid, sparsely covered by tough grass, dotted with scrubby mesquite and greasewood, and slashed by the occasional arroyo.

Hardly the oasis that Brigham Young had promised his followers, Conrad mused, but the Mormons had made their homes here in Utah anyway and in most cases seemed to be thriving, if bustling Salt Lake City was any indication. Conrad and Arturo had passed through the city a few days earlier and since then had been making their way around the huge salt lake that gave the place its name, following the railroad that skirted the northern end of the lake. At last they had left the vast body of water behind them and now angled southwestward toward Nevada.

Conrad rode a big, blaze-faced black gelding while Arturo handled the reins hitched to the four-horse team pulling the buggy. They had been together for several months after leaving Boston and embarking on a cross-country quest for Conrad's lost children, little Frank and Vivian. The children's mother, the vengeful Pamela Tarleton, had concealed their very existence from Conrad, who hadn't known she was pregnant when he broke their engagement and married Rebel Callahan instead.

A lot of time and tragedy had gone by since then. Rebel was dead and so was Pamela. But she had managed to strike at Conrad from beyond the grave when her cousin delivered the letter she had written revealing that Conrad had a previously unknown son and daughter, twins that Pamela boasted were hidden where Conrad would never find them.

It was a particularly vicious way of tormenting him, but Conrad wasn't the sort to suffer without trying to do something about it. His investigation had uncovered the fact that Pamela had taken the twins from Boston and started to San Francisco with them. Since then, Conrad and his friend and servant Arturo had been searching for them, following Pamela's route across the country. Conrad had no way of knowing whether she had taken the children with her all the way to the coast, so he and Arturo stopped frequently along the way to ask questions and find out if anybody knew anything about a woman traveling with a nanny and two small children.

But there wasn't really anybody to ask questions

of, out here in this thinly-populated wilderness. Often the steel rails of the Southern Pacific and the telegraph poles and wires erected by Western Union were the only signs that civilization had ever visited the area. No more settlements of any size lay between here and Nevada, at least none that Conrad knew of.

He was a tall, well-built man in his twenties, with close-cropped sandy hair under his flat-crowned black Stetson. Once he had been so handsome that he'd set the hearts of society girls all over Boston—and the hearts of their mothers—to fluttering, but time and trouble had etched character lines in his face. He wore a white shirt and black boots, trousers, and coat. A hand-tooled black gun belt was strapped around his trim hips. A meticulously cared for Colt revolver with a walnut grip rode in the holster attached to the gun belt.

In addition to the handgun, Conrad carried a Winchester repeater and a heavy-caliber Sharps carbine in sheaths lashed to his saddle. He was an expert with all three weapons but perhaps most deadly with the Colt, which was fitting since he was Frank Morgan's son and Morgan was one of the fastest men to ever strap on a six-gun. Morgan was known as The Drifter, and some called him the last true gunfighter.

That might have been true once, but no more. Now there was the man who called himself Kid Morgan, and while Conrad didn't go out of his way to keep it a secret, not all that many people knew that Kid Morgan and Conrad Browning were one and the same. He had invented the identity to help him track down Rebel's killers, and it still came in handy from time to time.

More than a month earlier, while they were in Denver searching for clues to what Pamela might have done with the children, Conrad and Arturo had gotten roped into some trouble that left Arturo with a wounded arm. Since then they'd been traveling at a slower pace so his injury would have more time to heal. Conrad had handled the buggy for a while. Now Arturo's arm was stronger and he had resumed his driving chores. That was fine with Conrad. He preferred being in the saddle.

"My word, there's really not much out here, is there?" Arturo said. "I thought Wyoming was godforsaken, but this is just depressing."

Conrad smiled. "I don't know, it has a certain stark beauty about it, don't you think?"

"For about the first ten minutes. After that it's just flat and empty and ugly."

Conrad couldn't argue with that. It seemed like a pretty accurate assessment to him. Still ahead of them in Nevada were areas like that, too, but eventually they would get into the prettier country around Reno and Carson City.

Carson City . . . Just thinking about the place threatened to send waves of melancholy sweeping over Conrad's soul. That was where he and Rebel lived when she was murdered. Later their home had gone up in flames, and for a while everyone believed that Conrad had perished in the blaze.

That was what he wanted them to think. That was when Kid Morgan was born and set out on his mission of vengeance.

Not unexpectedly, vengeance had turned out not to be very satisfying. Conrad had drifted for a while after that, but violence and death still seemed to dog his trail. Then the revelation about the twins had changed everything.

Arturo broke in on Conrad's thoughts by asking, "How long will it take for us to get to those mountains?"

Conrad studied the snow-mantled peaks. "Maybe late today, maybe early tomorrow. We'll have to follow the railroad through the passes. There may be other ways through, but I don't know them."

"We could be in San Francisco tomorrow if we took the train."

"Yes, we could, but what if Pamela hid the twins somewhere along the way?"

"Yes, I'm familiar with that logic," Arturo said. "I wasn't suggesting that we *should* take the train, but rather just commenting on the relative speed with which it could deliver us to our destination. Isn't it amazing?"

"Yeah," Conrad said. "Amazing." He was distracted as he spoke by a cloud of dust he spotted north of the railroad tracks. He squinted toward the dust and watched it drift closer.

Arturo must have seen where Conrad was looking, because he turned his head and studied the desert country in that direction, too. "Someone's coming," he said.

"Yeah," Conrad said. "Fast, too."

And that usually meant trouble.

Conrad reined in his horse and Arturo brought the buggy to a stop. As they sat there watching, the dust column continued to move toward them. Conrad's keen eyes made out a single figure at the base of the column. Then his gaze shifted and he lifted a hand to point.

"Even more dust back there," he said.

"What does it mean?" Arturo asked.

"Means that fella in front is being chased by at least half a dozen riders," Conrad said, "and I'll bet they don't have anything good in mind for him."

Arturo's eyes narrowed suspiciously as he looked at Conrad and asked, "What exactly are we going to do about it?"

With a faint smile, Conrad said, "Now that's a good question."

He reached for his Winchester and drew it out of the saddle boot.

"I knew it!" Arturo said. "Whatever this trouble is, you're going to get mixed up right in the middle of it, aren't you? You can't just let it gallop on past us."

Conrad didn't answer with words. Instead he heeled his horse into a run across the arid plains in a course that would intercept the fleeing rider.

2

Arturo yelled something behind him, but Conrad couldn't make it out over the thunder of the black's hoofbeats. He leaned forward in the saddle and urged the animal to greater speed.

He had been torn for a second between the two courses of action that lay before him. He and Arturo could have stayed where they were and allowed the pursuit to pass in front of them and continue on to the south. That probably would have been the smartest thing to do, since he was on an important mission of his own: finding his lost children.

Or he could give in to the part of him that didn't like six-to-one odds. That was the urge that won the mental battle. He had gotten in the habit of sticking up for anybody who was outnumbered.

Of course, it was possible the fleeing rider was a killer or a train robber or some other sort of outlaw, and that could be a posse on his trail. In that case, Conrad could stop the fugitive and do a favor for the law.

First, though, he had to get an idea of what was going on. He didn't hear any shots or see any puffs of powdersmoke from the pursuers. Evidently they weren't out to kill the person they were after.

Conrad suddenly realized he needed to stop thinking of that lone rider as a man. He was close enough now to see long, fair hair streaming out behind the rider's head. Some men wore their hair long like that, but Conrad's instincts told him this was a woman.

A woman being chased by that many men was bound to be in trouble. Conrad hauled back on the reins and brought his mount to a stop again. He levered a round into the Winchester's firing chamber and brought the rifle to his shoulder. Aiming high, he squeezed the trigger and sent a shot blasting over the heads of the pursuers, who were a couple of hundred yards away.

The woman was closer, maybe fifty yards from him. She changed course, veering toward him. The shot Conrad had fired at the men chasing her must have convinced her that he might protect her. Conrad levered the rifle and squeezed off another round.

The pursuers didn't return his fire. They still had to be worried about hitting the woman. She flashed past Conrad without slowing down. He caught a glimpse of her pale, frightened face. When he glanced over his shoulder after her, he saw that Arturo had followed him in the buggy and was stopped a short distance behind him. Arturo had jumped down from the vehicle and stood there with a rifle in his hands, ready to get into the fight if need be.

Conrad turned his attention back to the pursuers, who slowed their horses and then stopped, evidently unwilling to charge right into the threat of two Winchesters. They were far enough away Conrad couldn't make out any details about them except the broad-brimmed hats and long dusters they wore. The horses milled around as the dust cloud kicked up by their hooves started to blow away.

Seconds passed in nerve-stretching tension. Finally one of the men prodded his horse forward. Conrad stayed where he was, waiting in motionless silence, as the man rode slowly toward him.

"That's far enough," Conrad called when the man was about thirty feet away.

"Mister, I don't know who you are, but you're mixin' in something that's none of your concern." The spokesman for the pursuers was a thick-set man with dark beard stubble on his face. One eye was squeezed almost shut, no doubt from the injury that had left a scar angling away from it. "That woman belongs to us."

Conrad said, "You may not have heard, but it's almost a new century. Enlightened people are starting to believe that women don't actually belong to anyone except themselves."

The man grunted. "It don't matter what century it is. The law's the law."

"What law?"

"The law of God!" the man thundered.

With that, things became clearer to Conrad. "You're Mormons, aren't you?" he asked.

"Call ourselves saints," the man said. "Or in our case . . . angels."

Avenging angels, Conrad thought. Gun-packing enforcers for the leaders of the Mormon hierarchy. Conrad had heard stories about them, but these were the first he had encountered. When he'd been in charge of all the Browning business and financial interests—back in that other life of his before everything he held dear was ripped away from him—he had dealt at times with Mormon leaders. You couldn't do business in Utah without dealing with the Mormons. But they had been businessmen as much as they were church elders, their religious beliefs tempered by the desire to make money. These gunmen were very different sorts.

Despite being outnumbered, Conrad wasn't afraid of them. He said, "Chasing a scared girl across this wasteland doesn't strike me as being very religious."

The man scowled and jabbed a finger at him, as if to strike him dead. "Don't you presume to know the will of the Lord! The girl is ours and she goes back with us. She has defied the elders and must be punished!"

"You'll have to take her from us," Conrad said coolly.

"There are six of us and two of you," the man pointed out with a sneer.

"Yes, but we'll kill four of you before you put us down. Maybe five. Maybe even all six." Conrad smiled. "Not to brag, but I'm pretty good with a gun. Maybe we'll all wind up lying here, food for the buzzards, and then the girl will ride away. What good will that do your elders?"

The other men had been listening intently to the exchange. One of them spoke up now, saying, "Leatherwood, maybe we'd better not do this. We were just supposed to bring her back, not kill anybody."

The leader's head jerked around. "This man's not going to tell me what to do. Our orders were to fetch the girl!"

"We'll be able to find her later." The man waved a hand at the landscape around them. "Where are they going to go that we can't find them whenever we want to? This is our home."

The one called Leatherwood hesitated. He glared back and forth between his companions and Conrad. "Elder Hissop was clear about what we're supposed to do. I don't know about you, Kiley, but I don't much want to go back without doin' as we were told."

"They won't get away," Kiley said. "Besides, after these men have been saddled with that headstrong female for a while, they may want us to take her off their hands!"

Leatherwood nodded. "That's a good point." He turned back to Conrad. "All right, mister, if you want her, take her. But know that by defyin' us, you've signed your death warrant. Sooner or later we'll kill you, and the girl will go back where she belongs."

"Talk like that makes me wonder why I don't just go ahead and drill you right now," Conrad said.

The squint-eyed Leatherwood grinned, which

made him even uglier. "You're welcome to go ahead and try, mister."

Conrad began backing his horse away. Without taking his eyes off the six men, he raised his voice and said, "Arturo, take the girl and get out of here. I'll cover your back trail."

The Mormon gunmen stayed where they were. Conrad understood why the one called Kiley hadn't wanted to force the issue. Outnumbered, surrounded by miles and miles of nothing and no place where they could get any help, he and Arturo were at a definite disadvantage. The avenging angels could stalk them at their leisure, and Conrad and Arturo would have no way of knowing when or where the inevitable attack would come.

But for now, more gunplay appeared to have been headed off. Conrad had a chance to find out who the girl was and what was going on here, and he wanted to take advantage of that opportunity. He didn't mind fighting, but he generally liked to know what he was fighting *for*, especially when this trouble was delaying him in his efforts to find his missing children.

Conrad heard the buggy and the girl's horse departing behind him. He waited and continued backing his horse away from the gunmen. When he had put a hundred yards between himself and them, he whirled the horse without warning and kicked it into a run. As he galloped after Arturo and the girl, he looked over his shoulder and saw that the Mormons weren't giving chase. That surprised him a little, but obviously Leatherwood had decided they were going to bide their time.

Conrad was sure of one thing: This trouble was far from over.

Because Kiley was right. There was no place for them to go where the avenging angels couldn't find them.

3

Conrad, Arturo, and their unexpected companion didn't stop until they had gone at least a mile. Conrad kept checking behind them. He was ready to stop and throw up a screen of rifle fire to cover their getaway, but the gunmen didn't come after them.

When they finally reined in, the horses were all fatigued by the hard run. The young woman's horse was in the worst shape because she had been fleeing from her pursuers before Conrad and Arturo joined the chase.

The young woman wasn't in much better shape. When she tried to dismount, she half fell out of the saddle and had to grab hold of a stirrup to keep herself from dropping to the ground.

Conrad had already slid his Winchester into the saddle boot and swung down from the black. He reached out to grasp her arm and steady her. "Arturo," he said, "get one of the canteens."

Arturo turned around on the buggy seat and found a canteen in their boxes and bags of supplies.

He climbed down from the seat and brought the water over to them. Conrad unscrewed the cap and held the canteen to the young woman's mouth. She grabbed it with both hands and tried to gulp down as much water as she could, but Conrad pulled the canteen away after a couple of swallows.

"Take it easy," he told her. "You'll make yourself sick."

"I . . . I . . . Thank you," she gasped. "If you hadn't come along . . . I wouldn't have made it much farther."

While Conrad waited a moment before he gave her another drink, he took advantage of the opportunity to have a good look at her. She was tall and slender, and hair a little lighter in color than honey flowed all the way down her back to her hips. She wore men's clothing: a rough cotton shirt with the sleeves rolled up a couple of turns on tanned forearms, brown twill trousers with suspenders that went over her shoulders, and work boots that laced up. Despite the clothing, no one would ever take her for anything but female.

"What's your name?" Conrad asked.

She'd been breathless when she dismounted, but she was starting to recover. "Selena," she said. "Selena Webster."

"I'm Conrad Browning. This is my friend Arturo Vincenzo."

Conrad handed her the canteen, and this time he didn't have to take it away from her. She took a long drink, but not enough to make her sick. As she gave him the canteen, she said, "I can't thank you enough for helping me, but I'm afraid you've just doomed yourselves. Like Jackson Leatherwood said, when you interfere with Father Agony's men, you've signed your own death warrant."

Despite the perilousness of their situation, Conrad couldn't help but laugh. "Father Agony?" he repeated. "That's a pretty melodramatic name, don't you think?"

Selena smiled, but there was no real humor in the expression. "That's what some of his wives call him. His name is Agonistes Hissop."

"The man's parents had odd taste in nomenclature," Arturo said.

"Or else they were readers and admirers of Milton's *Samson Agonistes*," Conrad said. "Agonistes being from the Latin for 'one who struggles for a worthy cause.'"

Selena gave him an odd look. He didn't bother explaining that he had taken a number of courses in the classics during his university days.

"The man's parents raised a monster," Selena said after a moment. "His name is hardly the worst thing about him."

"He's the elder that Leatherwood and the others work for?" Conrad guessed.

Selena nodded. "He has a ranch about twenty miles northwest of here in a place called Juniper Canyon. It's more like his own little town, because a lot of his followers live there as well. He's a very rich, important man, and he doesn't let anyone forget it."

"You mentioned his . . . wives," Conrad said. "I

seem to remember reading in the newspaper that the Mormon Church outlawed polygamy almost ten years ago."

That brought a laugh from Selena. "Just because Father Agony is a saint doesn't mean that he agrees with everything the church leadership does. He believes that he's a prophet, like Joseph Smith, and that God has granted him the wisdom and right to make his own laws. He's always had multiple wives, and he doesn't want to give them up."

Conrad nodded. "And let me guess . . . he wants to add you to the number?"

The grimace that momentarily twisted Selena's face was answer enough to that question. She said, "I'll never marry him. He can kill me first, or more likely have Leatherwood and the rest of his avenging angels do it for him, but I don't care. That would be better than . . . than . . ."

"Maybe it won't come to that," Conrad said so that she wouldn't have to go on. "I don't like to brag, but Arturo and I are pretty good at handling trouble."

"Have you ever had an army of triggerites after you? Because that's what you'll be facing if you try to help me. I appreciate what you did, but you'd be better off if we went our separate ways. If Leatherwood and the others see that I'm not traveling with you, maybe he'll spare your lives. Maybe."

Conrad shook his head. "We're not going to abandon you. Once I take cards in a game, I like to play it out." He glanced toward the sun. "It's past the middle of the afternoon. We'll let the horses rest for a while longer, then we can start looking for a place to hole up for the night."

"Why don't you sit in the buggy, Miss Webster?" Arturo suggested. "The canopy provides a bit of shade from that brutal sun."

Selena smiled. "Thank you. You're very nice."

"Not really. I just know that having you suffer a sunstroke would only make our situation worse."

"Oh," she said. "Well, in that case, I appreciate it anyway." She climbed onto the buggy seat and heaved a weary sigh.

Conrad kept an eye not only on the area where they had left Jackson Leatherwood and the other avenging angels but also the rest of the landscape around them. He wouldn't put it past Leatherwood and the others to circle and come at them from a different direction. This vast expanse of Utah seemed as open and empty as if it had been on the moon, however.

Selena's exhaustion must have caught up to her. She dozed off with her head sagging forward. While she was sleeping, Arturo asked Conrad, "Are you sure that getting involved in this young woman's problems is a good idea, sir?"

"No," Conrad said, "it's a terrible idea. We need to get on about our own business. I know that. But . . . look at her. She's not much more than a girl."

"A very attractive girl."

Conrad shrugged. "Yes, but that doesn't have anything to do with it. She's in trouble, and if we don't help her, who will? Maybe we can take her someplace where she'll be safe from those men."

He didn't explain to Arturo how his dreams—and sometimes even his waking moments—had been haunted by Rebel for months after her death. Whenever he'd been faced by the decision of whether to help someone or just ride on, her sweet voice had seemed to whisper in his ear that he had to help . . . because that's what *she* would have done. Rebel wasn't here anymore, but Conrad could honor the life she had led and the legacy she left behind by not turning his back on people who needed a hand.

Or in his case, a gunhand.

After half an hour, Conrad tied Selena's horse at the back of the buggy. She could stay where she was and ride in the vehicle. She stirred when Arturo climbed onto the seat beside her.

Suddenly her head snapped up and she looked around, wide-eyed with terror. "It's all right, Miss Webster," Arturo told her. "You're among friends."

She looked like she wanted to bolt out of the buggy and take off running blindly. After a moment, though, her fear seemed to subside, and she sank back onto the seat.

"I'm sorry," she said. "At first I . . . I didn't remember what happened. I thought I'd passed out somewhere and that Leatherwood and his men were still after me." A laugh edged with bitterness came from her. "Which they still are, of course. They'll never give up. Not as long as they're alive." She looked back and forth between Conrad and Arturo. "Are you sure you want to take on my troubles?"

Conrad stepped up into the saddle. "We wouldn't have it any other way," he said with a smile.